MORE HARM THAN GOOD

ALSO BY ANDREW GRANT

EVEN
DIE TWICE

This is a work of fiction. All of the characters, organisations, and events portrayed in this novel are either products of the author's imagination or are used fictitiously.

MORE HARM THAN GOOD. Copyright © 2012 by Andrew Grant. Cover photo by George Cairns.

For Tasha, who shoots electrics.

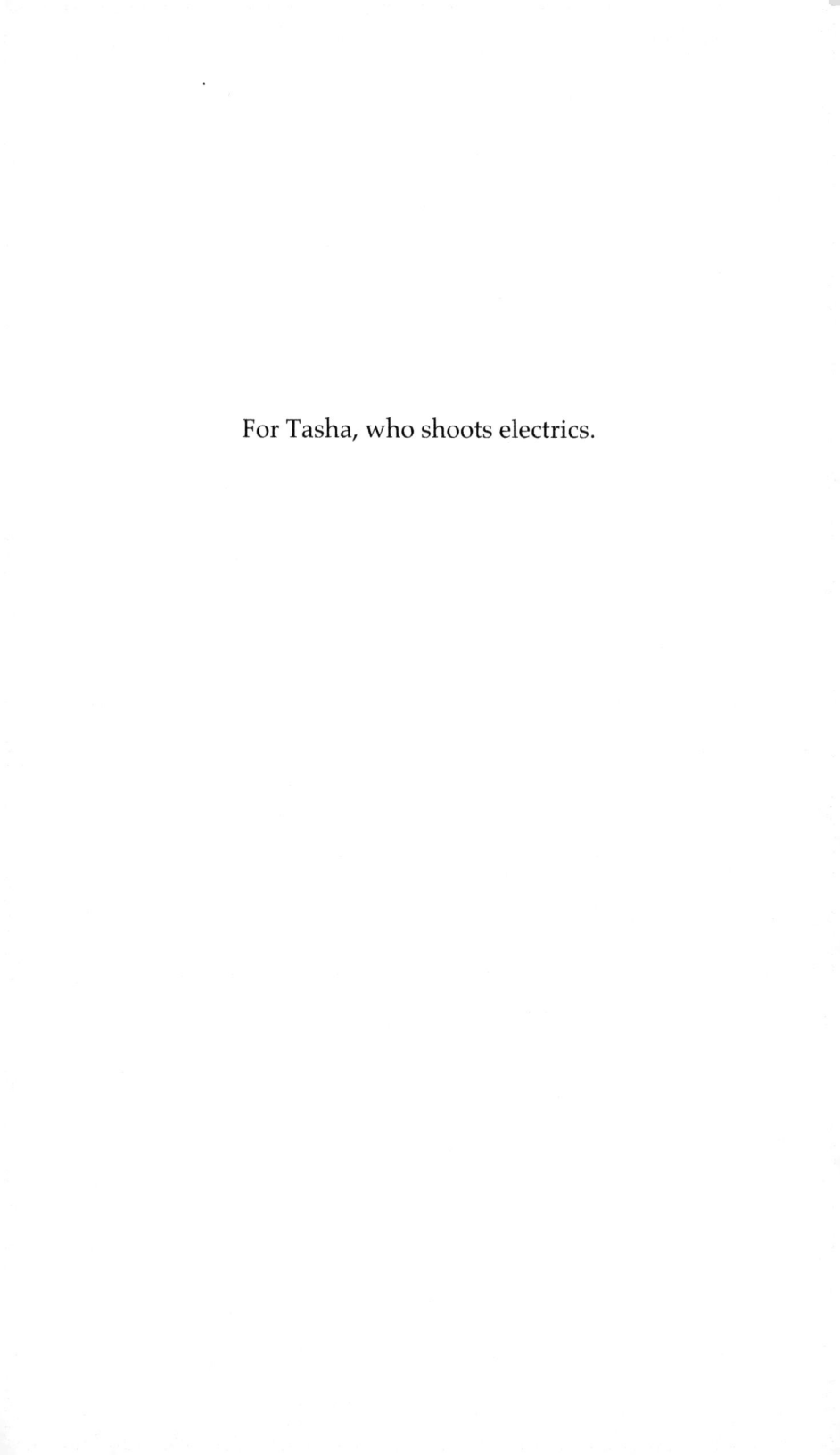

MORE HARM THAN GOOD

ANDREW GRANT

Chapter One

The man looked much older than his reputed thirty-five years. His hair was thinner, and his face was slacker and more sallow than his picture had suggested. I couldn't compare his height, though. Because he was on the ground, kneeling in front of two Royal Marines.

One of the Marines had a pistol levelled on the bridge of the man's nose.

And for a moment, I was tempted to let him pull the trigger.

There are dozens of different job roles in all the British Embassies and Consulates around the world, but one thing unites everyone who works in them. A phone number. During their training, everyone – from Ambassadors to janitors to chefs – has it drummed into them. The number to call if they come across anything remotely suspicious. An unfamiliar piece of IT equipment. A strange noise on the phone. An unrecognised entry in a fax journal. A ragged seal on an envelope. A change in a colleague's behaviour.

The first alarm call from the Boulevard Joseph II was made by one of the Embassy chefs. He was an eight-year veteran of the diplomatic service. Before that, he'd spent twenty-two years in the Navy, feeding multiple generations of Royal Marines. And after dishing out more than thirty thousand meals, he was pretty used to the amount they liked to eat. So when two of the younger guys from the guard duty detail starting sending their plates back hardly touched, he noticed.

The baton was passed to the Marines' CO, and it

didn't take him long to find out why his men had lost their appetites. The pair of them had been caught carrying on with a couple of local girls. But not by anyone from the Navy. By a man from Liverpool. He called himself Kevin Truly. And he had a simple proposition. Carry an extra rucksack each onto the military plane to England next time they were on leave - neatly sidestepping any customs checkpoints or police officers with sniffer dogs - and their wives need never hear what they'd been up to.

The analysts in London figured the danger most likely didn't extend beyond garden-variety blackmail, but they needed to be sure. Navy policy ensures every threat - however minor it seems on the surface - is taken seriously. So they told the Marines to play along. And when Truly next got in touch - with instructions to meet him the following night - they decided it was time to send someone in to take a closer look

That 'someone' was me.

It was less than a kilometer from the Embassy to the address Truly had given the Marines. It would have been a pleasant walk. Luxembourg City is beautiful. It felt like a scaled down version of Paris, crossed with Vienna, and set on a series of hills. The idea of taking a stroll through its elegant streets before getting my hands dirty was very inviting, but I couldn't ignore a nagging doubt at the back of my mind. Given the subject at hand, it seemed unlikely that somewhere so central - or public - was going to be our final destination. My Liaison Officer agreed, and without waiting for me to ask, she picked up her phone and called the car pool.

The rendezvous was set to happen at a trendy waterfront hotel. The building had recently been converted from a grand old department store. A new front entrance had been added, and this was separated from the River Alzette by a broad, block-paved promenade. The alleys on either side were too narrow for cars and vehicle access to the rear of the building was controlled by a secured gate, so I left my driver to his own devices and took a quarter of an hour to wander around the perimeter, observing the place from the outside. Then I made my way into the bar, ordered a glass of still water, and took the seat with the best view of the door.

There were twenty-seven people in the room, aside from me. A group of twelve - half men, half women, mixed ages from twenty to fifty - had pulled three tables together in the corner. They seemed comfortable with each other, and the volume of their conversation was rising steadily as the level of their drinks declined. Four men in their late thirties or early forties were sitting separately at the bar, quietly nursing bottles of upscale Belgian beer. A woman was reclining in an armchair near the window, on her own, sipping cappuccino and tapping away at a laptop. Four couples were huddled around tall, round tables. And a pair of twenty-somethings in suits was sitting near the door, holding cokes but not making much effort to drink them.

A quarter of an hour passed before I spotted the Marines. They strolled artificially slowly through the door, glanced around without letting their eyes settle on anyone in particular, then walked up to the table nearest the bar. They looked just like they had done in the photos I'd been shown, except for their clothes. One was wearing motorcycle boots, faded jeans, and a tasseled biker-style jacket. The other had Timberlands, grey cargo pants, and no coat. And as stipulated by Truly, both wore black Motörhead T-shirts.

Five people left the bar over the next twenty minutes. Three came in. But no one made any attempt to approach the pair. I finished my water and ordered a black coffee to replace it. The waiter brought me one with cream, but before he had time to take it away again a guy entering the room caught my attention. I guessed he'd be in his late teens. He was wearing jeans, trainers, an Ajax football shirt, and a denim jacket with a torn right sleeve. His skin was pale. His face was covered with freckles. His ginger hair was draped over his head in a kind of half-hearted mullet. But it was the way he moved that stood out the most. He shuffled into the bar like a sulky teenager at his parents' cocktail party. Then, as he drew level with the two guys near the door I saw him make eye contact with both of them. Brief, but definite. One of them nodded to him, very slightly. And after that he picked up speed, skirting round the remaining couples and walking straight towards the Marines' table.

I sent a text to my driver: Contact. Stand by.

The Marines watched the ginger haired kid approach, but neither of them got down from their chairs. He reached their table and stood and looked at the one in the biker jacket for fifteen seconds, fidgeting slightly as the bigger man returned his gaze. None of them spoke. Then he pulled a piece of paper from his pocket, laid it on the table, turned, and walked away.

As soon as the guy was half way to the door the biker Marine picked up the note he'd left. He glanced at it. Showed it to his friend. Then he dropped the paper back on the table, both of them stood and made for the exit themselves. I slipped some money under my saucer, waited until they were clear, then stepped across to where they'd been sitting.

The note was written by hand, in pencil, but it wasn't too hard to read:

Unit 4. Rue Robert Schuman.
30 minutes. Come alone. Take a taxi, don't use your car.
People will be watching.

I looked up and saw the Marines had just reached the door. The two guys who'd nodded to the ginger kid stood up and moved after them, their drinks still untouched. I scanned the bar for anything else that rang a false note. Nothing struck me, so I made my own way outside.

The Marines were striding away to my right, towards the nearest point where the promenade met the street. My car was already there, waiting, with its hazards on. The two guys were twenty feet behind, walking almost in step, hands in their pockets, not talking. And straight ahead, leaning on the railing that separated the river from dry land, was the ginger haired messenger boy. I strolled across and rested my forearms on the rail next to him, as if I was an old friend. No one was watching from the far side of the river. No boats were moored nearby. The lad started to fidget. I guess he was uncomfortable, being so close to a stranger. I turned so my back was against the rail. No one was paying us any attention from the hotel or the road, so I drew my right arm across my chest. I glanced around one more time, and rammed my elbow into the side of the lad's head. Then I stepped across and caught him before he hit the ground. He was heavier than he looked, but I was still able to support him with one arm while I reached into my pocket. I took out a flexicuff, fed one of his arms through a gap in the metalwork, bound his wrists together, and set off towards the road.

The drive took twenty-two minutes, which was plenty of time for me to call the Embassy and arrange for them to have to the police scoop the boy up and keep him out of circulation until we saw what happened next. It turned out that the Rue Robert Schuman was in an industrial area that spurred off one of the major arterial routes from the north west of the city. It led to a T-shaped development, probably built in the 1980s judging by the design of the small factories and warehouse units that were lined up on both sides. I counted twelve of them. Unit four was at the left-hand end of the crossbar. I couldn't help thinking Truly had chosen well. There were no houses nearby. No offices, or schools. With the nearby businesses closed for the night the whole area was deserted. An ideal situation, if he needed to move people and supplies around unnoticed.

Without waiting for me to tell him, the driver turned to the right and didn't stop until he'd gone another hundred yards. Then I climbed out and made my way back on foot. The other units all showed signs of occupation, but number four looked derelict. Its windows were boarded up. There was no company name. Patches of rust were showing through the peeling paint on the metal cladding. And there was only one vehicle – a jade green Ford Focus – parked anywhere near.

As I moved closer I saw the Ford was occupied. Two people were sitting in the front seats. They were both men. It was easy to guess who they were. And after another ten yards, I could confirm it. They were the two guys who'd been sitting by the door at the hotel bar.

I continued in the shadows at the edge of the pavement until I was level with the car. Then I drew my Beretta with my right hand, took hold of the passenger door handle with my left, and pulled.

"Good evening, gentlemen," I said, in French. "You now have two choices. Put your hands on the steering wheel. Or be shot in the head."

Neither of the men made a move.

I tried again in German.

They were both stock still for another 20 seconds. Then the driver put first his left hand, then his right, on the wheel. The passenger followed suit, very slowly.

"Very good," I said, pulling two more flexicuffs from my pocket.

I dropped one in each guy's lap.

"You first, I said to the driver. "Cuff your friend's wrists together."

He did as I instructed.

"Now, you," I said to the passenger. "Take care of your friend. Make it good and tight."

He also complied without a word.

I checked the cuffs to make sure they were secure, then patted the guys down for weapons. They both had 9 mm pistols. A Ruger P-85, and a Colt 2000. I took the guns, tucked one into the waistband of my jeans, and slipped the other into my coat pocket. Then I took their phones, switched them off, and slid into the back seat behind the driver.

"Did you see a taxi drop two men at unit four in the last few minutes?" I said.

Neither of the men responded.

I jammed the barrel of my Beretta into the bone just below the driver's right ear, and repeated the question.

"All right," the driver said. "Yes. We saw the taxi."

"You followed it here?" I said.

"Yes."

"Why?"

"We were paid to."

"Seems like a good enough reason," I said. "Now, think about when it arrived. Describe exactly what happened."

The driver shrugged.

"It pulled up outside," he said. "The door to the

building opened. A man came out. The men got out of the taxi and went inside with him. Nothing dramatic."

"Did it sound its horn?" I said.

"No."

So someone had seen it arrive. They'd been watching.

"Was the man who came out armed?" I said.

"Yes."

"What with?"

"The usual. An AK."

That sounded like overkill, for the suburbs. But then, we were talking about drug dealers.

"How many people are inside?" I said.

"Don't know."

I increased the pressure on the Beretta.

"I don't know," the driver said.

"Is Kevin Truly inside?" I said.

"I don't know who that is. You think the people who pay us tell us their names?"

"Were you told to expect any other people or vehicles?"

"Yes. Another taxi. The two men are supposed to leave in one."

"At what time?"

"We weren't told a time."

"What else were you told to do?"

"Wait here. Make sure... never mind."

I gave him another prod.

"Make sure no one was snooping around," he said. "Stop anyone who tried. Call a number if there was a problem."

"What number?"

He reeled off a series of digits.

"Is that their regular number?" I said. "The one you

normally use to contact them?"

"No," he said. "It's just for this job. For problems, only. It changes every time."

"Well, there's certainly a problem now," I said. "And the bad news is, the window for calling numbers has closed for the day. But it's not all doom and gloom. There's still something left for you to do."

Neither of the men responded.

"In fact, three things. And they're all simple. First, I want you to drive up to the building and stop in exactly the same place the taxi did, earlier. Second, wait for thirty seconds. And third, if no one has come out by then, sound your horn. Two long blasts. No more. Is that clear?"

"Yes."

"Absolutely, crystal clear? Because you'll need to do a better job than you did of stopping me from snooping around."

"We're clear."

"Do those three things, and nothing else. Nothing to warn whoever's in that building that something is going on. Because if you deviate in any way at all - do you know what will happen?"

The driver pressed his head sharply back against the Beretta for a second.

"You've got it," I said, sliding down low behind the front seats. "Now let's go."

I slipped out of the car the moment it came to rest and moved backwards into the shadows until my shoulders touched the wall of the dilapidated building. The two guys remained in their seats, sitting still, staring straight ahead, and doing nothing to invite a bullet. I counted the seconds in my head. Ten. Fifteen. Twenty. Nothing stirred. We reached thirty. The driver raised his hands from his lap and started to reach for the centre of the steering wheel, but before he made contact I heard a harsh metallic squeal to my left and the door to the warehouse was flung back on its hinges. The side of the car was bathed in light. Boots crunched on gravel. A man appeared. He was a shade over six feet tall, broad, with a completely shaved head. The reflection of his face in the car window put him in his early forties. His clothes looked expensive - black Armani jeans and a ribbed, zip up sweater made from ultra fine cashmere. He was holding a radio in his left hand. And a folding-stock Kalashnikov in his right.

The man paused for a moment, then approached the car. I fell in step behind him, and just before he reached the driver's door I reached my right arm over his shoulder, wrapped it across the front of his body and grabbed a handful of soft wool just below his left armpit. My left arm snaked up from the other side. My hand looped all the way around to the back of his skull. It kept going till I brushed his ear. Then my fingers clamped down and I pulled back hard in the opposite direction till I heard the telltale crunch of a pair of his cerebral vertebrae being torn apart.

Fresh bodies are always awkward to move on your own. They're slack and floppy - before rigor sets in, anyway - and their weight seems to multiply tenfold. That one was particularly uncooperative. I couldn't get a decent grip on it, anywhere. Its arms and legs kept escaping. The head was almost uncontrollable. In the end I felt like it took me an hour to bundle it in through the rear doors of the car.

"Is that the same guy who met the taxi, earlier?" I said, finally moving round to the front and pulling out two more flexicuffs.

"I think so," the driver said, after taking a deep breath. "But wait. You can't leave..."

"Hands out," I said, feeding the tongue of the first cuff through the one binding his wrists, then looping it around the steering wheel.

"You too," I said to the passenger.

He didn't argue, so I secured him in the same way.

"Now listen," I said, taking the keys then reaching across and wrenching the rearview mirror off its mounting. "I'm going inside. You're staying here. And you're going to stay silent. You're going to make absolutely no noise at all. Because if I hear one single sound, I'll be back out. And you'll both be joining that guy on the back seat."

Chapter Two

The sentry's Kalashnikov had fallen next to the car during the scuffle so I retrieved it, used the mirror to make sure no one unfriendly was lurking on the other side of the door, and then stepped through into a corridor. It was wide enough for two people to walk side-by-side, and extended all the way to an emergency exit at the far side of the building. A line of doors was set into the left hand wall. There were five. They were unevenly spaced, and all were standing open. The first led to an empty room. I guessed it had been an office, based on the shapes of the worn patches on the lino. A pile of squashed cigarette butts lay on the floor next to the window, and I saw that the board covering the glass had been pried away at both lower corners. That was probably where the sentry had been keeping his watch, but there was no one else in the room, now.

The remaining four rooms - a kitchen, two bathrooms, and one other, perhaps a staffroom - were deserted as well. That only left a pair of double doors on the opposite side of the corridor. They were closed. A keypad dangled on its wires from the frame, so I was confident they weren't locked. I stood and listened for a moment. There was nothing to be heard, so I moved silently to the far end, then turned, took out the phone I'd taken from the driver, and dialed the emergency number he'd given me outside.

The call was answered on the first ring.

"Yes?" a man said, in German. "What?"

"Quickly," I said, whispering to make my voice less recognisable. "Six guys. Front of the building. All armed. Looks like they mean business."

"On our way," the man said, then the line went dead.

I switched the rifle to semi automatic - Kalashnikovs are famously reliable, but notoriously hard to control on full auto - and lay down on my front. Five seconds passed. Then the double doors burst open. Two men charged though and started racing away from me, towards the exit. They were tempting targets, but I waited. They covered half the distance to the outside world. Three quarters. Then two more men emerged, running hard, and I finally squeezed the trigger. Four times.

The nearer pair had no chance to react. The other two slowed down a little. The final one even managed to half turn around before the three shells hit him. That was more of a chance than they gave their 'customers,' I thought, as I blew the stinging cordite out of my nostrils.

The main warehouse was a broad rectangular space, maybe 5,000 square feet all in. The walls and roof were bare metal, with an exposed skeleton of beams and girders. There was no merchandise left. No boxes, or containers, or even debris. Whoever had cleared the place out had been thorough. But they'd also been in a hurry. They hadn't unbolted the redundant shelf legs from the floor. They'd just chopped them off about three inches above the surface, leaving scores of jagged L-shaped uprights sprouting from the concrete like the shoots of uniform metal plants.

The only item not physically attached to the ground was the table that held the two piles of drugs. It was standing at the exact centre of the giant room, almost glowing in a pool of moonlight that spilled through a jagged hole in the roof. Three people were in front of it. The two Marines. And Kevin Truly.

"Good evening, gentlemen," I said, approaching the group.

"Sir," the biker Marine said, stepping back from Truly but not lowering the gun.

"Any more of his friends around here?" I said.

"There was one outside in the corridor, sir. And the four who just went running out of here, a second ago."

"They're all accounted for. Seen anyone else?"

"Not inside, sir. But I think our cab was followed by two guys from the hotel bar. They might be around somewhere."

"They're outside. Not in a position to trouble anyone, though."

The Marines glanced at each other.

"So, then, what we do with him?" the Marine said, gesturing to Truly.

"He's coming with me," I said. "A couple of my people are waiting to chat with him."

"Couldn't we just... you know?"

"You know, what?"

"Slot the bastard. Get it over with. Here and now."

I took a long, hard look at the Marine, and then turned to his colleague.

"After what he's done to us?" the biker Marine said. "He deserves it."

"And it's his gun," the other one said. "It's not traceable to either of us."

For people trained to find swift, decisive solutions to problems like this, you could see how the idea would appeal to them. Specially when their heads were on the block, and he was the star witness against them. So for a second, part of me – a tiny part – wished I could just look the other way.

"Not a chance," I said.

"With due respect, sir, you've 'accounted for' what, seven of the bastards already, tonight?" the biker said. "What's one more?"

"Asked, and answered," I said.

Neither Marine spoke for a moment.

"What if he tried to make a run for it?" the other Marine said. "We'd have no choice, then."

"OK," I said. "Tell me this. Who else at the Embassy is involved in this?"

The Marines glanced at each other again, but this time neither one spoke.

"What was going to happen next?" I said. "More drug shipments?"

The biker Marine shrugged.

"Or was this one just to get the noose tighter around your necks?" I said. "So you'd give them, what? The Ambassador's home address? Floor plans of the Embassy? Details of VIP visits?"

"Forget it," the biker said. "We'd never give them stuff like that."

"Spare me," I said. "And something else. He didn't do this to you. You did it to yourselves, by acting like morons. Killing him serves no tactical purpose. Not like the people outside. So if you expect any kind of leniency from the Navy, you'll help me get this guy safely out of here. Are we clear?"

"Sir," both Marines said after long a pause, but their body language made it clear they weren't happy.

"Time to move," I said. "Get him on his feet."

"On your feet, arsehole," the biker Marine said to Truly.

Truly didn't move.

"Feel free to encourage him," I said.

The Marine stepped forward and jammed the toe of his motorcycle boot into Truly's left kidney. He squealed and pitched forward, saving himself just before his face hit the concrete. The Marine grabbed him by the collar, hauled him upright, and sent him stumbling towards the exit. I stepped back to avoid his flailing arms, and then something caught my eye. Movement. Above me. From the hole in the roof.

"Gun," the other Marine shouted, spotting the same thing.

I threw myself forward, crashing my shoulder into Truly and sending him flying. We hit the ground together. I landed on top of him and the impact dislodged a lungful of his foul cigarette-breath, pumping it straight into my face. A bullet hit the ground near my feet, right where Truly had been standing. I grabbed him and rolled, not wanting either of us to offer a static target. I heard three more shots. They were coming from my left. I looked round and saw the biker Marine holding Truly's Colt two-handed, aiming at the hole in the roof.

"Don't think I got him," he said. "He might be running. Shall I go and see?"

"No, stay where you are and give us cover," I said, pulling out the Ruger I'd taken from the guys in the car and throwing it to the other Marine, who was closer to the exit. "You, outside, quickly. Find him."

The echo of his footsteps died away and for a moment the warehouse was silent, except for the slight whimpering sound Truly made as I lifted my weight off his chest.

"Come on," I said to the biker. "Let's get this idiot out of harm's way."

Truly's legs only managed a weak wriggle when he tried to move so I leaned down to lift him.

"Careful," the Marine said as I pulled Truly to his feet. "He's hit. His face is covered with blood."

I couldn't think how. I counted the shots I'd heard, and replayed what had just happened in my mind. Then I became away of a familiar throb at the back of my head. And a warm stickiness spreading down my neck. I looked down at the ground and surveyed the stubs of metal left by the shelf legs. It wasn't obvious at first, because of the lack of light. But if you looked closely, you could just see the tip of the nearest one was darker than its neighbours.

"Don't worry," I said. "It's not his."

St Joseph's Hospital London
Patient Admission Record
This patient, a telecommunications consultant who appears to be in his mid-thirties, presented this morning having been driven by his boss from work. He is complaining of a blow to the head suffered on a business trip to Europe. He appears to be moderately disoriented and is unable to state clearly the circumstances of the accident, his date of birth, or his health service no. *He is not happy about being admitted and has repeatedly stated his intention to self-discharge.*
This is the second occasion within the last 6 months that the patient has suffered a moderate to severe blow to the head. It is therefore recommended that an MRI scan be carried out at the earliest opportunity to assess the risk of permanent brain injury.

Chapter Three

I've ended up needing treatment many times, over the years. It's an occupational hazard. But I'd never been hurt saving a drug dealer, before.

I've found myself in all kinds of different medical institutions. Huge teaching hospitals. Tiny, charitable clinics. Sick bays on ships. Even a veterinarian's office on one unfortunate occasion. But never anywhere as picture-perfect as St Joseph's. It was made up of four matching buildings. They dated from the early eighteenth century, according to a round blue sign I saw on my way to the MRI suite, and were arranged symmetrically around a rectangular garden. Three of the wings contained the patients' wards and private rooms, plus operating theatres and suites for all the specialist treatments the hospital offered. The other housed the kitchens, offices, meeting rooms, and stores.

I'm usually desperate to leave hospital before the doctors want me to. I even had to break out of one, once. But I'd never wanted to be cooped up for longer. Not until that morning, after a bored technician had taken two hours to fill his machine with little electronic slices of my brain. Because someone had taken that time and used some of it to slip into my room. Poke around in my locker. Spill my water. Search inside my pillowcases. Scrabble around under my bed. Rifle through my clothes. Toss my keys and empty wallet onto the floor. And skulk out again, unnoticed.

But whoever this person was, and wherever they went, they didn't leave empty handed. They took something with them. Something that didn't belong to them.

A pair of boots.

Grenson brogues. In black. They were nice to look at. The leather was supple, so they were comfortable to wear. Even for days at a time. And the toecaps were solid - almost as good as steel - which is essential in my line of work.

I'd bought the boots in London, the last time I was here for more than two nights in a row. That was three years ago, now. Since then I'd worn them on four continents. In fourteen countries. During twelve jobs. And there's plenty of life left in them, yet. Enough that I'd figured to keep them another couple of years, at least. Till they got too scruffy. Or I found something I liked better. But either way, I was going to make the decision when to change them. It wasn't going to be forced on me by some small-time sneak thief. Not at home, in England.

I want to be very clear about those boots. They weren't government issue. There were no secret gadgets hidden in their heels. They weren't needed as evidence in any high stakes trial. They were simply my boots. Chosen by me. Paid for by me. And now stolen by someone I'd been injured while protecting. Which meant those boots represented something more than footwear. They represented betrayal. And that's something I'm never going to take lying down.

There was a practical aspect to the theft, as well. Consider the circumstances. What was I supposed to do without boots? Wander into town in a pair of disposable slippers? Hospital footwear was good enough to get me to the admin wing, though. And, appropriately enough, the first office I came to belonged to the Head of Security. But there was a snag. His secretary spilled the beans within twenty seconds of me approaching her desk. It turned out the guy liked playing golf more than he liked doing his job. Specially when the weather was good. It was unheard of for him to show his face in the office when the sun was out, she said. That doesn't happen all that often in England, particularly in late autumn. But it was everyone's bad luck that for the second day running, the sky was blue. So, having verified that his room really was empty, I moved on to the next door in the corridor. It led to the Chief Executive's secretary's desk.

Only she was missing, too.

I'd imagine Chief Executives aren't generally too concerned about pilfered footwear, unless it's their own belongings that have gone missing, but the whole boot situation – robbed by one of the people I'd been hurt looking out for – was making my blood boil. So, I didn't waste any time. I went straight for the inner sanctum.

For a moment I thought this office was empty, too, but then I saw the top of a bald head peeping out from above a huge computer monitor that sat on a desk at the far end of the room. The head was strangely pointed, and as I moved closer I could see that its owner was surprisingly young. Probably no older than his late thirties. He was tapping away at a wireless keyboard, and made no effort to look away from his screen even when I would have been near enough to reach out and wipe away the tiny beads of sweat that covered his shiny scalp.

"You're in the wrong place," he said after another fifteen seconds, still without even glancing at me.

I turned back, took hold of a wooden chair that was tucked under an oval meeting table by the right hand wall, brought it over to the desk, and sat down.

"What are you doing?" he said. He was looking at me now, and struggling to contain a slight tick in the corner of his left eye. "Don't waste time making yourself comfortable. You're not supposed to be here."

"Why not?" I said.

"Because I'm not a doctor."

"You think I'm looking for a medic?"

"Well, let's see. You're wearing Health Service pyjamas, which means you're a patient. And you're in a hospital. What else could you want?"

I took a moment to look around at the walls of his office. They were lined with motivational posters. Seventeen of them. All neatly framed. And all utterly nauseating.

"You're the Chief Executive of this place?" I said.

"Well, let's see," he said. "This is the Chief Executive's office. And my name's on the door. So, the answer must be yes."

"Then tell me something. To become the boss of a whole hospital, do you go through some kind of training?"

He nodded, very slightly.

"And when you were doing this training, did you pick up anything about making assumptions?" I said.

He didn't respond.

"It's a straight-forward question," I said. "Did your tutors recommend assumption-making? Or not?"

"OK," he said, after a long pause. "Point taken. You have another reason to be here. Let me guess. You want to complain about something. Another dissatisfied patient who thinks he knows best. What is it this time? The food not tasty enough? Pyjamas not comfortable?"

Before I could reply I heard a noise, behind me. It was the door opening. Someone came through. They were wearing heels. I looked round and saw a woman approaching. In her early fifties, I'd say, with a long blue skirt, cream blouse, and auburn hair cut into a neat, symmetrical bob. She held my eye as she moved, and couldn't help drifting wide of my chair as she passed me, as if she was afraid I'd pass on some revolting disease.

"Found it," she said, handing the manila file she'd been carrying to the man behind the desk. I could see a logo on the front - the words Human Resources formed into a circle around the hospital crest - but not anyone's name.

"Sebastian had it?" he said.

"He did," she said. "Just as we thought. He was off-site today, but I had to wait for his assistant - that useless Julie - to nip out to Starbucks."

"They both denied having seen it. Idiots."

"They always do."

"It was in his bottom drawer?"

"Where else? And look," she said, pointing to a coffee stain on the folder's tattered front cover. "See the state it's in? It wasn't like that when we sent it back to them, last time."

"Well, that's the least of our worries," he said. "Good work, finding it. And Mags? Keep your ears open. Any more complaints about *you-know-who* - any incidents at all, however small - I want to know."

The woman started back towards the door, but stopped after one step.

"Your visitor," she said. "He doesn't have an appointment. Is he...? Or do you want me to...?"

"What do you think?" the man said, turning back to me. "Are you...?"

"Don't worry," I said, after a moment. "You clearly have bigger problems than me. Lost files. Coffee stains. The stuff nightmares are made of. I'll be getting out of your hair now. So to speak. And I'll find someone else to help me."

"Good idea," the man said. "Best of luck with that."

"I think I'll start with the police. I'm sure they'll be much more interested."

I wasn't even half way out of my chair before the man spoke again.

"Wait," he said. "You're calling the police? Here? To the hospital? Why? What's the problem?"

I lowered myself back down and met his gaze, but I didn't reply.

"Look, maybe we got off on the wrong foot," he said after a few seconds, then flashed me a sickly smile. "Why don't we start this conversation all over again? If there's a problem, I'd be more than happy to help. That's what I'm here for, at the end of the day. There's no need to go calling anyone else. So, please. Tell me what's wrong."

I didn't answer. His change of heart wasn't fooling anyone. I was inclined to just walk out and let him believe I was following through with the police. The local plod was unlikely to spring into action over a pair of stolen boots, obviously, but the prospect of a horde of uniforms descending on the place seemed to have got him pretty rattled. In another second I'd have been heading for the exit, but then my eyes were drawn to the poster above the man's head. It showed a huge shark about to snap up a tiny minnow, with the caption, "AMBITION - If you can't swim with the big fish, stay out of the water."

"Can we at least start with your name?" he said.

I decided to stay. Partly to give him the chance to atone for the posters. But mainly because old habits die hard. I wanted to see why he was so worried about the police.

"David Trevellyan," I said, after a moment, and went on to explain the problem with the missing Grensons. He listened carefully, without interrupting, and looked increasingly confident as I went along.

"OK," he said, when I'd finished. "No worries. I have people who can take care of this for you, quite easily. Mags, could you get Stan on the phone for me, please?"

"Um, Mr Leckie is out of the office today," she said. "A very urgent family situation unexpectedly cropped up, again, I understand."

"This is the Head of Security we're talking about?" I said.

The man gave nothing away.

"Because I heard all about his urgent situation," I said. "It was him I originally went to see."

"Well, it's nothing to worry about," the man said. "Mags, can you get Lydia for me, instead?"

The woman nodded and made her way back out to her own desk, once again keeping a wide berth as she skirted around me.

"Lydia's our Deputy Security Chief," he said. "She's very thorough. This kind of thing is more in her remit, anyway. Probably better that she handles it, in reality."

"I'm putting her through," the woman said from the outer office, and after another split second the man's phone began to ring.

"Ready?" he said, pressing a button. "I'm putting her on loudspeaker."

"Lydia McCormick," a younger woman's voice said, sounding tinny and disembodied through the low-quality equipment.

"Lydia, this is Mark Jackson," the man said. "I'm here with one of our patients, a Mr David Trevellyan."

I didn't correct him.

"David's staying in one of the observation rooms on B wing, and he has some concerns over the security of personal possessions in that area," he said.

"What kind of concerns?" she said. "Can he be more specific?"

"Theft," I said.

"Then there's no need to worry," she said. "There have been no thefts reported from any of our primary patient accommodation units in over eighteen months. None at all since I've been here, in fact."

"Well, there's been one now," I said.

"When?" she said, above the distant rattling of a computer keyboard. "I can't see any record of anything."

"There won't be a record yet," the man said. "That's why David's here. His boots were stolen from his room this morning, apparently. While he was in the MRI suite. So we do at least have a clear window of time to focus on. He's understandably upset about this - and I'm disturbed about it too - so I'd like you to look into it, Lydia. As a matter of urgency."

"Of course," she said. "I'll jump on it straight away. Can you just tell me what happened to the S103, though? I'll need someone to track it down, and get it on the system as quickly as possible."

"What's an S103?" I said.

"It's our basic Security Incident reporting form," she said. "You have completed one?"

"No, I haven't," I said.

"Do you have a copy over there, at least?" she said.

"No." I said. "I've never set eyes on one."

"Well, that's not a problem," she said. "Just ask Mags to print one out for you - she can pull one off the intranet - then ask her to whizz it over to me once you've filled it out, and I'll get the wheels in motion."

"What information do you need for this form?" I said.

"Oh, not much," she said. "It's not hard. Just the basics. What happened. Where. When. Brief descriptions will be fine."

"I've already told you more than that," I said. "I've detailed exactly what happened. And given you a precise description of the boots."

"I know," she said. "But that was an oral report. We need it on paper."

"What other questions are on the form?" I said.

"Oh, none really," she said. "There's not much to it."

"So if you already have the information, and the form doesn't give you anything new, why do you need it?" I said.

"Because we need the form itself," she said. "That's what kicks the process into gear. We can't move without one."

"Why not?" I said. "Why can't you start now?"

"Because we don't have the form," she said.

"But the form doesn't tell you anything you don't already know," I said. "It's pointless."

"It isn't pointless," she said. "It's the start of the process. There's no case without one. Nothing for us to work with."

"OK," I said. "How about this. You make a start now, before the trail goes completely cold, and I'll get the paperwork across to you as soon as I can."

"No," she said. "I need the form first. That's how the system works. We can't do anything without one. We can't be fully accountable, otherwise."

"Mark?" I said, looking directly at the man on the other side of the desk. "This is crazy. Help me out, here."

The man put both hands over his face and then pulled them sideways for a moment, spreading his skin and stretching his eyes into narrow slits.

"Sorry," he said, letting go of his cheeks again. "If my Deputy Head of Security says we need a Form S103 before we begin, then we need a Form S103 before we begin."

"Thank you, Mark," she said. "It isn't hard to fill in, Mr Trevellyan. And believe me, nothing can be done without one."

"Is that right?" I said, standing up to leave.

"Where are you going?" the man said.

"Back to my room," I said. "I feel like I might need a second assessment for my head wound, after all. I'm going to get that taken care of, then see about what you've been telling me."

"Sounds like a plan," the man said. "Let me know if there's anything more I can do. Lydia - anything to add before Mr Trevellyan leaves us?"

"No, nothing else from me," she said, then there was a click, and her voice was replaced by a harsh, grating dial tone.

"Well David, I'd like to thank you for coming in," the man said, pressing a button on his phone and shutting off the irritating noise. "I appreciate the chance to clear this matter up. I'm sure you'll be satisfied with the outcome - Lydia really is good at what she does - and I'm glad she was able to clarify the process for you. Good luck with the rest of your treatment. And please, check back with me at any time."

I turned my back and walked away, thinking that Mark Jackson had actually been right. The conversation with Lydia really had clarified things for me. But probably not in the way he'd expected. Because from the moment she'd mentioned the S103, I'd been absolutely certain about one fact.

No one in that place was going to give me any meaningful help. So, if I ever wanted to see those boots again, I was going to have to get them back by myself.

Chapter Four

It took a full quarter of an hour for me to retrace my steps through the hospital's maze of colour-coded corridors, but when I reached my room I found that someone had at least come by and cleared up the mess while I'd been gone. I hit the button to call for a nurse, and with nothing else to do while I waited, lay on the bed and flicked through a dozen channels of daytime television. I rejected the soap operas straight away. And the quizzes. There were no news or current affairs programmes to be found. A cooking competition seemed vaguely promising for a while, but I finally settled on a talk show where a seventy-year-old man was being taken to task for sleeping with his thirty something sister-in-law. The host was adamant this was wrong, but the guy himself was standing his ground. He insisted he was entirely justified. He'd already got his third wife's teenage daughter pregnant, after all. And with the girl temporarily off-limits, how else were his prodigious needs to be met? The audience was still grappling with that one when his wife made her entrance. Things were shaping up nicely, but before I could see whether she would make good on her threat to kill him with her bare hands, there was a knock on my door. It was time to be a patient again.

The nurse - the same one who'd admitted me that morning - stayed in my room for twenty minutes. Fifteen for her to re-appraise my condition and take note of my dramatic decline. And five for me to subtly pick her brains about the whereabouts of any other new arrivals. Because it seemed to me that anyone with a mind to help themselves to other people's property would want to get in early, while the richest pickings were still available. Like they'd done to me. So if I wanted to track them down, the new patients' rooms would be a good place to start. Which was fine, in theory. It only had one snag. The nurse told me that no one else had been brought in for four days. And as the unit only catered for trauma patients, it wasn't possible to predict when any more would arrive. Unless I went out and bashed someone over the head, I thought, but that seemed a little extreme. I kept on pressing, but the best lead she could give me was that there were only two empty rooms left. They were both at the far end of the corridor below mine.

The rooms were easy to find. They were opposite one another, and you could tell they were still not being used because their doors were propped open and you could look inside. The nurse had told me they always filled these ones last, because their location made them the least convenient for the staff to reach. But that also made it impossible for me to stake them out. There was no cover of any kind. Any potential thieves would see me a mile off, so I decided to scour the rest of the hospital for anything useful, then come back and check on developments.

One area I didn't have a clear picture of was the top floor of the admin wing. The MRI technician had mumbled something about steering clear of it, so I decided to head there next. I thought his warning referred to boredom when I peered through the first few doors. An abandoned classroom, choked with dust. Two storerooms, with half their shelves left empty. A cupboard, full of filing boxes. And then I found what he must have really meant. Tucked away in the far corner, hidden behind an unmarked door, was a kind a macabre museum full of grotesque anatomical specimens in ancient glass jars.

A breath of fresh air seemed like a good idea in the circumstances, so I made my way to the nearest exit and stepped outside into the garden. The ground was strewn with twigs and branches. There must have been a storm recently. A big one, judging by the amount of debris. I hadn't known anything about it. Maybe it had happened when I was over in Luxembourg. Or before that, in Tokyo. But either way it had passed me by. The thought made me strangely uncomfortable so I made for one of the benches that lined the path around the centre of the lawn and perched on the edge, suddenly feeling sickened, and almost light headed. If I was unaware of something simple, like the state of the weather in my home city, what else was I in the dark about? What else was I missing about the place? And what about the people? What was going on with them? Was I perpetually bouncing from country to country, putting myself in harm's way on their behalf, just so they could rob each other blind? Steal from me? Fill their veins with drugs? Or carry on like the family on that TV show?

I woke up in the dark. I was lying on my back. On a bed, but not under the covers. Still wearing my pyjamas and slippers. My head was back to normal, and no other parts of me were showing any signs of damage, so I sat up and waited for my night sight to adjust. Objects and shadows gradually took shape around me, and after a couple of minutes I realised I was back in my hospital room. I tried to focus, and managed to coax a few vague pictures out of my recent memory. I was fairly certain I could recall getting up from the bench in the garden. Picking my way through the detritus. Coming in through the main entrance to the north building. Hauling myself up two flights of stairs. Drifting down the corridor, making doubly sure I selected the right door. And doing something else. What was it? The curtains. For some reason I'd closed them before lying down. I felt my way across to the window and tugged them apart again. They must have been thicker than I'd realised because with the street lights on it turned out to still be fairly bright outside. I turned and checked the clock on the wall above the bed. It was ten past six in the evening. I'd only been asleep for around an hour. That wasn't too serious. And it wasn't too late. There was time to nip downstairs, check the vacant rooms, and still be back in time for dinner. If there was anything on the menu worth eating.

I could tell from the second I stepped into the lower corridor that something was different. The shadows at the far end had changed. One of the doors - the one on the left - had been closed. No one else was around so I approached, silently. I heard a voice from inside. A woman's. Then another woman answered it. I didn't recognise either one. A nurse, perhaps, or a doctor, speaking to a patient? A reasonable guess, I thought, but I had no way of knowing for sure. Not without seeing them. And I couldn't afford for them to spot me, so I slipped into the empty room opposite, closed the door, and stooped down far enough to fit my eye to the peephole.

Nothing happened for eleven minutes, then the door I was watching swung open. A woman shuffled into the corridor. She was a nurse, but not the one who'd helped me, earlier. She took one step to her left and stopped, staring into the distance. Another thirty seconds ticked away, then she moved back and a man appeared. He was in his mid twenties, I'd guess. Thirty at the outside. It's hard to be precise through a fish-eye lens. He was wearing a porter's uniform. The material was faded and the trousers looked too tight in several places, but he didn't seem concerned about it. The pair conferred for a minute, then disappeared into the room.

They were out of sight for less than a minute. The nurse re-appeared first. She positioned herself near the hinges and reached back into the room to stop the door from closing. Then I saw the porter again. And realised why the nurse had waited for him. The person I'd heard her talking to was using a wheelchair, and she wanted someone to help push it. But the patient's condition wasn't relevant. The important thing was - she was a new arrival.

All I had to do now was wait for the thief to show his face. That wouldn't be too hard. Waiting is one thing I've had a lot of practice at. It's easier than chasing. And that night, I was in luck. Because it took less than four minutes for my trap to spring shut.

I saw a man enter the room across the corridor. He was also dressed as a porter. Only his uniform was subtly different from the guy's who'd been pushing the wheelchair. The material was in better condition. It looked brand new, in fact. It had no hospital logos. And it fitted him way too well.

I guessed from the mess he'd made in my room that the thief would only be inside for a couple of minutes, so I didn't waste any time. And it wasn't like I needed to catch him in the act. All I wanted was to get my boots back. I was planning to have the same conversation with him regardless of what he was doing when I walked through the door. So the fact that I found him sitting in a visitor's chair, fiddling with the combination on a black leather briefcase was of no concern to me at all.

The fact that he pulled a Sig Sauer pistol from his overall pocket a second later was a different story altogether. A P226. It looked clean. Factory fresh, even. A nice weapon. I remember thinking it was a little extravagant for a low level burglar even as I kicked it out of his hand. It flew across the room and crashed against something metal - maybe the radiator - but I kept my eyes locked on the man. I was worried he'd pull out a knife or a backup piece. But that didn't seem to cross his mind. There was no hesitation. He just dropped the briefcase and came at me with his fists, relentlessly combining flurries of sharp jabs and hooks.

I carried on moving and blocking, trying to frustrate him and wear him down, until he finally pulled away about eighteen inches. He dropped his head and let his shoulders slacken, but I also saw him shift his balance. It was a feint. I guessed he was looking to change tack and catch me with a kick so I stepped aside, then as he came forward I moved straight back in and swept his standing leg. He crashed down onto his back and immediately rolled to his left. But he wasn't just trying to get away. He was trying to retrieve the Sig. He landed with his fingertips two inches from the grip and started to wriggle frantically forward so, short of options, I snatched up the chair he'd been sitting on and smashed it down across the back of his head.

The guy was left completely still. He was touching the gun with his right hand, and his upper body was surrounded with splintered fragments of the chair's wooden frame. Only its seat remained intact, and that had come to rest upside down near the foot of the bed. Someone had drawn a frowning face on the underneath in white chalk. I knew how they felt. Because my chances of asking any questions had been pretty much destroyed, too, along with the furniture. There was no hope of the guy waking up before anyone raised the alarm, with the amount of noise that had been made. Lydia McCormick would try to bury me with her forms. And the police would have a field day, as soon as they heard about the firearm. My only hope was to find something that I could follow up on my own, like a name or address or phone number, then make myself scarce. I could see the guy's wallet peeping out from one of his pockets. I figured that would be a good place to start, so I reached down and worked it free. And at exactly the same moment, I heard the door crash open, behind me.

I'd expected to see a hospital security guard standing there, or possibly a medic. But I was wrong. It was the woman in the wheelchair. She was on her own this time, with no sign of a real porter to push her.

"Evening," I said. "Is this your room? Sorry about the mess. Things got a little out of hand."

"A little?" she said, looking at the guy's prostrate body.

"It's not as bad as it looks. We'll soon get everything cleaned up."

"I don't think we'll soon do anything. What are you doing here?"

"Well, I just was passing by and saw this chap trying to steal your briefcase. So I stopped him."

"Really?" the woman said as she wheeled herself forward, coming fully into the room. "I don't believe you. So let's try this, instead. I want you face down, on the ground. Fingers laced behind your head. Legs spread. And I want you there right now."

"I beg your pardon?" I said.

"You heard."

"You're right. I did hear. Only I was expecting something more along the lines of a 'thank you' for stopping your stuff from being taken."

"He wasn't trying to take anything. And you're the one holding somebody else's wallet in your hand. So, get on the ground. Face down. Now."

"OK. Maybe I should try a different question. Such as, why would I want to do a thing like that?"

"You took the wallet from the man on the floor?"

"I did. I was looking for some ID."

"Then go ahead. Look inside."

I was curious, so I looked. I found six credit cards. Two ten pound notes. An Oyster card, for the London

Underground. And an official identity card.

"See that?" she said. "Read the name."

"Timothy Jones," I said.

"No. The name at the top. His employer."

"The Security Service."

"Correct. He's an MI5 Intelligence Officer."

I didn't respond.

"Have you seen one of those cards before?" she said.

I didn't answer.

"I have one just like it," she said. "Do you want to see that, too?"

"Not especially," I said.

"Are you surprised?"

"A little."

"Do you like surprises?"

"Not really."

"Well that's a shame. Because I've got three more for you. Tell me when you're ready."

I said nothing.

"One," she said anyway, and pulled a matching Sig from beneath the folds of her sweater. "Ready for the next one?"

I shrugged.

"Two," she said, effortlessly standing up and stepping away from the wheelchair. "Don't worry. It's not a miracle. And the next?"

"Why not?" I said.

"Good sport," she said, pulling a pair of handcuffs from her belt and dangling them off her left index finger. "Guess who these are for?"

Chapter Five

The MI5 agent was about five foot eight when she wasn't sitting in the wheelchair. She was wearing dark skinny jeans with black ankle boots - flat enough to run in - and a long grey sweater that was sufficiently baggy to hide the holster for her sidearm. There was no sign of any jewellery. Curly blonde hair reached down beyond her shoulders. She wore no make-up, and her face looked like it could be quite pretty if she hadn't been scowling so vigourously.

I let her cuff me - she was still holding a Sig, after all - and I didn't interfere when she called a medevac team for her partner. It was a little ironic, given that we were in a hospital, but I knew she wouldn't be ready to drop her cover just yet. I also knew what her next move would be. To summon a snatch squad to spirit me out of there, and without any ID it was the devil's own job to convince her I was from Royal Navy Intelligence and that we were on the same side. The best I could do was persuade her to hold off calling the cavalry until she'd at least run my code words past her liaison duty.

"Wait by the wall," she said, eventually, then prodded a number of keys on her phone before holding it to her ear.

Someone answered inside ten seconds, and it took her another minute to pass on her request. Then she raised the gun and held it steady, centred on my chest, while the person at the other end ran the necessary checks. She was silent for another three minutes, occasionally glancing down at the guy on floor. He was twitching slightly now, and moaning quietly to himself. She took a step towards him but stopped abruptly, concentrating on the phone again, then lowering the Sig to her side.

"You're to go to your room," she said, ending the call and retrieving the handcuff key from her pocket. "Don't go anywhere, and don't contact anyone. They're going to talk about us, your people and mine. They don't want anyone disappearing. And they don't want anyone muddying the water."

Julie Smith, the nurse who'd admitted me, was standing in my room when I got back. I opened the door and the initial look of panic on her face turned to anger when she saw it was me.

"And where do you think you've been?" she said. "Do you think I've got time to hang around patients' rooms, waiting for them to decide whether to show up?"

"Sorry," I said. "I didn't realise you were coming back, tonight."

"I told you I was."

"Really? I don't remember. And the truth is, I've got a bit of a problem."

"I'm sure you do."

I took two halting, half steps backwards then sat down heavily on the bed, my right hand settling against my temple for a couple of seconds before I let it fall back to my side.

"Are you OK?" she said.

"Not really," I said.

"How are you feeling? Can you describe it to me?"

"Tired. Absolutely exhausted. It just came over me. I feel like I need to sleep for a week."

The nurse's hands didn't move from her hips but her head tipped slightly to the side, she let out a long, slow, breath, and the harsh expression on her face began to gradually soften.

"Heightened fatigue is perfectly normal in these situations, Mr Trevellyan. Your body's trying to repair itself. That takes a lot of energy. So try not to fret. Everything will sort itself out, in time. And for now, we'll keep a really good eye on you. At least you're back in the right place."

"Thank you. I do appreciate the care you're taking of me. But now, I really need to get off to sleep."

"You're probably right. But let's have a look at you, first. Best to be sure, you know."

"Couldn't we leave that till morning? I'm honestly fit to drop."

"No," she said, reaching for the chart which was hanging from the foot rail of the bed. "I've got to do your obs' now. Those are the rules. Now come on. Play along, and I'll be as quick as I can."

Nurse Smith was true to her word. She wasted no time with her poking, prodding, and scribbling. But fast as she was with her observations, I was faster to grab my phone from the bedside table drawer the second the door closed behind her.

There was a knock on my door at 9.35 the next morning, but it wasn't one of the nurses coming to check on me. It was the MI5 agent. She was back in her wheelchair. Her blonde hair was straighter than before, making it appear slightly longer. The blue of her eyes seemed a little more pronounced. A hint of lavender and bergamot washed over me as she opened the door. And surprisingly after last night, I saw she was smiling.

"Question for you," she said, from just inside the doorway. "Destiny. Do you know what determines it?"

"That's profound for this time of the morning," I said. "Do they serve coffee early, on your floor?"

"Coffee, no. And it's not so profound, either. The answer, apparently, is 'the choices we make, and the chances we take.'"

"Oh, OK. I'm with you. And I'm getting a vision. An old rowing boat, painted white, tied up on a deserted sandy beach. Crystal clear water lapping against its picturesquely weathered sides. Some kind of weird big rock in the background..."

"In a cheap, cheesy frame, hanging over a visitors' table."

"Exactly. So, you've had the pleasure of an audience with Mr name-on-the-door Jackson as well?"

"I have," she said, resting her hands in her lap. "First thing this morning. I got the job of smoothing over the rumpus about that spontaneously self-collapsing chair, since its suicide occurred in my room. That wasn't the kind of low-profile insertion my people were hoping for. They wanted me to throw a couple of buckets of iced water around, if you know what I mean. Make sure none of the neighbours were getting too nosey."

"Were you successful?"

"Time will tell. And don't worry – I kept your name out of it. Can I come in?"

"Be my guest."

"So I'm told you're here because you're sick," she said, crossing to the foot of the bed and unhooking the clipboard that held my charts.

"Injured, actually, rather than sick," I said. "See for yourself."

"This looks convincing enough," she said, studying the papers.

I shrugged.

"One more question for you," she said. "What were you doing in my room, last night? I mean, what were you really doing?"

"I saw that guy go in. Jones. I followed him. I thought he was a thief."

"The elusive boot thief, perhaps?"

"You know about that?"

"I took a peep at Jackson's email while I was waiting for him to turn up, just now. There was one from a woman called Lydia. She was refusing to officially record the theft - alleged theft - of your boots because you wouldn't fill in some form."

"According to her, if it's not down in black and white, it didn't happen."

"So, your boots get stolen and you do what? March barefoot all the way to the CEO himself. You don't think you could have been over-reacting, just the tiniest bit?"

"There was no one else around to talk to."

"This isn't some elaborate cover for what you're really doing here?"

"No. They were just nice boots. I wanted them back."

"Listen, David. Your name actually is David? Please. I'm in a bind, here. We both could be. The people above us may not play well with others, but that doesn't mean we can't. We're the ones at the sharp end. And we both have reasons to be here. They could be separate. Or they could overlap. Yes? So I'd like to know. I don't need specifics. But tell me - should I be looking over both shoulders, now? Or only one?"

"Only one," I said, after a moment.

"Really?"

"Really. I'm here because I hurt myself. I was busy making a serious mess of someone else's day when a metal spike did the same thing to my head. So now, I'm waiting for test results. I'm not working. And I'm not going to interfere with what you're doing - whatever that may be - in any way."

"Are you sure? Cause you pretty much interfered the hell out of Tim."

"That was an accident. He was in disguise. I didn't know who he was."

"Some accident. The guy's young. He's fully fit, and he finished top of his class in training school. Which means I'm struggling to see someone with brain damage demolishing him in two seconds flat."

"It took longer than two seconds."

The agent didn't reply.

"Look, the truth is, I don't have brain damage" I said. "And I may have prolonged my stay here a little because I want my boots back. It's outrageous they were stolen, given how I got here, and the hospital suits won't do anything to help. But that's all."

"Give me your word on that?" she said.

"I do."

She didn't look convinced.

"OK," I said. "If you don't believe me, look around for those boots. Any footwear, in fact. If you can find a single thing in this room I could wear on my feet, you can call me a liar."

She glanced at the locker at the side of the bed, then shook her head.

"It's all right," she said. "I do believe you."

"Thank you," I said. "And I'm sorry about your guy, Jones. I didn't mean to hurt him. I wouldn't have, if I'd known who he was. How's he doing, anyway? Will he be OK?"

"Don't worry. He'll be fine in a little while. He'll recover, and he'll have learned a useful lesson."

"And I'm sorry for throwing a spanner into whatever you're working on."

"Thanks. I'm trying to keep the lid on a powder keg here, and flying spanners are the last things I need. Plus I've been stuck with mentoring Tim. That's another reason I was a little crabby last night. I hate baby-sitting. Specially when the baby ends up in Intensive Care."

There was a sharp knock at the door before I could reply.

"Come in," I said, reluctantly. I was enjoying the conversation, and I wanted to find out more about what she was doing at the hospital. Hints about powder kegs with loose lids can have that effect.

The agent broke eye contact as the door swung open and a nurse I'd not seen before stepped into the room.

"It's me, Suzanne," the nurse said. "And you have a visitor, I see."

"Don't mind me," the agent said. "I can't hang around, anyway. Just one more question for you, though, David, before I go. Your boots. If you got them back, would you hang around?"

"Are you joking?" I said. "You wouldn't see me for dust."

Chapter Six

The new nurse held the door for the agent until she'd negotiated her way back into the corridor, then strode over to the bed and started her routine mauling. She was alarmingly enthusiastic.

"Your temperature's OK," she said, making a note on my chart. "Blood pressure's a little low, but nothing to worry about. Same for heart rate. Now let's talk about what really matters. Your head. How is it? Have you had any pain?"

"I had a pretty bad headache last night," I said, thinking back to the conversation I'd had with my control once Nurse Smith had left me alone. They appreciated the heads-up, I suppose, but that didn't outweigh their irritation at having to mend fences with MI5. "It's a little better now, but it hasn't quite gone away completely."

"That's understandable. And what about nausea? Have you been feeling sick at all?"

"I had one pretty bad episode," I said, picturing myself surrounded by Jackson's display of management-speak posters.

"And did you actually throw up?"

"Not quite. I managed to restrain myself."

"You shouldn't do that, you know. If you feel like vomiting, your body's telling you something. You shouldn't hold back. If there's something bad in there, it needs to come out."

"I'll remember that, next time," I said, suppressing a smile as I pictured how that would go down with Jackson's prim secretary.

"Any memory loss, while you've been here?"

"Not that I'm aware of."

"That's a difficult question to answer, isn't it? How do you know you've forgotten something, until you've remembered it again? Or someone reminds you? But still, it's important, so anything like that, we need to know. Now, concentration. How are you finding that?"

"Sorry, what was the question?"

"Concentration. Have you - oh. I see. Never mind. So, what's next? Your sight. Any problems with focussing, field of vision, anything like that?"

"I feel like I've maybe had a bit of tunnel vision since I've been here," I said, thinking about my missing boots. Then the MI5 agent's intense, worried face floated into my mind. "Although, that might be easing a little, now."

"Good. Now, one last thing. And don't take offence at this, but you're a man, so I want you to take a moment and think before you answer. I want you to be honest. It's about your emotions. Don't deny having any. I know you do. So just think, and tell me if you've had any mood swings in the last twenty-four hours. Or if you've felt angry. Or frustrated. Or even just a little bit cranky."

The truth was I had been pretty irritable since I'd got there - with the betrayal over my boots, and having to deal with the unhelpful Jackson and obstructive Lydia. And the way I felt had suddenly changed, as well - since this morning's encounter with the MI5 agent. So this time when I answered, I wasn't just angling to be kept in the hospital.

"Yes," I said, after a suitable delay. "I think so. All of the above."

Suzanne scribbled deliberately on the chart for another couple of minutes, then hung the clipboard back in its place. But instead of leaving like the other nurses had done at that stage, she crossed to the window and gazed out across the square. Thirty seconds passed in silence, then she started talking. About the storm, and the damage it had caused. About her children. Her husband. Their neighbourhood. The TV shows she liked. Where she'd been on holiday. On and on, until a quarter of an hour had dragged by. I was beginning to wonder if it was some kind of technique to assess my mental state - seeing how long I could stand her babble before strangling her and hiding the body in a laundry cart - when someone tapped on the door, breaking her off mid sentence.

"Who is it?" I said, before she could get back into her stride.

The door opened and a man stepped into the room. I'd guess he was probably in his late sixties. He was tall - around six foot three - with immaculately combed silver hair, an elegant, plain grey three piece suit, and black Oxford shoes that were polished like crystal. If someone had told me he was an ex-Guards officer I wouldn't have been surprised. He paused to gently close the door, and when he turned back to face me I saw he was holding a green plastic bag in his right hand, low down by his side.

"Would you by any chance be Lieutenant-Commander Trevellyan, sir?" he said, looking straight ahead.

"I would," I said, glancing at Suzanne to see if she reacted to the way he'd addressed me.

"In that case, I have a delivery for you," he said, handing me the bag.

"Thank you," I said, relieved that she was just staring out of the window again, not paying much attention. "Who's it from?"

"I have no idea, sir. Perhaps there's a note inside the package? Such an arrangement is customary, I believe."

"Very kind of you to point that out. That's the first

place I'll check."

"Very good, sir," he said, reaching back for the door handle. "Now if there's nothing else, I really must excuse myself."

"What are you waiting for?" Suzanne said, the moment the door had shut behind him. I guess she had been listening after all, but if she was more interested in the parcel than me, then I was happy. "Open it. Open it. What's inside? Let me see."

The bag contained a white cardboard box, five inches by eleven by fourteen. Three quarters of the lid was covered by a logo - a stylised Tudor rose with a capital 'G' in the centre - and on both long sides the words 'Grenson, England 1866' were printed in bold red ink. I opened it and unfolded a double layer of tissue paper. There was a brand new pair of boots nestling beneath it. They were black leather. Lace up. With a classic brogue pattern.

"Oh, they're lovely," Suzanne said. "Are they like the ones you lost?"

"Almost identical," I said, checking to see if the design had changed much over the years. "Only mine were stolen, not lost."

"I bet they were expensive. Does it say who they're from?"

By now I had a pretty good idea, but I fished out a little card that had slipped down between the tissue and the side of the box, just to be sure.

I hope these help you get back on your feet. Best wishes, M. PS - check your phone.

"Who's M?" Suzanne said.

That was a good question, I thought. How should I answer? Assuming I was right, I could tell her it was the woman she'd just seen in the wheelchair. Hint that she was an MI5 agent. Or just say it was someone trying to do a difficult job, which I'd inadvertently made worse.

It took another five minutes of grunted 'yes's and 'no's before Suzanne finally left and I could get to the drawer and retrieve my phone. A single text icon was bouncing around the screen. The message was from my control. It said he wanted to talk. Immediately.

The signal in my room was weak so it actually took three attempts to reach him.

"Trevellyan?" he said with only a trace of last night's annoyance in his voice when we were finally connected. "How's the head?"

"Not too bad," I said. "Not quite one hundred percent, yet, but it's getting there. Thank you."

"Wrong answer."

"I beg your pardon?"

"Your head isn't improving. It's getting worse. You'll have to stay in the hospital. And the medics can't put their finger on the problem, so you could be there for a while."

Had he somehow heard about my boots? Normally the prospect of open-ended incarceration would fill me with gloom, but this sounded like excellent news.

"Worse?" I said. "OK. I can do that. Only, what's the real story?"

"Remember the girl from Box, from last night?" he said.

Box is inter-service slang for MI5, based on their wartime address – PO Box 500, London.

"Yes," I said. "Why?"

"Well, after your inadvertent introduction, our two head-sheds have been talking," he said. "And the long and short is - they want to borrow you."

"What if I don't want to be borrowed?"

"Let me rephrase. They're borrowing you."

"I see. It's like that. OK. But why? And how long for?"

"For as long as they want you. They think one of their people might have been to Cambridge, so they want some eyes they can trust from the outside."

Going to Cambridge is MI5 slang for turning traitor after Anthony Blunt, Kim Philby and co. were recruited by the NKVD – the forerunner of the KGB – when they were students there in the 1930s.

"And they're putting me in the middle of it?" I said.

"It makes sense," he said. "You're on the scene. You've got a reason to stay there. They're a body down, thanks to you. And infiltration's your specialty."

"It is my specialty. Which is why this makes no sense at all. You can only infiltrate a group if everyone in it takes you at face value. This girl knows exactly who I am. She's no fool. There's no way she'll confide in me, and she'll not incriminate herself with me watching. Even assuming her hands are dirty, which they might not be. No. What they need here is Internal Investigations."

"They want you."

"This won't work. It's a mistake. I'm the wrong man for the job."

"Why are you talking as if you have a choice?"

I didn't reply.

"Look, I know this isn't ideal," he said. "It'll no doubt be awkward. You'll have to improvise. But since you set foot in that hospital, you've done more harm than good. This is your chance to atone. And given what you did to their man, frankly, you're getting off lightly."

"OK," I said, after a moment. "I'll bow to the inevitable. So what happens from here? What's the rest of the story?"

"I've got no idea. It's not my department. You're to liaise with their girl. She'll fill you in."

"OK. I'll talk to her."

"Good. Only, David - one last thing. You're probably right about this girl. She probably won't open up to you, but we don't know anything about her. I'm trying to dig up some background, and in the meantime, watch your back. Their brass is ready to ask for help, remember. What does that tell you?"

"Someone's closet is about to burst open."

"Exactly. So just make sure the skeletons don't land on you. Whoever they belong to."

I hung up, and bundled the boots back into their box, ready to leave the room. They still looked nice. But after that phone conversation, I wouldn't be able to look at the agent in the same way. Not now that I had to work with her. Watch her, to see if she was a traitor. Maybe end her career. Or even her life.

It made me think that why she'd sent the boots was a more relevant question than who had sent them. Could it be something to clear the air, after last night's fight? An indication of the kind of influence she could bring to bear, ahead of us working together? Or a little demonstration that I was playing on her turf, and she was planning to call the shots?

The only way to find out would be to talk to her. I didn't have her number so I made my way down to her corridor and walked to the far end. The door to her room was closed, and there was no reply when I knocked. I thought about waiting in the room opposite, which was still vacant, but decided against it. The sickly disinfectant smell that hung in the hospital air was making me queasy, so if I had to hang around anywhere, I wanted it to be outside.

I'd planned to return to the bench I'd used yesterday, but when I reached the garden I quickly changed my mind. Three people were sprawling all over the one next to it. They were all male, in their early twenties. Their jeans were ripped and stained, and their T-shirts were covered with vulgar slogans and logos of bands I'd never heard of. Their pale, pointy heads were shaved. They were making enough noise for a dozen people. And even though it was still morning, they were already acting like they were drunk. Crumpled beer cans lay in a broad circle around them. I counted thirteen. Then the tallest of the group added a fourteenth as I settled on the bench furthest away from them.

"What're you looking at?" he said, when he realised I was watching him.

I stayed silent, but held his gaze until he eventually looked away.

The sun was shining weakly through the light, fluffy clouds. It wasn't warm, but it would still have been a pleasant morning if I'd had the garden to myself. Or to share with people I'd chosen to be with. Although, if I was honest about it, there weren't very many of those left.

"Oy!" a male voice said, breaking my chain of thought.

A man had entered the garden from the opposite side and was gesturing half-heartedly at the three lads. He was wearing a uniform, of sorts. A security guard's. From a private company rather than the hospital itself, I'd say, judging by the logo on his chest.

"Yes, you," the guard said. "All of you. I've told you before. This garden isn't for you. It's for patients. Visitors. Hospital staff. And that's all. You're trespassing. So. Stop what you're doing and get lost."

The guy who'd spoken to me picked up an empty can from the ground, tossed it in the air, and headed it into a bush.

"Going to make us?" he said.

One of the others climbed on the back of the bench and started to tight-rope-walk from one end to the other. The third stood up and looked a little lost for a moment. Then he pulled a flat, half-size bottle of generic supermarket whisky from his inside pocket, twisted off the lid, and took a long swig.

"I've warned you," the guard said, after staring at each one in turn. "I've given you a chance. Be gone in five minutes or I'll be back with the police."

"He won't," the tallest one said in my direction as the guard slunk away. "He always threatens us. But he never comes back."

I sat in the garden for another twenty minutes, and saw that the lout was right. The guard didn't return. I was wondering whether he'd ever intended to, if this was such a frequent occurrence. Or whether he always tried, but could never get the police to show any interest. They must have bigger fish to fry than a trio of half-hearted vandals. And the more I thought about it, the more I began to suspect the threat was just an excuse to walk away.

Two minutes later a pair of nurses opened the door the guard had used. They paused for a moment while they took in the way the group was behaving, then backed away. That meant no fresh air for them, after all, which didn't seem right. It made me wonder whether I should have given the guard a hand, earlier. I could have shown him a more practical approach to the problem. I was still mulling this over, debating whether to have a little word with the lads before heading upstairs to see if the MI5 agent was back in her room, when the door opened again. And, as if she'd known I was thinking about her, the agent appeared.

She wheeled straight out onto the path. It seemed like she was looking in my direction, but I knew her peripheral vision would be locked onto the yobs. The residual twigs and broken branches made it hard for her to move, and as she struggled forwards the three lads stopped what they were doing and stared at her. She drew level with them, and the tall one reached into the bush to retrieve the can he'd headed there earlier. She kept going, apparently oblivious, until she was fifteen feet beyond their bench. Then the guy threw the can. It looped up in the air, in a big lazy arc, and crashed down against her right shoulder. She stopped. I held my breath. I guessed it would be too much to ask for her to stand up, draw her Sig, and scare the life out of them, but I was sure she'd do something to bring them into line.

She stayed still, and did nothing.

Then it dawned on me. She wouldn't want to blow her cover. I didn't have to worry, though, so I shot her a look:

Want me to care of this?

She shook her head, and started moving again. So did the hooligans. Two of them caught up with her before she'd traveled three more yards, and the third - the one with the whisky bottle - was only a couple of paces behind them. They shadowed her for a moment, looming over her from behind, leering at their prey, then the tall one took hold of the chair's hand grips. He pushed down and the chair tipped, its front wheels leaving the ground. The agent let out a little scream and the idiots around her grinned. The one holding the chair spun her round in a complete circle and then let go, leaving her to crash down and roll diagonally until her wheels became snagged with debris once again.

She glanced round, checking on their positions, then looked straight at me.

Stay where you are. Don't interfere, her eyes were saying.

I didn't understand. I assumed she was getting ready to make some kind of move, but she showed no sign of responding. And I couldn't help thinking that if she gave them much more rope, it wouldn't be themselves they'd be trying to hang.

The guy who'd been standing on the bench moved around behind the agent's chair and pushed down on her shoulders, pinning her in place. Then the taller one stepped across in front of her and began to unzip what remained of his jeans. The agent's eyes registered nothing until she realised I was moving. The yob noticed me coming towards him a moment later. He glanced at the wall behind me, then took a large step to his left. I adjusted my course to follow him, but as I drew close he didn't make an attempt to defend himself. Or even to argue with me. He just threw himself backwards, going down like he'd been shot and almost burying the side of his head into the ground.

Chapter Seven

The two yobs that were still on their feet converged on their friend, then together they hauled the idiot up off the ground. The three of them stood still for a moment, arms around each other like exhausted runners at the end of a marathon. Then the tallest one broke free and started for the exit at the far end of the garden. Little pieces of gravel were still sticking out of his scalp and blood was oozing over the folds of his neck onto his T-shirt. The others followed him without a word. I watched until the door closed behind them, then became aware of the agent maneuvering her chair past me as she wheeled towards the nearest bench.

I walked across and sat next to her, expecting her to say something, but she seemed content to wait in silence.

"What was that all about?" I said, eventually.

"A couple of things," she said.

"The guy just threw himself on the floor."

"I know. He was playing to the camera. But don't worry. It won't do him any good."

"What do you mean, 'playing to the camera?'"

"You saw where it was mounted on the wall, right? Over there, behind the bench you were sitting on?"

"I saw it."

"And you saw how he lined himself up, with you between it and him? He was trying to make it look like you assaulted him. Probably looking for compensation, from somewhere. But he won't get any."

"Of course he won't. I didn't touch him."

"Ha. That's not the reason. It's because the camera's not working. I had cause to check it, very recently."

"I thought those cameras were to protect innocent people."

"They are."

"But now the criminals are using them to their advantage? That's crazy."

The agent shrugged.

"Criminals have rights, too," she said.

"You know what they call us, in the States?" I said. "One nation, under CCTV. I used to think they were joking. Now I can see why."

"They do a lot of good, too," she said, after a moment. "The cameras. When they're working. Did the boots arrive yet, by the way?" I told them to put a rush on the delivery."

"So you are M," I said. "I thought so."

"You were right. I am."

"Is that the whole of your name?"

"No. It's Melissa. Melissa Wainwright."

"Pleased to meet you, Melissa. I'm David Trevellyan. But you already knew that. You knew a lot about me, in fact. Including my shoe size, it seems. Unless that was a lucky guess."

"I saw the notes that Jackson had made after your meeting. Our pencil-pushing friend is very thorough. He'd written down the size. The brand. The colour. Everything."

"Well, thanks for sending them. That was another surprise you sprang on me. A nice one, this time, though."

"I'm glad you like them. I wasn't sure they'd be an appropriate 'welcome to the team' present, in the circumstances, though."

"Why not? What's inappropriate about boots?"

"Well, I remember you saying you couldn't wait to leave the hospital. Now, here you are, having to stay."

"True. But it's not a problem. I've been stuck in

worse places. And I'm very adaptable."

"Can you adapt to working with us, do you think?"

"Why shouldn't I? Or are you unusually hard to work with?"

"I wouldn't say so. But from what I hear, teamwork isn't normally your forte."

I shrugged. Working in teams wasn't usually a problem. It was leaving them intact when I'd finished that was the issue. Specially if one of the team members was hiding any unsavoury motives, which they usually were, if there was a reason for me to be involved. And looking across at the agent, I couldn't help wondering if that would be case, here.

"How many times have you operated in the UK before?" she said.

"I never have," I said. "Does that matter?"

"I think it might. Look at how you just responded to those cameras. And our CCTV's just the tip of the iceberg. I've seen a list of the places you've been posted to lately, and I don't care where your passport says you were born. There are very real ways the UK's going to be the most foreign place you've ever worked. I don't think you're going to like it."

I didn't say anything, but I was beginning to think she might be right.

"I don't want to be lumbered with a fish out of water," she said. "Specially not an angry, violent one. Because there are laws here. Laws that are enforced. That'll make your usual methods impossible. That frown on people who pulverise everyone they come across who they don't like."

I played back how things had got started with the three yobs, and realised it was no coincidence. Following the debacle with Jones she'd set out the field deliberately to see if there'd be a repeat of the violence. That made her supremely opportunistic. Maybe even manipulative.

The more I saw of this woman, the more I liked her. How typical that she came with a health warning.

"Those guys who were hassling me?" she said. "You wanted to stop them, didn't you? You wanted to hurt them. And you would have done, if that one hadn't taken a dive."

"Maybe," I said. "Someone had to do something about them. And it fell to one of us."

"Why?"

"Think about it. They pick on the disabled. Damage public property. Spoil this garden for others. They're like a cancer."

"That's a little harsh."

"I don't think so."

"Then why didn't you call security?"

"A security guard was here before you arrived. He tried, but he couldn't do anything about it."

"So call the police."

"He did. The police aren't interested."

"That doesn't make dealing with it your job. Or mine."

"Not our jobs, no. But it's still an obligation. We were here. We could have done something. Turning a blind eye was wrong. And... forget it."

"What?"

"Well, you know who I work for."

"Obviously."

"Then you know I've been lucky. I'm still here. But a lot of my friends aren't."

"The Security Service loses agents too. What's your point?"

"I'm asking a question. These people – yours, and mine. The ones who've given their lives, defending this country. What did they die for? To build a safe haven for thieves and drug addicts? Or for vandals, like the idiots we just let walk away? Degenerates who rot the place away from the inside, little piece by little piece. It makes me wonder, why do we even bother?"

She didn't answer.

"Don't you ever feel that way?" I said. "It must be worse for you, having to live here with them all the time."

"It doesn't strike me that way at all," she said. "Where there's freedom, there'll always be crime. That's how societies work. The big problems, we deal with. Other than that, it's about finding a balance, and most of the time we do that pretty well. You've got to keep things in perspective. And guys like them? They're not threatening anything fundamental. They're not smart enough. They're morons. Who cares?"

"So, freedom and crime, two sides of the same coin. Don't you find that depressing?"

"No. I don't. It's a glass half full, as I see things. It gives me hope."

I caught some movement to our left. The door had opened again. A doctor and a nurse were looking through, but when they saw the garden wasn't vacant they turned and disappeared back down the corridor.

"You know, my stomach's telling me it's nearly lunchtime," I said. "Are you hungry?"

"Maybe, a little," Melissa said, after a moment.

"Fancy helping me hunt down a sandwich?"

"That might be nice," she said, hesitantly. "But I need to make a couple of calls first. Check up on a couple of things. I'd do it later, only it can't wait. You can come with me, if you like."

I thought her offer over for second, but decided to decline. There was no point looking over her shoulder. Not when she was expecting me to, anyway.

"No thanks," I said. "Why don't we meet somewhere when you're done?"

"Deal," she said. "How about the hospital canteen? Half an hour?"

Chapter Eight

I found the hospital canteen on the top floor of the wing that contained the offices. Outside, a plaque said it had been opened eighteen months earlier by some junior minister from the Department of Health. Inside, it looked like it had been transplanted from a mid-scale department store. Circular tables, each large enough for four people, were scattered seemingly at random throughout half of the space. A sweeping, curved counter provided shelter for the people serving the food, and behind them were three parallel rows of shiny stainless steel kitchen units. It all looked good - very sleek and industrial - though there was no sign of anyone doing any actual cooking.

Around half the tables were occupied. I could see little knots of nurses. Physiotherapists. Doctors. Clerical workers. Each group was set apart by their clothes and separated by where they sat, as if they were divided into hostile clans. The only exception was the occasional huddle of patients or visitors who had managed to find their way into the place. Several of them scrutinised me as I bought a mug of coffee, presumably categorising me by my hospital pyjamas. But I belonged to none of the groups, so I just collected my drink, retreated to an empty seat in the corner furthest from the door, and settled down to wait.

A quick inspection the other customers' footwear revealed no sign of my boots, so I turned my attention to the garden. It was deserted. I wondered if that was because no one wanted to be there, or whether people were put off by the kind of yobs we had encountered earlier. I was still feeling surprised by Melissa's attitude to the situation. I hadn't expected her to accept the hooligans so readily. I thought back to the other MI5 people I'd crossed paths with over the years, and couldn't imagine any of them seeing things that way, either. Especially not the field agents. Either she was the exception that proves the rule, or the Security Service had changed dramatically in recent times. And I certainly couldn't see her point of view finding much favour in Naval Intelligence. In my world things were much more black and white. There was a threat, or there wasn't. Someone needed to be eliminated, or they didn't. I was beginning to think that spending time with Melissa could be interesting, if only for the shades of grey she brought with her.

I was half way across the room with my third cup of coffee when two shrill, angry voices caught my attention. They were coming from a table to my left. Two women had started to argue. I sat down and watched them out of the corner of my eye. They were both smartly dressed. In office clothes, not medical uniforms. I guessed that one was in her mid thirties, and the other no more than early twenties. Their postures suggested that the older woman had started the ball rolling. The younger one looked like she was reaching the end of her tether. She fell silent for a moment, then sprang to her feet, sending her chair skidding away behind her. She lent across the table, palms flat on its surface, her nose almost touching the other woman's. Her voice dropped to a whisper, and for the life of me I couldn't make out what she said. Then she turned and flounced away, almost falling into Melissa's lap as she chose that moment to wheel into the room.

"Everything OK?" I said, as Melissa reached my table a few moments later.

"It is with me," she said. "But what was that all about? I nearly ran that woman over."

"I don't know. Some kind of argument, I think. I couldn't hear the details."

"Damnation. I always miss the excitement. Was it a good one?"

"No. Quite tame, really."

"Any punching?"

"No."

"Scratching?"

"No."

"Eye gouging?"

"None. Nothing like that. You really didn't miss much."

"Who was she arguing with?"

"Another woman. She's still here. Grey cardigan, white blouse. Three tables behind you. Seven o'clock."

Melissa looked up slightly towards the window, trying to catch a reflection in the glass.

"It must have been quite a good one," she said. "That woman's hand is still shaking. Ten quid says she'll spill her tea."

I didn't reply.

"I wonder what they were rowing about?" she said. "Work? What do you think? Football? Or maybe a man?"

"No idea," I said.

"I bet some guy's at the heart of it. An office romance. Never a good idea."

"I wouldn't know."

"Well, have you ever heard of one working out well?"

"Actually, no," I said. "Although, it's not a field I have much experience in."

"Me neither," she said.

"So, tell me, how did your phone calls go?"

"Oh, OK. Frustrating, more than anything. I had to

follow up on a few things. I made some enquiries before I arrived here, and a few of the responses aren't coming through quickly enough. I had to light fires under a couple of people."

I looked out of the window for a moment, trying not to take her bait.

"You want to know what we're doing here, don't you?" she said.

"No,' I said. "I honestly don't have the slightest interest."

Melissa tipped her head to one side, like she'd done in the garden, and waited a few seconds before saying anything else.

"Do they have good sandwiches here?" she said.

"A couple looked quite reasonable," I said. "There was a prosciutto and goats' cheese panini. That was probably the best of the bunch."

"OK, then," she said. "You grab us each one of those. We'll eat. Then we have an important meeting to go to. But before that, there's something I want to show you, downstairs. It'll help you make sense of everything."

Melissa told me to hit the button for the basement, and when the door opened I saw that instead of a single corridor as there'd been at ground level, we now had a choice of four.

"It's like Hades, only with colour-coding," she said as she emerged into the stale air, nodding towards the broad stripes that were painted on the pale green walls. "I mean, as in the underworld, not the god of the dead."

"I don't care about the dead," I said. "Just as long as there are no three-headed dogs down here."

"Don't worry," she said, starting off down the corridor to our left. "There are no dogs of any kind. Except maybe some Guide Dogs, and you hardly need worry about them. So, are you coming? It's this way. We want the purple route."

I caught up with her and took hold of the chair's handles, but didn't need to actually push. She was happy to keep the speed up on her own, running her hands rhythmically around the rim of the wheels. The corridor she'd chosen was long and straight. The light grey on the floor was peeling in places, allowing the concrete to show through, and the walls were plain except for the slightly wavy navigational line that ran all the way down the right hand side. A mess of cables and ventilation ducts dangled from angled brackets above our heads, along with a row of caged-in fluorescent lights. They were evenly spaced, one every ten feet, so there was no relief from their harsh glare.

As I trudged forward I noticed that one of Melissa's wheels was developing a squeak every time it turned. She was going to need some oil pretty soon if she didn't want to announce her arrival everywhere she went, and I was still wondering where she could get some when I realised the smell of the air was changing, too. The stagnant odour near the lift was gradually being replaced by something with a sharper, harder edge.

"What is that?" I said. "It smells like chlorine."

"I think it is chlorine," Melissa said.

"Where's it coming from?"

"The swimming pool, I expect."

"Which swimming pool?"

"The hospital's."

"I didn't know it had one. Where is it?"

"Round the next corner."

"But wait," I said, taking a moment to make sure I had my bearings straight. "Wouldn't that bring us up into the street?"

"If we went up," she said. "Yes, it would."

"You've lost me."

"The pool's down here. Underground. Between the hospital and the nurses' home."

"I didn't even know there was a nurses' home."

"Oh, yes. That big, ugly, modern building on the opposite side of the road. The pool's actually bang in the middle, twenty feet below street level."

"Are you sure?"

"I am. And just think. All those stressed out office workers heading home every evening. What would they do if knew they were a few yards above a horde of student nurses in tiny little bikinis?"

"Do people use it much?" I said, trying to imagine how it would feel to be in a pool of water beneath one of the busiest commuter streets in London.

"Actually, I have no clue," she said. "I've only seen it on the plans. And don't get any ideas, cause we're not going that far. There's something else you need to look at."

After another thirty yards the corridor made a ninety-degree turn to the left, but we didn't follow it.

"Can you get that for me?" Melissa said, nodding towards a door set into the right hand wall. It was painted the same shade of grey as the floor, and the purple stripe continued straight across it. There was nothing to indicate what it led to. And there was no handle attached to it, either. I glanced down at Melissa, then gave it a push. It opened easily, and beyond it was another featureless corridor. This one was about eighty yards long, and slightly narrower than the first. Its walls were the same pale green, but there was no sign of any coloured lines. The floor wasn't as worn. There was less junk hanging from the ceiling, and the lights were spaced further apart, making the place noticeably dimmer. But the main difference, as far as I could see, was the CCTV cameras that were here. There were two. Both in protective, wire mesh cages. One was facing me, to monitor anyone entering the corridor. The second was focused on the only other possible exit - a single door about half way down on the right hand side.

I shrugged, stepped into the new corridor, and held the door for Melissa. She wheeled past me and kept going, faster than before, till she was level with the door. Then she spun her chair hard to the right and waited for me to catch up.

"This is it," she said. "This is why I'm here. And you, too, now."

The door appeared to be made of wood. Pale, maybe ash, with a delicate grain running from top to bottom. It didn't look very robust. You'd think that one decent kick would be all you'd need to open it. I'd seen ones like it in offices all over the world, right down to the flimsy metal handle and standard wall-mounted keypad to the left. There was only one unusual aspect. The surface had been damaged. There were three gashes, almost parallel, roughly at shoulder height. Each one was about five inches long, but they were surprisingly shallow. Only about an eighth of an inch deep. And even in the low light you could see a hint of something metallic, glinting, just below the surface.

All was clearly not as it seemed, but without the cosmetic damage, you'd never have known.

"See those dents?" she said. "What do you think happened?"

"I'd like to think that a bad tempered T-Rex had tried to claw its way through," I said. "But I guess I'll have to settle for something more mundane. How about a bad tempered human with an axe?"

"Right second time. Although I can't be certain they were bad tempered."

"Who was it?"

"We're not sure."

"When did it happen?"

"The afternoon before you arrived."

"And why this door?"

"We have two theories."

"Which are?"

"The first is that it was an innocent mistake."

"OK. And option two?"

"That someone wanted what's on the other side."

"What is on the other side?"

"As far as I know, there's the entrance to a World War Two air raid shelter, now bricked up. A standby electricity generator, now disused. And one other thing. The largest repository of Caesium-137 in the south of England."

Chapter Nine

Melissa put a little more meat on the bones for me as I followed her back towards the lift.

"Caesium-137 is a kind of medical waste," she said. "It's extremely radioactive. And it stays that way for a very long time. More than thirty years."

"Nasty," I said. "What state is the stuff in?"

"It's a metal, which is liquid at room temperature. So it has to be stored and transported in special containers."

"What happens if it gets out of those containers?"

"Nothing good. It's incredibly soluble, so it gets into everything, all over the place. It starts by seeping into the ground water, and then Mother Nature takes over and distributes it through the rain cycle. After Chernobyl it was found over ten thousand miles from the accident site, to give you an idea. From there it gets into the food chain. Animals. Fish. Fruit. Vegetables. Everything. And if it gets into the body, through eating or drinking something contaminated, you're in real trouble. It's much worse than other radioactive agents because for some reason your organs treat it like potassium, and absorb it incredibly easily."

"And if that happens?"

"You die. A slow, hideous, drawn-out, agonising death. And children are particularly vulnerable. Specially their thyroids."

"So if I was a terrorist, I'd have a special fondness for this stuff?"

"Definitely. Its effects are deadly. They're invisible. They spread naturally over huge distances, and once the genie is out of the bottle it's impossible to put back in. Put it this way - when Bin Laden was caught, caesium was needed for nine of the thirty-four schemes he was working on. And you know what else? The other reason terrorists love it?"

"What? Why?"

"If you can get hold of some, you can use it within seconds. You don't need complex delivery systems. Advanced technology. Special training. Or lots of people. You just take the lid off the container and pour it on the floor. Or down a drain. Or into a reservoir. And that's it. Hundreds, maybe thousands of people will die."

"And there's a lot if it here?"

"Stacks of it. Because this place isn't just a regular hospital. It's the central holding facility for all the hospitals in the region."

"How many?"

"Seven, altogether. The waste from all of them is brought here. It's broken down by a couple of factors – type of contaminant, degree of toxicity, that kind of thing – then consolidated. Special technicians take care of that. And when they're done, it's sent to the relevant places for reprocessing."

I paused for a moment, trying to think of a tactful way to say what I was thinking.

"Please don't take offense at this," I said. "But you're painting a picture of moths and flames, here. And you don't seem to be doing much to keep them apart. What am I missing?"

"Nothing," she said. "If you're talking about me, personally. But what do you expect to see? Caesium is a priority one threat. Safeguarding it isn't just down to Jones and me. We're only one small part of a huge machine. The visible tip of a tried-and-tested iceberg. We're sent in after a possible incident to make absolutely certain nothing's slipped through the cracks. We're a duplicate resource, but the stakes are so high we can't afford to take any risks."

"And in this case, nothing's slipped through? Are you sure?"

"Here's another thing about caesium. It doesn't occur naturally. So, if you want some, you have to make it, buy it, or steal it. And if this was anything, it was an attempt at stealing, yes?"

"It looks that way."

"Now, we don't just wait around for someone to snatch a barrowful, and then run around trying to catch them. We stop them before they get the chance. We have the snoops at GCHQ on the case, listening in to everything, 24/7. Plus a whole network of agents and specialised, dedicated informers. If there's as much as a whisper of anything related to caesium, they'd know. And none of them heard a thing."

"What if it's someone new, who's not on the radar yet? Or someone good enough to disguise what they're doing?"

"It could be someone new, I guess. But they're certainly not good. Attacking that door was stupid. You couldn't get through it with a hundred axes, let alone one."

"Maybe the axe thing was a diversion, to make you take the attack less seriously. Maybe they got in another way."

"There are no other ways. And the door's security log shows no one opened it."

"Couldn't the log have been hacked? Or fiddled?"

"There's an outside chance of that, yes. Which is why a hazardous materials team is coming tomorrow to do a full inventory. But based on the sum total of all the data from all our avenues of enquiry, I believe they'll prove the correct amount of caesium is here, and put the whole question to bed."

"Why wait till tomorrow?"

"We need a team with special equipment. You can't just pick this stuff up and count it, obviously. And tomorrow's the soonest they can be here."

"Aren't there emergency crews?"

"For containing leaks, and urgent relocation from compromised facilities, yes. But not for inventory work. And don't forget, the scene of crime report showed no evidence of any tampering and no manic axe men were picked up anywhere on the CCTV, so it was more likely to be a badly trained fireman who damaged the door."

"Why would a fireman have been here?"

Melissa stopped her chair in the centre of the corridor and looked up at me.

"Oh," she said. "David, I owe you an apology. I forgot you weren't in this from the start. The marks on the door were discovered by the hospital technicians when they tried to go back in after a fire alarm. Standard procedure calls for them to report any damage, then lock down the site so it can be investigated."

"Was there actually a fire?" I said.

"No. And I know what you're thinking. But remember your Freud, David. Sometimes a false alarm is just a false alarm."

I thought about what Melissa had told me, and I had to agree - you couldn't rule out the possibility that nothing nefarious was going on. Not yet, anyway. There was plenty to be skeptical about - someone attacking the one door in the hospital which led to the radioactive waste - but that was circumstantial. I could think of several occasions over the years when I'd scratched the surface of something suspicious and found only chaos, not conspiracy. But those judgments had been based on evidence, and evidence was one thing that seemed to be lacking here.

"You mentioned CCTV," I said. "There's a camera pointing at the door. Doesn't it show who did the damage?"

"It should," Melissa said. "And that would make my life a million times easier. But on the night of the fire alarm, it wasn't working."

"Just that one?"

"No. That would be too coincidental, for sure. Four separate zones were down, spread randomly across the site. And that's what our next meeting is about. It's with the hospital security chief. I'm going to rattle his cage about his maintenance record, and see how he reacts."

"Should be fun. But what about the firemen, themselves? Could we talk to the ones who were on duty that night, and see if any of them own up to it?"

"I'm sure we could. And then we could check the geriatric wards for grandmothers, in case any want to learn to suck eggs."

I didn't reply.

"Obviously, we spoke to the firemen," she said. "But here's the problem with them. All the crews from all four stations that cover this place are supposed to know that they never, ever, under any circumstances, try to open that door. So you're asking them to land themselves, and probably their commanders too, in seriously hot water."

"So you think we're either dealing with an over-ambitious terrorist, or an under-attentive fireman."

"I know that's what I'm here to deal with," she said, turning her head again to look me straight in the face. "With thousands of lives potentially in the balance. But I'm not so sure about you."

"Then why do you think I'm here?" I said.

"We all know what it means when someone from another agency is brought in to 'help' on some flimsy pretext. The rat squad are behind it. They don't want to show their nasty little rodent faces, so they're staying in their sewer and using you to do their dirty work."

I didn't reply.

"It's true, isn't it?" she said. "There's no point denying it. That's not going to change what I think."

"You can think whatever you like," I said, after another moment. "I'm not going to comment."

"Thank you. Only, it goes further, doesn't it, what you're here to do?"

"What do you mean?"

"They're after me, specifically."

"Not as far as I know."

"So they didn't spell that part out. So what. Think about it. Only two people from Box were assigned to the hospital. And since Jones is (a) too new to have had time to get his nose dirty, and (b) not here cause you conveniently took him out of the equation, who else does that leave under the microscope?"

Put like that, Jones's injury did look a little coincidental. I was pretty sure I'd have reached the same conclusion, in her shoes. You don't last long in our world, taking coincidences on blind faith.

"You can rule someone out, as well as in, you know. If they're even a suspect in the first place."

"In theory. But here's my problem. I've been doing this job for twelve years. It's my life. It's the reason I'm not rich. Not married. Not a mother. And don't have many friends. But it's what I love doing. I'm good at it. I've never once turned a blind eye or slipped a hand into the till. And if anyone says I have, I want to look them in the eye. I want the chance to prove them wrong. I don't want to wake up one morning with a blade in my back, and no way to pull it out."

"I understand."

"Look, I realise you have a job to do. It's not easy, and I'm sure you didn't volunteer for it. I wouldn't have said anything, only back in the garden it sounded like you care about doing the right thing, and I just wanted you to know - well, I do, too."

We swung by my room so I could change into something more business-like than my hospital pyjamas, then headed to the next building to meet the Head of Security. He wasn't there when we arrived, two minutes early for our appointment.

"Mr Leckie will be here very soon," his secretary said, as she showed us into his office. "Please, take a seat. Can I get you some coffee? Tea?"

"No, thank you," Melissa said.

"I hope there's not been another urgent family situation," I said. "What's the temperature like outside?"

The secretary flushed slightly and scampered from the room, but she couldn't keep her eyes from flicking up to the array of pictures on the wall above Leckie's desk as she went. They were all of golf courses. I recognised St Andrew's in Scotland, plus one in Karlovac, Croatia, where I once had to arrange the disappearance of a corrupt Serbian diplomat. I had no idea about the other dozen. They could have been anywhere.

Melissa pushed one of the visitors' chairs aside and wheeled around so that her back was to the side wall, which was covered with more pictures. Paintings, this time, of birds of prey. I wondered if Leckie was into shooting.

"It must be nice to have time for a hobby," I said. "It's so annoying when work gets in the way."

"Did anyone brief you about Leckie?" Melissa said, with an eye on the door.

"No. But I did pick up some office gossip.

Apparently he's not the world's most conscientious employee."

"That must be a recent development."

"How do you know?"

"He's ex..." she said, then mouthed the word, "Box," as the door swung open.

"Afternoon," he said, as he strode into the centre of the room. "Sorry to keep you. Melissa, still using the prop chair, I see. And you must be our cousin, Commander Trevellyan."

We shook hands, then Leckie dumped a pile of paperwork on his desk and flopped down into his chair.

"Did Ms. Wainwright tell you much about me?" Leckie said.

"No," I said. "Should she have?"

"Well, you see, the thing is, I'm a bit of a mind reader. And I'm going to go out on a limb and say she's here to tear a strip off me cause these wretched faulty cameras of mine have turned what should have been a simple job into a bit of a ball-ache. Am I right?"

I looked at Melissa, and wondered if this was the kind of cage-rattling she had in mind.

"Yes," she said. "You took the words right out of my mouth."

"It's my fault entirely," he said, holding up both his hands. "The buck stops with me. All I can do is apologise. And let you know that in fact five zones were down on the night of the non-fire, not four as originally reported."

"Five?" Melissa said. "What kind of outfit are you running, here, Stan?"

Leckie let his hands flop into his lap.

"What can I tell you?" he said. "Civilians."

"That's not good enough. What are you doing about it?"

"I've fired the people who dropped the ball, obviously," he said. "And brought contractors in - the best in the country - to get everything straightened out, double quick. Two zones are already back up and running. They're busting their guts on the others. And I was thinking, given what's at stake here, once the dust has settled your people and mine should get together and come up with a way to avoid this kind of cock-up in the future."

A classic exercise in blame sharing, I thought. How long till the whole fiasco turned out to be MI5's fault?

"When will the other three zones be fixed?" Melissa said.

"Close of play tomorrow at the latest, I'm told."

"Is the camera outside the caesium vault one they're still working on?"

"Yes. I believe so."

"Well, your people can't be anywhere near that corridor between noon and 4.00pm. The hazmat team will need free access to do their inventory."

"They're doing that tomorrow? So soon? I'd stretch it out another couple of days, if I were you."

"Good golfing weather, is it?" I said.

"I like the way our new friend thinks," he said. "But sadly, no. You know what I mean, don't you Melissa?"

"Stan always found the rules a little restrictive," Melissa said. "And he had a theory - the greater the level of threat, the more you could get away with bending them."

"Exactly," Leckie said. "As long as you know nothing's really wrong, drag the panic out as long as you can. Use it to your own ends. Walk a little less softly, and carry a bigger stick for a while."

"I don't think so," Melissa said.

"Oh, come on," Leckie said. "There must be all kinds of doors you're knocking on, but can't quite risk kicking down. This is your chance. It's the upside of the pain my antiquated systems have inadvertently caused you."

"Thanks, but I'll pass," Melissa said. "The inventory's tomorrow."

"They're going to confirm that no caesium is missing," Leckie said. "We all know they will, cause we all know there's no way anyone got through that door. Then you'll be back on a much shorter leash. Are you really going to throw away such a golden opportunity?"

"I just want to get this mess squared away, as quickly and cleanly as possible," Melissa said, turning to look at me. "And the thing I don't want to throw away is my job."

The admin building was crawling with people when we left Leckie's office, so we made our way back out to the garden to talk.

"Tell me something, Melissa," I said, lowering myself onto the nearest bench. "Hypothetically speaking. If I hadn't been there, and you hadn't felt like you were in the spotlight, would you have been tempted to follow Leckie's advice? Use the threat of missing caesium to buy you a little leverage elsewhere? I'm sure that's been done before."

"No," she said. "Now, don't get me wrong. That approach does work, sometimes. Leckie certainly brought down some major villains that way while he was with us. But look at the end result. He was shown the door. And how much good is he doing now, playing golf and presiding over a broken down CCTV system?"

"He was thrown out? Why?"

"The word on the street was brutality."

"Do you believe it?"

Melissa rotated her chair a quarter turn to the left, on the spot, and then straightened up again before answering.

"It's ironic, isn't it?" she said. "Given someone's

shoving me towards the same door, with no good reason. But yes. I believe it. He was always pushing the limits, and I think one time he pushed that little bit too far."

"Did he get a result, that time?"

"Well, yes. But you still can't condone it."

"I'm not condoning it. I'm only asking."

"Not morally. And not practically. It does more harm than good, nine times out of ten. Look at the situation we're in now, with the firemen."

"What's Leckie got to do with the firemen?"

"It's his fault they're being so uncooperative."

"Did he brutalise one of them?"

"Not physically. But verbally, yes. He was furious when he heard what had happened during the alarm, so he got the chiefs of all the fire stations together on a conference call. Then he bawled each one out, one after the other, in front of their peers."

"Not the most constructive of approaches."

"No. What we needed was trust and openness, but because of him, that ship's not just sailed. It's been torpedoed and gone down with all hands."

"Maybe he should spend more time playing golf."

"Maybe he should. Seriously. Normally I hate the game. But if it means golf balls are the only things Leckie hits in future, that's something I could get behind."

Chapter Ten

Under different circumstances I'd have been happy to stay in the garden with Melissa all afternoon, but that day it wasn't to be. She had several more phone calls to make, she said. Plus some preparations to complete for tomorrow, when the hazmat team would arrive. And of course, the inevitable reports to file, to keep her boss safely out of her hair.

She invited me back to her room while she worked, but again I declined. Admin's bad enough when it's your own. She'd already shown herself to be too smart to give anything away in front of me, even if she was tainted. And the stakes were too high to waste time going through the motions, or trailing other people around like a nursemaid. Instead, I needed the chance to weigh up what I'd learned, see what was missing, and figure out what to do about it.

We agreed to meet at 6.00pm, assuming everything went smoothly, and take stock again then. It was just after 3.00pm, so that gave me almost three hours. I thought about staying in the garden, but the rain had grown heavier and there's no fun in getting wet on your own. The coffee I'd had in the canteen was surprisingly reasonable so I thought about going there, but in the end I just made my way back to my room. I slipped off my new boots, then picked up the remote control and flopped down on the bed.

The TV came back on to the same channel I'd been watching yesterday, but somehow I couldn't make myself concentrate on the show. My thoughts kept homing in on Melissa. I pictured her six rooms across from me, one floor below, phone pressed to her ear, taking care of business.

Yesterday, I had no idea who she was. Today, it was down to me whether she kept her job or went to jail. I was starting to like her, and she certainly came across as honest. But in our business, I knew those things count for nothing.

Most of what Melissa had told me down in the basement made sense, but I still wondered what the inspection team was going to say in the morning. And if the inventory checked out, whether she'd be happy. I knew I wouldn't be, if I was in her shoes. The fact that no caesium was missing wouldn't prove there hadn't been an attempt to steal some, however inept. So whatever she learned tomorrow - theft or no theft - Melissa would have some work to do. Her only way out was to prove that the armoured door had been damaged by a fireman, and that he'd done it by mistake.

I switched off the TV and made for the door. The basement was calling me back. Because it struck me that Melissa had focused on two factors - the human elements, and the technology. She had those well covered. But there was another angle to consider. Logistics. I didn't know much about caesium, but clearly it was a volatile substance. You couldn't just pick some up and walk away with it, even if you could get into the vault. Which meant you'd need special clothing, to handle it. Maybe something to transport the containers she'd mentioned, depending on their size. And you'd need an escape route. Getting inside the hospital under cover of the fire alarm was one thing, but getting out again with such volatile loot was another.

The next two hours were lost underground. I must have walked at least two miles without setting foot outside even once. It was stifling, and the whole time I couldn't shake the thought that during the cold war, people actually believed they could live like that for years at a time. Every time I passed the junction of the four corridors I was tempted to jump in the lift, head up to ground level and grab a breath of fresh air. But I resisted. I stuck to the task at hand, and in the end I was glad I did. Because the hospital may have looked picturesque from the outside, but it was in the basement where it really became interesting.

The swimming pool was my first port of call, but I spent more time in the machine room that lay behind it. There were dozens of drums of chemicals stored there, bristling with toxicity warnings, which would have been heaven for anyone with a mind to cause trouble. I found three boiler rooms. Each had miles of inviting, vulnerable pipework, which would be a gift for anyone wanting to cause a diversion. There were four separate storage areas. Each one was large enough to hide a dozen men. Or all the supplies they'd need to lay siege to the whole complex. An office belonging to the hospital's security firm was down there, too - tucked in between a standby generator room and a tool store - which didn't recommend working for them. But the thing that sounded the most interesting of all, I didn't even get to see. It was sealed away behind a rusty, steel door. I only found out about it from a maintenance guy who saw me trying to pry it open. He swore it was the entrance to a fully equipped World War II rifle range, and that he knew this because his father had been inside. The government had built it in 1940, he said, when they were more worried about improving the hospital workers' ability to shoot invading Germans than their skill at patching up injured Londoners.

That maintenance worker wasn't the only person I spoke to. I also talked to five of his colleagues. I found them in a huddle, sneaking crafty cigarettes in a room at the far end of the red corridor. It was full of ancient-looking ventilation equipment. The old machinery appeared basically redundant, with just enough life left in it to dissipate their smoke. I asked if they'd rigged the place back up specially for that purpose, and one of them admitted they had. Then the subject of the recent fire alarm came up. That wasn't much of a surprise, given the cigarettes in their hands and the piles of flammable debris on the floor. The biggest talking point wasn't whether the hospital had been in danger of burning down, though. It was the attention they'd attracted from the police, afterwards. All of them seemed pretty indignant about the implied stain on their characters, but one guy's complaints were particularly strident. He was standing furthest from the door, so when the others made a move to leave it wasn't too hard for me to head him off. I penned him back in the corner, and when the sound of footsteps had died away in the corridor outside, I asked him his name.

"Elvis Presley," he said, without irony. "What's it to you?"

"Just being friendly," I said. "I thought maybe we could talk."

"Haven't got time," he said, eyeing the narrow gap behind the largest machine. "I've got work to do."

"It won't take long," I said, stepping to the side to show how easily I could block his escape route if he tried to worm his way out. "Give me a minute. I think I might be able to help you with something."

"Help me? How."

"Let me give you my card," I said, reaching into my jacket pocket, then pulling a frustrated frown. "Oh, damn. They must all be upstairs, in my room. I'll get one for you later, if you're interested. In the meantime, let me tell you what I do. I'm a lawyer. And I specialise in police brutality cases."

"You're a lawyer? Good for you. Why would I care?"

"Because I saw how you reacted when your friends

mentioned the police, just now. I know the signs. If the police are giving you a hard time, I can make them stop. And if they've crossed any lines, I can make them pay."

"Why should the police be giving me a hard time? I haven't done anything."

"I'm not saying you have. But I've been cooped up in this place for a few days, now. I know about the fire alarm. I know some hospital property was damaged. And I know the police are looking for someone to pin it on."

He didn't reply.

"How many times have they questioned you?" I said.

He looked away from me.

"How many times?" I said.

"None," he said.

"And you'd like it to stay that way?"

He nodded.

"Were you working that night?" I said.

"No," he said.

"So where were you?"

He didn't answer.

"You can tell me," I said. "Anything you reveal to me is privileged information, because I'm a lawyer. It can't get you in trouble. But it might make it easier for me to help."

He looked at the ground, and remained silent.

"You were at the hospital, weren't you?" I said.

He nodded.

"Down here?" I said.

"Yes," he said.

"What were you doing?"

"Collecting something. Then the alarm went off. And I saw firemen all over the place. I thought it was for real."

"So what did you do?"

"Tried to get out without any of them seeing me. I wasn't supposed to be here, remember."

"Did you make it?"

"Almost. Then two of them practically fell on top of me."

"Where was this?"

"At the end of the hot corridor."

"The hot corridor?"

"Where they keep the hot waste. Along there."

"Why were you in that corridor?"

"I wasn't. I was passing the end of it, and I heard voices. Two men, arguing. I paused for a moment, curious, like an idiot. Then the door opened and they burst out, one dragging the other by the arm."

"Could you hear what they were arguing about?"

"The door to the hot room. One had tried to get through it. Whacked it with his axe. And the other was tearing him a new one for it. No one's supposed to touch that door, ever. Anyone working here should know that."

"So, it was one of these firemen who'd damaged the door."

"Right."

"Are you sure they were firemen?"

"What kind of question is that? There was a fire alarm. They came in a fire engine. They had firemen suits. Yes, they were firemen."

"OK. So why didn't you tell the police what you saw?"

"They didn't ask."

"Because you weren't supposed to be here that night?"

"Right."

"And you didn't volunteer the information because that would have revealed you were here when you shouldn't have been?"

"Right."

"And is that such a big deal? Being at the hospital when you're off duty?"

"It is, lately. The rules changed. There've been some thefts, and stuff."

"How do your chances look, keeping the police off your tail?"

He shrugged.

"Not good, I guess," I said. "They're still crawling all over the place. And it won't be long before they start pulling everyone in, not just the ones who were working that night."

"Do you think so?" he said.

"I do, based on my experience of these things. It's how they operate. They're like clockwork. They have a procedure, and they follow it. But you don't need to worry about that. There's a way we can shield you from it."

"There is? How?"

"There's a special kind of statement you can make. An Incoactus Inviolati. Don't worry about the weird-sounding name. It's from the Latin, and it just means that because you voluntarily provided information which was helpful to the case, the circumstances which led you to be in possession of that information – even if they were in and of themselves illegal – will be excluded from the resulting investigation."

"Really? Are you sure?"

"I'm a lawyer. It's my job to be sure. The Inviolati is a very useful tool for the police. Without it, they wouldn't be able to get half their informants to come forward."

"How come I've never heard of it?"

"Well, they don't exactly advertise. They don't want people trying to use it to wriggle out of crimes that aren't really related. But in your case, it's completely legit. We could get it done in five minutes."

"We could? How?"

"Well, I'll be out of this place probably the middle of next week. I should be able to fit you in a couple of days after that, if you don't mind coming over to my office."

"Wait, wow, no way. Far too long. The police will come knocking long before that."

"There's not much I can – oh, hang on. It's a little unconventional, but my assistant is here at the hospital, too. We were in the same car, you see, hit by one of those dodgy new bendy buses. She has all the basic forms with her, in her briefcase. We could head up to her room, right now? Take care of it straight away?"

There was no answer at Melissa's door when we knocked, ten minutes later. Elvis's resolve wasn't dented, though, and he was happy to head back down to my room and pass the time till she returned. Happy, until I stood back and let him cross the threshold in front of me.

A man was already inside my room, waiting. A uniformed police officer. I'd guess he was in his mid forties. I couldn't get a good sense of his height, though, because he was sitting on my bed, his helmet at his side, brushing sandwich crumbs off the front of his tunic. He looked up as we appeared in the doorway and locked eyes with Elvis, who promptly turned on his heel and took flight down the corridor. I spun around and went after him. We were less than half way along when a second police officer appeared. He was coming towards us, from the direction of the staircase, holding a polystyrene takeaway cup in each hand. Elvis and I covered three more strides, still at full speed, then the policeman bent down and placed the drinks neatly on the floor by the left-hand wall.

"Stop him," I said, slowing down to avoid a collision.

The officer straightened up, stepped into our path, and stretched his arms out wide like an angry bear. He looked me straight in the face, and dodged to the side, letting Elvis race past him. Then he launched himself forwards, wrapping his arms around my knees and bringing me to the ground in a classic rugby tackle. He held on tight despite my protests, and by the time I'd rolled over and wriggled myself free, the two of us were alone in the corridor.

"You moron," I said, getting back to my feet. "Which part of 'stop him' did you not understand?"

The officer also stood up, and took a step closer to me, blocking my path.

"Is your name David Trevellyan?" he said.

I didn't reply.

I heard a sound behind me. It was the door to my room almost being ripped off its hinges. Then the officer who had been sitting on my bed marched into the corridor with a strange, twisted look on his face. I couldn't tell if it was anger, or embarrassment, or a mixture of both.

"Are you David Trevellyan?" the officer who'd tackled me said. "Come on. Yes? Or no?"

The officer from my room pushed past us and picked one of the cups up from the floor.

"Is this one mine?" he said.

"They're the same," the other officer said.

"Thanks, Dale," he said. "That's good. I'll take things from here."

He took a long swig, nodded his head like he was some sort of connoisseur, then made a show of looking me up and down.

"Tut, tut, tut," he said, after a moment. "Oh dear. Running from the police. Not a good idea. What was that all about, eh?"

"I don't know," I said. "I think you frightened him."

"Frightened who?"

"The guy who ran away from you. And now we need to get him back."

"Who was he?"

"He calls himself Elvis. I don't know his real name."

"Well, we don't care about him. We're here for you. Your name is David Trevellyan?"

"It is. And I'm really happy you're taking the theft of my boots so seriously - I honestly didn't think you would, or I'd have called you myself - but right now, finding that guy is more important."

The office shot a quick glance at his colleague, then turned back to me.

"This has nothing to do with any boots," he said. "Or with finding Elvis impersonators. What it does have to do with is us taking you into custody."

"What?" I said. "Are you insane?"

"David Trevellyan, I am placing you under arrest for occasioning actual bodily harm, disturbing the peace, and aggravated assault. You are not obliged to say anything, but anything you do say will be taken down and may be used as evidence against you in a court of law. Understand?"

"I haven't got time for this nonsense," I said. "We need to get after the guy I was chasing. Quickly. Before he disappears back down his rabbit hole."

The policeman handed his coffee to his colleague then reached around behind him and took a pair of handcuffs from his belt. I didn't like the way things were heading. They clearly had the wrong end of the stick, and I knew if I let them continue, things were only going to get worse. That's a road I've been down before.

"OK," I said. "I have no idea why you think I've done anything wrong, but we need to turn this around before you have a real problem on your hands. The guy you just let escape? He's a witness. A very important one. In fact, he just hit the top of the Security Service's hot list. So if you know what's good for you, you're going to stop talking about arresting me and start searching for him."

"Listen, David," the policeman said. "Can I call you Dave?"

"No."

"Well, Dave, let me tell you something. You're not doing yourself any favours here. You need to stop talking and come with us."

"I don't think so. You need to help me, right now. Otherwise this moves from a minor bollocking into full-scale arse kicking territory."

The policeman took a step towards me, still swinging the handcuffs between his finger and thumb.

"Look," he said. "Come quietly, and we'll let you stay on your feet. Keep shooting your mouth off, and we're going to drag you down the station. Your choice. But just so you know - there's lots of concrete staircases between here and there. Going down those when you're not properly balanced? Bad idea."

"You're not going to bring those cuffs anywhere near my wrists," I said. "You might as well put them away, right now. And give me some space. I need to make a call."

"You can call from the station. Now. Last chance. What's it to be?"

I've known people resort to assaulting police officers in nine or ten countries, over the years. I've aided and abetted them in four or five. I've done it myself, in two. But never until that moment had I been tempted to take a swing at a British bobby.

"We don't seem to be communicating very effectively, do we constable?" I said. "I need to make a call, and I need to make it now."

"Enough is..." he was saying, when his radio

crackled into life. He stepped away, unhooked his handset, and spoke to someone for forty-five seconds. Then he turned to his colleague.

"Dale," he said. "We're going to forget about this joker. Come on. Let's go."

"What about my witness?" I said. "You frightened him off. You need to get him back."

"Mr Trevellyan," the officer said, scowling at me again. "Something you should know. This time, you're lucky. But I never forget a face. If I see you again, you won't like what happens."

"How do you know?"

"What?"

"How do you know what I like? And don't like?"

"Well, I... "

"There's no sugar in this one, right?" I said, leaning down and taking hold of the remaining polystyrene cup. "What about milk?"

Neither of the policemen answered.

I pried open the lid and looked inside.

"Good," I said. "Thank you. Now, goodbye, gentlemen."

Chapter Eleven

I'd been back in my room for less than four minutes when I heard a squeak outside in the corridor. There were two urgent knocks, then the door swung open without me saying a word. It was Melissa, still in her chair.

"David," she said. "Are you all right? The police? Have they…?"

"They were here," I said. "Then they left. Someone called them off."

"That was me. Well, not me directly. I got word they were going to arrest someone because of those idiots in the garden, and I figured it had to be you. I insisted they drop it."

"Who told you about it?"

"A sergeant at the local station. I made them aware we were working here when I first arrived. It's standard procedure. They're supposed to keep us in the loop about anything they're doing in the vicinity, and luckily this guy was on the ball. I'm just sorry I couldn't get to them before they showed up here."

"Me too."

"They didn't get rough, did they?"

"Not even close. But they did cause a little bit of fall out."

"What do you mean? What kind of fall out?"

"I'll get to that in a second. What I want to know is, why did they come after me? Did those idiots actually file a complaint?"

"Yes, they did."

"And the police listened to them?"

"Unbelievable, isn't it?"

"And those morons were able to describe me so accurately the plod came straight to my room? Seems like a bit of a stretch."

"There's a little more to it than that. David, remember how I told you that CCTV camera wasn't working?"

"Clearly."

"And remember how Leckie told us two zones had been repaired again?"

"The garden was one of them?"

Melissa nodded.

"But I don't want you to worry," she said. "When we tell the police to forget something, they forget it. This won't come back to bite you, David. I guarantee."

"I hope not."

"It won't. So. This fallout you mentioned. What was that all about?"

I told her about Elvis.

"Damn," she said. "Five minutes with him and I could have gone home happy."

"That's what I figured," I said.

"Oh well. Thanks for finding him, anyway. That was good work."

"My pleasure."

"What are the chances of putting your hands on him again, do you think?"

"How quickly?"

"Let's say, before the sun rises?"

"I'd say, somewhere between zero and zero."

"That's what I was thinking. OK. So this is what we'll do. I'm assuming Elvis Presley isn't his real name?"

"I'd say you were on pretty safe ground, there. Although, he didn't sing anything, so I can't be sure."

"Right. So, we'll pull all personnel records for the maintenance staff. We can eliminate everyone who shows up for work in the morning. We'll give the details of the others to the Met, and they can scoop them up, pronto. In the meantime the hazmat team will hopefully prove there's no caesium missing. Then, if we can get Elvis to ID the fireman, that should get the job done."

"Sounds like a plan."

We chewed things over a little longer, and came to the conclusion that there was nothing to be gained by hanging around talking, and nothing to be lost by finding something decent to eat. It turned out that Melissa's favourite food was steak and kidney pie, and she knew a little pub that made their own less than a quarter of a mile away. That wasn't far, but she decided to abandon the wheelchair for the trip down the bumpy footpaths and narrow passageways that ran alongside the river.

"My sister used a chair," she said, when we'd been going for a little over five minutes. "I don't know if I told you that before."

"Is that the place?" I said, nodding towards a half-timbered building at the corner of the next street. "The Frog and Turtle?"

"She was in a motorcycle accident when she was seventeen. She never walked again. And I'd watch people looking at her, time after time after time, and only seeing the chair. They had no idea who she was. How smart she was. How beautiful she was. So that made me think. Any time I need cover, I'll use a chair, too. And hey presto. I'll be invisible."

"Is that the only reason you use one? Or is it a kind of tribute to your sister?"

"That's the only reason. It's entirely practical."

"Is she younger than you? Or older?"

"She was older."

"She's no longer with us?"

"No. She got hit by a fire engine, would you believe? Four years ago. Crossing the road. About a mile and a half from here, as it happens. It was late at night. A streetlight was broken, and it turned out the driver was just someone else who didn't see her. Or the chair."

"I'm sorry for your loss, Melissa. Truly. That's a terrible story."

"The Frog and Turtle?" she said, after a few seconds. "Yes, that's the place. Strange name. Good pies."

"You'll get no argument from me," I said. "You can't eat a name."

There were no free tables when we arrived at the pub, so we made our way over to the bar. A woman was sitting in the booth nearest the door. She was on her own. There was only a quarter of an inch of wine left in her glass, so I took my time to deliberate over the eight kinds of beer they had on draught, watching her in the big mirror on the wall. I finally bought a pint of Timothy Taylor for myself, and a bottle of hard cider for Melissa. The woman took a final sip of her wine, so we wandered across and loitered close by till she got up and left. Then Melissa slid her legs under the table and I settled in opposite her.

The place was busy and the rumble of background conversation was correspondingly loud, but Melissa still leaned in close before speaking.

"How long are you going to stick around?" she said.

"Tonight?" I said.

"You know what I mean."

"That's not up to me. I'll be here till I'm told to be somewhere else."

"Another country?"

"Always is."

"Must be strange, never being in the same place very long."

"Must strange, always being in the same place."

She took a couple of long pulls on the cider, then turned back to me.

"There'll be more to this than just finding Elvis, you know," she said.

I nodded.

"Hopefully he'll lead us to the fireman, but that won't be the end of it, either," she said.

I took a sip of my beer.

"We'll have to run his background," she said. "Even if he's a genuine firefighter it doesn't mean it was a genuine misunderstanding with the door."

"It doesn't," I said. "And here's another thing. You guys have been obsessing over whether this really was a robbery attempt. I guess that's what your procedures set you up to do. But have you ever wondered whether actually stealing the stuff was never part of the plan?"

"What do you mean?"

"It could be someone just wanted to do enough damage to cause a radiation scare. Even if none actually leaked out, it could trigger an evacuation. Of the hospital, maybe the whole area. Then, who knows what would be possible. Are there any high profile patients, who are normally guarded? What buildings are around here? What's stored in them? What about access to infrastructure, that could be sabotaged? Perhaps the attack on the door is the tip of the iceberg, not you."

Melissa smiled.

"All good points," she said. "But we haven't just fallen off some collective turnip truck. I told you, there's more to our operation than meets the eye. Your eye, anyway. Remember all the phone calls I've been following up? Well, every patient; every employee; every structure, current and abandoned, above or below ground; every phone, power, gas, water, TV, and traffic signal network; every London Underground line; even the old pneumatic pipes the Post Office used to us - all of that's been checked and risk-assessed. We're not worried."

I shrugged.

"But I am worried about starving," she said. "Are you ready to eat?"

I nodded.

"My treat," she said, and wriggled out of the booth.

Melissa eased her way through the crowd at the bar, and realised I wasn't the only one watching her. A couple of city boys liked the look of her, too. They were perching on stools with champagne flutes in their hands, with the rest of the bottle on the bar between them in a black plastic ice bucket.

Melissa spoke to the barman, and while she was waiting for our drinks to be poured one of the city boys slithered off his stool. He straightened his tie, ran one hand through his hair, and sidled up to her. He said something to her and she moved half a step to her left, away from him. I could see her upper lip curling into an expression of distaste. He moved after her and said something else. She looked away. He leaned in close, and presumably kept up his pursuit in a more intimate tone. He'd have been better advised not to because she spun around towards him, shot out her right hand and took hold of his ear. I knew what was coming next. She was going to gouge her thumbnail into his lobe. It was a simple move. Innocuous, on paper. But agonising in the flesh. And judging by his scream, she executed it perfectly. She held on for a couple of seconds, then picked up our glasses and moved back to the booth.

"The food'll be here soon," she said as she sat back down. "And I got you a pint of something called Old Peculier to go with it. I thought it would suit you."

"Thanks," I said. "Good choice. And more popular with you than champagne, tonight."

She shrugged.

"Morons," she said.

"Are we going to have trouble with them, later?" I said.

"I doubt it."

I glanced across, and saw the barman filling their glasses from a fresh bottle of Krug.

"They're sucking down that bubbly pretty enthusiastically," I said. "And the one you didn't pinch is wearing a rugby club tie."

"Well, if he tries anything, I'll give him a taste of my nails too," she said. "And watch as he runs home crying to his mummy."

The conversation moved away from work when the food arrived, but Melissa paused half way through her pie with a thoughtful look on her face.

"Interesting point you made about following procedures, before," she said. "Because you're right. There are so many, it's easy to switch into robot mode. And it's left me with this sick feeling that I'm missing something. And if I am, you know it'll be blindingly obvious with hindsight."

"Easy to be wise, after the event," I said.

She nodded, and took another bite.

"What if you were in my shoes?" she said. "How would you approach this? Have you dealt with anything like it before?"

"Not really," I said. "But you've discounted any idea

of the whole thing being a diversion, you told me. Which means we're stuck with an attempt to steal the caesium. So, what happens if you put yourself in the burglar's shoes, instead? Assume you've done your homework, and you know the vault is basically impregnable. What do you do?"

"Try a different vault?"

"Could do. Or maybe you'd try and get this caesium moved to a different vault, where it's easier to steal?"

"Interesting. But that doesn't work. The secondary site is equally secure."

"OK. But would the burglars know that?"

"If they'd done their homework, they might."

"What about when it's in transit?"

"Between sites? It'd definitely be more vulnerable then."

"Maybe that was the idea, then. To make you move it, and snatch it on the road."

"Maybe. But if that was the plan, it failed. We haven't moved it."

"What about after the inventory, tomorrow?"

"I can't see any need to move it then, either. Unless - I suppose it'd depend more on the prognosis for repairing the door. If that has to be taken out of service..."

"If that happens, we should go with whoever moves the canisters. If I was going to steal them, that's when I'd do it."

"We can't ride in the hazmat truck. You'll love this - procedures. But I could arrange extra escorts. And it's unorthodox, but we could follow in a separate vehicle."

Melissa stuck her tongue out at me, took the last of my fries, and then nodded to the waitress to clear our plates. She came over straight away, and I noticed the city boys leering at her as she leaned over the table. The clientele had changed during the course of the evening – office workers stopping in for a quick drink on the way home had given way to people getting fueled up on their way out to the local clubs – and the atmosphere in the place had changed with them. I looked at my watch. It was pushing ten o'clock.

"Do you want to get another drink here?" I said. "Or shall we try somewhere else?"

"Actually, would you mind if we called it a night?" Melissa said. "Tomorrow's going to be fraught, no doubt."

"That works for me," I said.

"I need to quickly powder my nose, then what? Meet by the door?"

"Deal."

The city boys watched Melissa wriggle into her coat, and their eyes followed her as she made her way across the room. They exchanged a glance, nodded, and slid down from the their stools. The guy who'd approached Melissa earlier counted out eight notes - presumably fifties - and threw them down on the bar next to his glass. It still was half full. The other guy had a final try at draining the last drops of champagne from his, then they set off together. They both gazed at the sign to the women's bathroom, but kept going towards the exit, slightly unsteady on their feet. I watched till they were safely outside, and kept an eye open in case they came back in.

When Melissa was ready I held the door so she could go through first, but as soon as her feet reached the pavement she stopped moving. I came up alongside her, and could immediately see why. It was the two city boys. They were standing five feet in front of her, leaning against the wall. The one who'd spoken to Melissa was smoking a cigarette. The four of us stayed still for a moment. No one spoke. Then the guy levered himself upright and stepped forward, blocking our path. I'd guess he was bang-on six feet tall. He had a mop of blond hair, all unruly curls, which didn't blend well with his conservative charcoal grey suit, white shirt, and striped tie. And it was picking up an orange hue from the streetlights, which made him look like a clown.

The guy took another drag on his cigarette, then flicked the butt at my right foot. It missed, sending a little shower of sparks dancing across the pavement.

"There's nothing quite like trying to be cool, but falling a little short, is there?" I said.

The guy glared at me, then turned his attention to Melissa.

"My ear's a little sore," he said.

"Why?" she said. "Did you feel a little prick when I grabbed it?"

The guy's eyes narrowed a touch.

"I was thinking," he said. "Maybe you want to kiss it better."

"That's fascinating," she said. "Do you seriously think there are any circumstances in which I'd want to kiss a part of you?"

"Well, you better think of some circumstances, you bitch. It's time to pucker up, and let me see you're sorry. You've got thirty seconds."

"Oh, really? And if I don't?"

"If you don't, I'm going to beat your boyfriend's brains out on the pavement."

"That's going to be a little tricky, you know."

"I don't think so," the guy said, looking me in the eye.

I smiled back at him.

"In fact, it would be impossible," she said. "Because I don't have a boyfriend."

Melissa shifted her position, readying herself, and

the back of her left hand brushed against mine. I felt the hairs on my arm stand up all the way to my elbow.

"I'm talking about him," the guy said, nodding towards me.

"Him?" Melissa said. "You're threatening to beat his brains out? Oh dear."

"It's not a threat," he said. "It's a promise."

Melissa had to stifle a laugh.

"David?" she said. "How do you want to handle this? I've had a nice evening, up to now. I don't want to end up dealing with the police again."

"There may be no way around the police," I said. "Let me just check my understanding of the situation. This guy's offered to beat my brains out. Is that right?"

"It is. I heard him."

"And you confirm that?" I said to the guy.

He nodded a little half heartedly, and I saw that confusion was starting to replace the anger on his face.

"OK," I said. "I accept your offer. Which means we just need one more thing."

I reached into my pocket, pulled out a handful of coins, and selected a penny piece. Then I reached out and dropped it into the breast pocket of his jacket.

"Hey," he said. "What are you doing?"

"It's called a consideration," I said. "It's a legal term. You haven't heard of it?"

The guy looked blank.

"It means a form of payment," I said. "You need an offer. An acceptance. And a consideration. Take those three things, and do you know what you have?"

He didn't reply.

"A contract," I said. "Legally binding, under English common law. So. Come on. Time to deliver."

He didn't move.

"Thirty seconds," I said. "That's the timeframe you promised, just now? Which means you have thirty seconds to beat my brains out, if my friend doesn't kiss you. Otherwise, you're in breach of contract. And I don't know about you, but I take breaches of contract very seriously."

I held my left wrist out in front of me, pulled back my sleeve, and looked at my watch. Or at least pretended to. I was actually counting the seconds in my head, and focusing all my attention on the guy.

He did nothing.

I gave him an extra ten seconds, but he still didn't react.

"OK," I said. "That's it. You're in default. Time to make the call."

I pulled my phone out of my pocket, dialed three consecutive nines, then looked the guy straight in the eye. And paused without hitting the green button.

"Although, we do have one alternative," I said. "We could think about an alternative form of penalty."

The guy stepped back towards his friend.

"Stop," I said. "I'm not going to hurt you. But I want to know how much money you've got in your wallet."

He didn't answer.

"How much?" I said.

"I don't know," he said. "Three hundred. Four, maybe. Plus credit cards."

"I don't want the cards. Just the cash. Give it to me. Now."

The guy reached into his jacket and produced a shiny, black leather wallet. He opened it, took out a fat wad of notes, and handed it to me.

"Good," I said, putting my phone away. "I'll consider that the first installment. Any time I see you in the future, you're going to give me the same amount again. Understand?"

The guy nodded.

"Now leave," I said. "And take your friend with you. I'm sick of looking at you."

We watched them all the way to the end of the street, and when they turned the corner Melissa set off in the opposite direction.

"You coming?" she said.

I had to pick up the pace to keep up with her.

"I have to ask, David, mugging someone?" she said after we'd covered fifty yards in silence. "After everything you spouted off about in the garden? Was that all lies? Or have you switched sides? Honestly, I'm a little shocked."

"Mugging that little weasel? Is that what you thought I was doing?"

"Wasn't it? You threatened him. And you took his money. That sounds pretty textbook, to me."

"I took his money, yes. But not for myself. I'm going to give it to the first homeless person I see."

"Seriously?"

"Absolutely."

She slowed down a little.

"David, stealing from the rich and giving to the poor – that's not your job," she said. "In fact, that's not anybody's job."

"Well, it should be someone's job," I said. "You saw how that guy behaved. Do you think it's OK to treat people that way? To take whatever – or whoever – you want, just because you're rich?"

"Of course not."

"The guy was a bully. Someone needed to stop him.

Or else why would he think twice, next time?"

"And you were the person to do that?"

"Yes."

"Why?"

"Because I was there. And it was the right thing to do."

"But who gave you the right to decide?"

"You don't think I did the right thing? You think I should have sent him to the hospital, instead?"

"No."

"Look, I let him walk away. I saved the country the cost of an ambulance and a hospital bed. I made it so that Christmas is coming early for some tramp, tonight. And do you know why?"

"You have a soft spot for tramps?"

"No. Because you told me to."

"Wait. Let me think. No. It's as I thought. I did no such thing."

"You did. Back at the hospital. After I finished 'spouting off' in the garden. Remember?"

"I told you we had to find a balance," she said, after a moment's thought.

"Exactly," I said. "And that's as balanced as it's going to get."

Chapter Twelve

I usually fall asleep within seconds of my head touching the pillow, but that night my eyes would not stay closed. I lay awake for two hours, and even after I dozed off, I only slept fitfully. I couldn't stop dreaming. A woman was in most of them. A Navy Intelligence Liaison Officer. We'd been close from the moment our paths first crossed in Madrid, then again in Morocco, and more recently in New York. So when Melissa appeared next to my bed – fully dressed, and with no sign of the wheelchair – I thought for a moment she'd taken her place. Then she reached out and shook me by the shoulder, and I knew it was no dream.

"David," she said. "Wake up. Quickly. Get your clothes. Something's happened."

"What is it?" I said, sitting up and instinctively smelling the air. "What's the problem?"

"There's been an explosion."

"Where? In the hospital?"

"Yes. In the basement."

"The room with the caesium?"

"We're not sure. That corridor, definitely. But there's a lot of smoke, so no one can see anything."

I slid out of bed and crossed to the window, then drew back the heavy curtains.

"Is the fire brigade on its way?" I said.

"They're already here. The fire engines are round the other side. They aren't visible from here. But there's not much they can do, anyway. Because there's another problem. The radiation alarms have gone off."

"Meaning what? That the caesium vault has been

breached?"

"It looks that way. We'll know for sure in an hour or so."

"What about the hazmat team? Can you bring them forward?"

"No. They wouldn't be any use. They do inventory control. Too specialised. But another team is on its way, in their place. An emergency response crew."

"Is the hospital being evacuated?"

"Not yet. That's a last resort. They avoid it at all costs. Unless the fire spreads, the patients are safer on the wards than out on the street."

"What about the radiation?"

"It's seems to be a small leak. Very localised. Any further action depends on what the emergency team finds."

"Is there anything we can do in the meantime?"

"Yes. Two things. Check the CCTV to see if it caught anyone suspicious coming in. And fetch some tea. My mouth is as dry as a bone."

We agreed on a division of labour. Melissa and the people back at her office would chase up the surveillance tapes, and I would head to the canteen - which was supposed to be open twenty four hours a day - in search of the tea. It was a reasonable plan, on the face of it. I had further to walk, and I wasted a little time watching the emergency crew Melissa had mentioned crossing the garden with their equipment, but it seemed like I had the easier job. And this impression was made stronger when I pushed open the door to her room and caught sight of the expression on her face.

"More bad news?" I said

"I just got off the phone," she said. "Not bad news, exactly. Not good news, either. The hazmat guys are here. They were out of the traps pretty fast. I spoke to the team leader just before you got back. He says their operation's already underway."

"They aren't hanging around. I saw them, on my way back. And they looked like they knew what they were doing. But what about the CCTV? Is anything doing there?"

"No. A big fat zero. It's the same story. None of the cameras that are working picked up anything. The ones in places that would have helped us aren't back in service yet, despite Stan Leckie and his 'best in the country' contractors. He probably meant 'cheapest in the country.' We're going to have a serious conversation when this is over, he and I."

We sipped our tea. Melissa put her cup on the table and wheeled restlessly backwards and forwards, her gaze flicking from a window to the door to her phone and back again. I sat on her bed, and waited.

"No sign of a new chair, then," I said.

"What?" she said.

"They didn't give you a new chair. For the desk. To replace the one that got broken. You told me you'd spoken to Jackson about it."

"Oh. No. I guess they didn't think they could trust me with one."

Melissa stopped moving and looked at me.

"I'm surprised you're still here," she said.

"I haven't finished my tea," I said.

"I mean, because of that girl. The one in the Frog and Turtle."

"Which girl?"

"Oh come on. You know which girl. The tall brunette at the far end of the bar."

"The one with the interesting blouse?"

"Yes."

"What's she got to do with anything?"

"She liked you."

"She didn't like me. You're making that up."

"Did you at least get her phone number?" she said.

"Why would I want her phone number?" I said.

"I saw how you were looking at her. Don't try to deny it. At one point I thought I was going to have to reach across and wipe the drool off your..."

Melissa's phone interrupted her so she grabbed it from her lap, talked for three minutes, then got to her feet.

"That was the hazmat team leader again," she said. "Come on. We have to go."

"What's happening?" I said. "Was it a deliberate attack?"

"They can't be sure. They're looking at some worn out insulation they think came from the old generator equipment. It's soaked in oil residue, and they say a spark from some kind of electrical short circuit might have been at the root of it."

"Is the fire out?"

"Not yet. But here's the thing. They had to move the caesium out of the way before the fire crew could get to work. They've no way of telling how long it'll be before it can go back in the vault. And they can't tell why the radiation alarm sounded, because none of the canisters appear to be damaged. So guess what they're doing with it?"

"Moving it."

"Correct. They're doing exactly what you said would make the stuff most vulnerable."

The hazmat truck was sandwiched between four police cars when it pulled out of the service entrance at the side of St Joseph's, ninety minutes later. You could hear its engine rumbling from a hundred yards away. Its six spherical wheels could have been taken from a moon buggy, and its high, rugged bodywork looked like a Hollywood version of an armoured personnel carrier.

"If this pays off, I've got to warn you, I'm taking the credit," Melissa said, easing the black Ford Mondeo away from the kerb. "It was hell, putting all this together with ten seconds notice. But if nothing happens, and anyone starts asking where all the money went, you're taking the blame."

"Wait," I said, as she shifted into second gear. "Stop the car."

"Come on, I was only joking. It's not like the government can't afford it. Austerity hasn't gone that far. Not yet, anyway."

"What have you got covering that thing, aside from the police?"

"Four unmarked cars, with two agents in each of them, and a helicopter."

"And the real truck?"

"It has one car, which is standard."

"OK. I think we should change our plan. We should follow the real one instead."

"Why?"

"The decoy sounds like it's well taken care of. If anyone hits it, having us there won't make any difference. But the caesium is vulnerable, just like someone wants it. That's where we should be."

Melissa was silent for a moment, then swung the car back to the side of the road.

"This is insane," she said, coming to rest again. "And all the more reason to blame you. I hope you realise that."

For fifteen minutes we sat and listened as the agents tailing the decoy van called in their movements. Street after street, turn after turn, as central London began to give way to the outlying districts, they had nothing untoward to report.

Then the hospital gate opened again and a plain white, long wheel-base Mercedes Sprinter emerged, closely followed by a silver Vauxhall Insignia. Melissa let the pair of vehicles pass us and make their way around the next corner before pulling away herself, guided by a new voice on the radio.

The agent in the chase car spoke calmly and clearly, giving precise details after each junction, and Melissa's driving reflected his tone. She drove slowly and smoothly, making sure we were always at least two moves behind, worrying more about being spotted by anyone watching the truck than getting held up by the sparse traffic that was left on the road at that time of night.

The decoy convoy was making better time than us, and after another twelve minutes we heard them report their arrival at the Queen Elizabeth II Hospital in Croydon. The threat wouldn't be over till the real truck caught up and the caesium was locked in the back-up vault, but a disappointed expression started to spread across Melissa's face anyway. She glanced at me, and I thought she was about to say something when her phone began to ring.

"OK," she said, ending the call after two minutes. She was breathing hard now. "Let me think for a minute. David, can you look at the map? We need a place to stop the van. As close to here as possible, but where the other units can quickly get back to, and nothing too near any housing. And we need it quickly."

"Stop the van?" I said. "Why?"

"That was Jones on the phone. He's back at St Joseph's. All hell's broken loose over there. A fire crew's just discovered the hazmat team. The whole of it. In the basement. Knocked out. Tied up. And stripped of all their kit."

"So who are we following?"

"That's a very good question. Someone with the

savvy to trick us into giving them a ready made caesium removal machine, I guess. Oh my God, David – you know what this means? This is it. The nightmare's begun. The caesium's gone. We don't know who's got it. Or what they're going to do with it. Or when. All we know is how they got it."

Melissa's words raised the hairs on the back of my neck. Someone had seen the logistical problems of removing caesium from the hospital, just like I had. And they'd realised it would be easier to take the stuff if it was already outside the vault. But when they'd joined the pieces of the puzzle, they'd come up with a subtly different solution. One that could be even more effective. And in a case like this, effective equates to lethal.

"Where's the helicopter got to?" I said.

"Half way back to base by now, I should think," Melissa said. "Why?"

"Well, I know you're desperate to get your hands back on the caesium as quickly as possible. But here's a thought. Are you sure you want to stop the van right away? Why not follow it? See where they're taking the stuff. That way, maybe we could scoop up whoever they're planning to hand it off to, as well."

"That's risky," she said, after a moment. "I don't like the idea of that stuff on the loose for any longer than it needs to be. But I guess you're right. Jones is already whistling up another hazmat crew. I'll have him get the chopper back, and see if he can get hold of any more of our people, pronto."

Melissa picked up her phone and was half way through giving Jones his instructions when we reached a roundabout. It came sooner than I'd expected, because it was the last point on the route the MI5 agent had reported. He'd called in a right turn. Melissa was driving much faster now, and she had to hit the brakes hard as we came to our exit. Because the road was blocked. By a car, slewed sideways across the carriageway. A silver Vauxhall. The driver's side was completely caved in. Both windows were smashed, and two male figures lay slumped in the front seats.

Melissa swerved and came to a stop behind the remains of the car. She glanced back at the agents. Then looked forward, along the road. It was completely empty. There was no sign of the vehicle that had caused the accident. And no sign of the white Mercedes van.

Chapter Thirteen

There are times when improvisation is your only option. There are times where you have to just cross your fingers and ride your luck. But nine times out of ten - as my father used to say - you can't beat having the right tools for the job. And in this case, Melissa and her people had the right tools. A GPS transponder concealed in the truck carrying the caesium, and a helicopter to track its signal.

We drove for three more miles, then left the car next to a wrecked phone box and covered another hundred yards on foot. It was dark. None of the streetlights were working, and we had to move slowly to avoid tripping on the cracked and cratered road surface. The weather wasn't extreme enough in that part of Croydon to account for the damage, so I put it down to abuse from the trucks that used to serve the abandoned freight depots we passed on both sides.

The eight agents who'd been following the decoy truck were waiting for us, weapons drawn, bodies tense, pressed up close to the eight foot wall at the far end of the street. No sound reached us from the other side, but we knew we were in the right place. The MI5 technicians had supplied the co-ordinates they'd derived from the van's transponder signal, and the helicopter pilot circling high overhead had visually confirmed it was still there. The four occupants were still with it, but there was no sign of anyone else in the surrounding buildings. That meant there was a good chance we'd found them before they'd rendezvoused with their contacts. Now we just had to find a way into the compound without giving them the chance to raise an alarm. And without damaging the caesium containers.

Melissa told four of the agents to prepare their Kevlar blankets for spreading over the glass shards embedded on top of the wall. Then she dispatched the other four to the far side of the compound, to mop up anyone who tried to escape. "Squirters," she called them.

It took the first agent three minutes to report he was in position. The next two confirmed within another thirty seconds. That just left one more to call in, and Melissa was starting to get a little jumpy when the helicopter pilot cut across him.

"Hold, hold, hold," the pilot said, on the radio. "Movement."

Everyone froze.

"Two suspects," he said. "Breaking away from the van. Heading for the rear wall. No, ignore that. For the main building. They're going inside. I'm switching to heat-sensing. OK. They're still moving. Slower now, though. Looks like they're starting a room by room search of the place."

"Where are the other two?" Melissa said.

"No change," he said. "Holding position at the van."

"OK," she said. "Change of plan. This is what we're going to do."

The agents huddled for a moment while Melissa ran through her new instructions, then one pair moved away towards the heavy double gate set into the wall forty feet away. They looked back, checking their colleagues were ready, then one of them banged twice on the wood.

"Movement," the pilot said. "One suspect. Leaving the van. Approaching the gate."

"The two in the building?" Melissa said.

"No change," he said. "Looks like they're continuing to search. OK, the first suspect's reaching the gate... now."

"Who is it?" a man's voice said from inside the compound.

"Who do you think?" the agent who'd knocked said. "Open the gate."

"Where have you been? You're late."

"Took longer to get here. It's all kicked off at the hospital, apparently. Had to make sure we weren't followed. Now let's get this over with. Open the gate, or I'm out of here and you'll be the one holding the baby when the police turn up."

I heard a rustling sound as the stiff Kevlar blankets were eased into place, behind me. There was a pause, followed by an angry squeak as the gate was jerked back a couple of inches. Then the nearest agent raised a square, yellow and grey handgun and fired through the gap.

"Suspect one down," the pilot said, and I turned just in time to see the other pair of agents disappear over the wall.

"Suspect two down," he said, a second later. "Compound clear."

Melissa and I hurried to the gate, and I saw a man lying in our path on the far side, twitching slightly, still attached by the neck to the agent's gun with a pair of transparent wires. Melissa glanced at him, then hurried towards the van where the other pair of agents was waiting. They were standing over another man's body. This guy was wearing similar overalls, but he was completely inert. It looked like they'd taken care of him the old-fashioned way.

"Have you looked inside?" Melissa said.

One of the agents nodded.

"And?" she said.

"They're all there," he said. "Four canisters, battened down, safe and sound."

Melissa let out a long, slow, sigh of relief, but I have a

less trusting nature. I felt compelled to look for myself. The rear cargo doors were standing open, and the space inside was dominated by eight pairs of metal arms. They were bolted to the floor via heavy duty rubber shock-absorbers, twelve inches from the van's reinforced sides, and each pair met in the centre, three feet above the armoured floor. The jaws at the top of the four outer sets were empty, but the others were clamped around shiny metal canisters. They looked identical to the ones I'd seen being wheeled through the hospital garden, except for the coloured discs that had been attached to the seam where the lids met the bodies. They were radiation indicators. And all four were green.

"It looks good," Melissa said, stepping across to join me. "We'll get the new hazmat team to check them, though. To make sure they're the real deal. In the meantime, we just have to flush the other two out of that building. Then we can see about scooping up their contacts, like you suggested."

Melissa asked me to keep an eye on the two prisoners. It didn't seem like too hard a job. Neither had regained consciousness, and both had been dragged into the space between the wall and the van and were lying on their backs, secured at the wrists and ankles with flexicuffs. She checked that the four agents were still in place on the far side of the compound. Then she approached the building, a pair of agents fanned out on either side of her, and signaled for the helicopter to descend to a level where its rotor blades were clearly audible.

"Armed police," the pilot said, his voice amplified through the speakers on the outside of his aircraft. "The building is surrounded. Throw your weapons through the main door, and come out with your hands in the air. You have thirty seconds."

Melissa kept her Sig trained on the door. The other agents covered the windows on either side, methodically scanning the six windows on each of the three floors.

No one showed themselves.

"I repeat," the pilot said. "Armed police. We have you surrounded. This is your last chance to surrender. Leave the building immediately. If we have to come in after you, we will shoot on sight."

Five more seconds crept past in silence, then I saw the agents stiffen. I heard footsteps. They were coming from the main doorway to the building. There were two sets. They hesitated, then stopped altogether. An object flew through the air and crashed on the ground. A handgun. It was followed by a second one. Then the footsteps started again, and two men shuffled reluctantly into the courtyard, one in front of the other.

"Good," Melissa said, taking a step towards them. "Now, get on the ground. Face down. Hands behind your heads. Do it now."

Neither man moved.

"Face down, on the ground," Melissa said, raising her Sig and lining it up on the closer man's forehead. "You can do it while you're still breathing. Or while you're not. Either way works for me."

"Wait," he said, taking a half step forward. "Please."

"Stop," Melissa said. "Get on the ground."

"I will," he said. "I will. We surrender. We're unarmed. But please, listen to me first. There's something you need to know. About what we took from the hospital. It's urgent. I swear. We're in danger. All of us."

"Why?"

"Those big flasks?" he said, inching a little closer to Melissa. "They're not stable. They've been sabotaged."

"How?" she said. "When? By whom?"

"Before we left the room, in the hospital. The driver did it. He's the technician."

"What did he do?"

"Attached some device."

"What kind of device?"

"It's on a timer. The people who are supposed to meet us have a key to deactivate it. A radio thing. But if they don't do it by..."

The guy raised his left arm as if to check his watch, and when it was at chest height he sprang forward, reaching for Melissa's throat. I expected her to shoot him on the spot but instead she swatted away his outstretched arms and drove the heel of her left hand into his jaw, knocking him flat on his back.

"How about you?" she said to the second man. "Have you got any urgent information for me, too?"

The guy shook his head and got down on his knees. He paused, then pivoted as if to lie down. But instead of hitting the ground, he used the momentum he'd created to close the gap with Melissa, regain his feet, coil one arm around her neck, wrap the other around her waist, and spin her round to shield him from the other agents' Sigs.

"Give me your gun," the guy said to Melissa.

She dropped the weapon and kicked it away.

The guy tightened his grip around Melissa's neck and reached into his overall pocket with his other hand. He withdrew it a moment later and stretched his arm straight out to the side. His fingers were clenched around a narrow, white tube and his thumb was pressed hard against the top end.

"That was stupid," he said. "You've forced me to do this. Now all our lives are on the line, not just yours. Tell your people to drop their pistols."

Melissa didn't respond.

I looked down at the two guys tied up next to the van. They were both still completely inert, so I tucked my

Beretta into the back of my jeans, reached through the door, and picked up one of the handguns the agents had recovered when they'd entered the compound.

"Your weapons, gentlemen," the guy holding Melissa said. "On the ground. Quickly."

The agents who'd been on either side of Melissa remained still, but the two on the outside of the line started to move forward, looking for a clearer shot. It was an obvious ploy, though, and the guy responded by dragging Melissa backwards until his back was safely pressed against the wall of the building.

"OK," he said. "No more second chances. You see what I'm holding? It's a remote trigger. You see my thumb is pressing the button? That means the system is armed. If I let go - boom. There'll be clouds of caesium over half of South London. Is that what you want?"

The agents stopped moving.

"Good," the guy said. "So, this is what I want. Put your guns on the ground, now. Then back off, and do not interfere while this nice lady and I get into the van and drive away. And when we're gone, do not call anyone for thirty minutes. Remember the button. If I see anyone following, I'll let go."

The agents stayed where they were and showed no sign of lowering their weapons, so I stepped out from the shadow of the van. I was holding the borrowed Colt out to my side at shoulder height, with its grip between my finger and thumb.

"It's OK, lads," I said, throwing the gun down in front of me. "Do as he says."

It took a few seconds, but eventually the agents' Sigs rattled to the ground.

"Everyone, stay calm," I said, then turned to the guy holding Melissa. "We've done what you asked. No one's armed, and no one's going to do anything stupid. You're free to take the van. But how about this? Take me with you, instead of her?"

"No chance," the guy said. "I'm taking her."

"That's fine," I said. "There's no problem. You can take her. We're not going to call anyone, when you do. And no one's going to follow you, so there's no need for anyone to get hurt. OK?"

"OK."

"Good. Now look, we're giving you what you want. Everything you asked for. But I just have one thing to ask in return. Later, when you're in the wind and we recover the vehicle, our people will have to make it safe. So can you tell me, are all the canisters booby-trapped? Or just some of them?"

He didn't answer.

"We could always leave it an hour before we call this in," I said. "Give you twice as long to get away. It would be worth it to know what we're dealing with when we get our hands back on that van. And no one would ever know you'd told us anything."

"Two," the guy said, after a moment. "Two canisters are wired."

"Definitely two?" I said.

"Definitely."

"Which two?"

"I don't know."

"So how do you know there are two?"

"I saw the driver rigging the devices at the hospital. But I didn't load them into the van. I don't know which order they loaded them in."

"You saw him open them?"

"No. The devices are attached to the outside. Just tell your people to look for the wires."

I took a moment to reconstruct the interior of the van in my memory. The exact appearance of the canisters. And to push the thought of their contents out of my mind.

"OK, thanks," I said, when I was ready. Then I reached behind me, took hold of my Beretta, and shot a glance at Melissa.

It's OK. He's bluffing.

"Agent Wainwright," I said. "Would you like me to shoot him?"

Understood, her expression replied.

"No need," she said, smashing her the back of her head into the guy's face, then stamping down on his right knee and driving her elbow in his abdomen. "I think he's changed his mind about that drive."

Chapter Fourteen

Hurry up and wait. That's how my father used to sum up the routine of life in the army. An unbroken cycle of frenzied action followed by long periods of doing nothing. He warned me to expect the same when I joined the Navy, but my experience has been pleasantly different. For one thing, I've had very little time on my hands over the years. And for another, the Navy really does try to keep what we call the 'dead time' - the meetings and the paperwork that follow every assignment - to an absolute minimum. But as I sat with Melissa in an office at Thames House the next morning, I began to suspect that things weren't quite the same at MI5.

The chair I picked was still warm when I sat in it, but the man at the end of the table - the Deputy Director General, the officer in charge of the day-to-day running of the whole organisation - showed no sign of having noticed the person occupying it had changed. He was too busy cleaning his half moon reading glasses, carefully spraying them with clear liquid from a tiny silver aerosol and buffing them with a square of bottle-green silk.

Melissa took the seat next to me and we waited in silence until two more men came into the room. The first was the agent who'd fired the tazer through the gate at the compound in Croydon, and Melissa whispered to me that the other was her boss. They took seats with a space in between them on the opposite side of the rectangular table, but before they'd settled themselves the door opened again and Tim Jones appeared. Melissa beckoned him in, and he hurried to sit down at her side.

The Deputy DG moved his head for the first time as

soon the door had swung closed. He held his spectacles up to the light, nodded, then used them to gesture towards Melissa's boss.

"Introductions," he said. "Chaston, get the ball rolling, will you?"

"Colin Chaston," Melissa's boss said. "Central Counter Terrorism Unit."

"Phil Green," the agent said. "Field Operations."

"I'm Arthur Hardwicke," the Deputy DG said. "I'm taking a personal interest in this mess. Our friend on the other side of the table is Commander Trevellyan, who's joining us temporarily from Navy Intelligence. And everyone knows agents Wainwright and Jones, yes?"

Everyone nodded.

"Good," Hardwicke said. "Now, we had a very close shave last night. A very uncomfortably close shave. Chaston – how do we smell this morning? Of roses? Or of the stuff they grow in?"

"I'm quietly optimistic, actually," Chaston said. "We already knew we'd recovered the right number of containers, yesterday. Well, the lab boys have been burning the midnight oil, and they've now confirmed the correct amount of caesium was inside them. None had been syphoned off, diluted, stolen, or in any other way tampered with. So, any immediate threat has been avoided."

"That's good. But what worries me most about this whole bag of spanners is that we didn't see it coming. It landed on us completely out of the blue. So, what else do we know? Who's behind it? What were they planning?"

"Well, we're progressing on three fronts. The hospital crime scene. The vehicle. And the criminals we apprehended with it."

"That's not what I asked."

"Well then, the simple answer is we're in the dark."

"Start with what's happening at the hospital. Wainwright, that's your bailiwick, yes?"

"Yes sir," Melissa said. "Jones and I became involved when axe marks were discovered on the door to the caesium vault. These did not represent a credible attempt to gain access, so we're working on the theory that persons unknown were attempting to cause the caesium to be removed, thus rendering it more vulnerable."

"This was not successful?" Hardwicke said.

"No sir. The damage was only cosmetic, so there was no need to move the caesium at that time."

"Who wielded the axe?"

"A fireman. Or someone dressed as one. We haven't yet been able to establish his identity. Or, if he's a real fireman, whether he was bribed or coerced."

"Why not?"

"I'm sorry to report this sir, but the Met allowed the only witness to escape."

Hardwicke picked his glasses back up from the table and carefully sprayed more fluid onto each lens.

"I assume you're doing something about getting him back?" he said, catching an excess drop of liquid with the cloth before it could hit the table.

"Yes sir," Jones said. "I'm taking personal responsibility for that. I'll ensure he's found."

"Very good," Hardwicke said. "And what about last night's episode? A second try?"

"We believe so," Melissa said. "It seems that someone learned their lessons and tried a more refined approach. The fire brigade believes the fire was started deliberately with some wads of insulation from a disused generator. The stuff was soaked with oil, so it gave off copious clouds of very dense smoke. And it was arranged around some pieces of an old x-ray machine, to give off enough of a radiation signature to prompt us to call the emergency hazmat team."

"Ingenious."

"Very. It was improvised, and highly successful. And because all the components were sourced from the hospital itself, it gives us very little to trace."

"I see. And what about the van?"

"Nothing constructive, I'm afraid sir," Green said. "The van, the tools, the hazmat suits, all completely clean. There were no prints, other than from the four individuals we apprehended at the scene, and nothing with any DNA."

"Was it rigged in any way?"

"No sir. We don't think it was intended as a come-on. Based on how the thieves reacted when we arrived, we think they were just waiting to hand it off to someone else."

"Who?"

"We don't know. We kept the location under observation for another four hours, but no one showed their face."

"What are the thieves saying?"

"Nothing. But they may well not know anything. Whoever planned this is clearly too sophisticated to allow any of the pawns to know anything about their set up."

"You're probably right. But I want them sweated, anyway. Any other observations?"

"Yes sir," Melissa said. "We're talking about the thieves and the people they were apparently handing the caesium over to as if they're separate groups. And yet we haven't heard a whisper of either one. Doesn't that strike anyone as strange?"

For a moment there was silence.

"Continue," Hardwicke said, when no one else responded.

"Here's what I'm thinking," Melissa said. "What if

we're actually dealing with a single organisation? With one team to steal the caesium, one to turn it into whatever kind of weapon they're planning on using, and maybe another to take it to their target. Feasible?"

No one spoke, but Green and Jones nodded their heads.

"Now, let's stack up what we know about this organisation, so far," Melissa said. "They're determined. They misfired with their first attempt on the vault, but that didn't put them off. They adapted and tried again. And they're resourceful. Look at how they used the junk they found in the hospital basement. It certainly fooled us. We played right into their hands, by sending the emergency crew. So alongside what we're already doing, I think we should prioritise the key piece of the puzzle we're missing."

"That piece being?"

"What they're targeting. And I think we should bring in additional resources specifically to help in this area."

"I'm not sure," Chaston said. "We can't afford to dilute the operation, or lose focus or control. The consequences would be too dire. We have a plan, and we should follow it through with maximum expedience."

"I think we should do both things," Melissa said. "And here's why. We can see how this group responds to setbacks. So, the failure to secure the caesium may well not stop them. They've probably got a plan B, ready to roll. They could just press ahead, only with a different weapon. And they could easily shut down this whole arm of their operation, leaving us high and dry if it's the only thing we're looking at."

"There's the timescale to think about, too," Jones said. "The second attempt on the caesium was so hard on the heels of the first, it suggests they need it urgently. Which means we may not have long to unravel this thing. They could be preparing to strike at any moment."

"I agree," Hardwicke said. "This has all the hallmarks of something spectacular. I'm determined that we stop it. But if we don't, I'm not going to tell the PM we backed away from the Hydra that caused it after only cutting off a single one of its heads."

Chapter Fifteen

The Naval Intelligence Division's offices in their bleak, unmarked building in Tottenham Court Road were nowhere near as plush as the ones in MI5's headquarters. The chairs were not as comfortable. The dull orange carpets were worn through in places. There was no restful view of the Thames from the unwashed windows. But they did have one advantage. There was a Caffe Nero almost next door. And the strong cappuccino they sell made recounting recent events for a second time that day much more palatable.

"So what's your next step?" my new controller said, when I finally wound up the summary.

"Box want me to stay on at the hospital, and help them dig into the theft," I said. "But I was thinking along different lines."

"Really? Such as what?"

"I think we've reached the point where I'd be more useful on our side of the fence again."

The controller reached into his briefcase, took out a bottle of water, and drained the remaining two inches in a single swig.

"Out of the question," he said, tossing the empty bottle into an overflowing rubbish bin next to the door then turning back to me. "Your job with them isn't close to being done."

"I don't agree," I said. "The caesium's been recovered. None of it's missing. It's all under lock and key, somewhere else. The people who stole it are in the bag. Box have got all their available resources trying to find out what the target would have been, in case someone tries to hit it another way. All the bases are covered. They don't need me anymore."

"Maybe not, from that point of view. But you were never there to find caesium or catch thieves, Trevellyan. Or even to stop the thieves using the caesium to kill people. Your job is to find out whether anyone from Box is bent. And judging by the picture you painted, I'd say their brass is right to be worried. Something is very definitely rotten with the state they're in."

The problem was, I knew he was right. But it had been unpleasant enough the various times I'd had to wash the Navy's dirty laundry, in the past. I didn't relish having to do the same for MI5, now. Not because I had a particularly soft spot for them as an organisation. But because I had to admit, there was something about Melissa I liked. I was going to be genuinely disappointed if I found she'd crossed the line.

"Let me ask you this," he said. "Box have sketched out a pretty convenient connection between the first time the vault door was damaged and the successful theft. But what do you think? Are you buying it?"

"I'm not convinced of it," I said. "But I'm not convinced it was a coincidence, either. That's why I went looking for witnesses. The key will be getting our hands back on that janitor. He saw what happened. His story should throw a little more light on things."

"It might, I suppose. If you can trust him. He might be a plant."

"He might be."

"You're looking to him to explain that connection. Well, something smells off, and that's where the stench started from, for my money. I mean, I understand the idea of someone learning lessons. But think about how much the M.O. changed. And when."

"What do you mean?"

"Scratching a high security door and expecting it to trigger an evacuation of such a closely monitored substance? That's totally naive. But compare it with what happened, only a couple of days later. It wasn't just in a different league of sophistication. It smacked of specialised knowledge."

"It was a step change, for sure."

"It was. So, ask yourself, what had changed between the attacks? Two agents turned up, on the scene. And all of a sudden this mystery group that no one had heard of before went from amateur hour to knowing exactly how to press all Box's buttons. How's that for a coincidence?"

"It's a stretch, I grant you. But I don't see Melissa Wainwright's fingerprints on it."

"Why not?"

"Because one of the thieves, posing as the hazmat team leader, called her and told her they were moving the caesium. We can prove that."

"So? What's your point?"

"How did they get her number? Someone from Box must have given it to them."

"Unless she gave it to them herself, to create her own alibi? Did you consider that?"

I didn't answer.

"And can you be sure it was one of thieves who called her?" he said.

"I was there when she took the call," I said.

"But could you hear who she was talking to?"

"No."

"So it could have been anyone. Like, Jones, for example. Where was he when the theft took place, by the way?"

"Still out of the game after his accident."

"Was he? Are you sure? Because he was back at the

hospital later that night, wasn't he? Wasn't he the one who told Wainwright about the Fire Brigade finding the hazmat team all tied up?"

"He was."

"Right before someone told the thieves. I wonder who that could have been?"

"We don't know anyone told them."

"No, you're right. It could have been a complete coincidence, them choosing that particular moment to knock out their escort."

"Well, Melissa Wainwright couldn't have warned them. I was sat next to her in the car."

"And the buyers. Or whoever was supposed to pick the stuff up. Who warned them? Not the thieves. What did they say when the Box agent knocked on the gate? 'You're late?'"

I was silent for a moment.

"I know you agree with me," he said. "Otherwise, why did you risk turning Croydon into the new Chernobyl to stop Wainwright leaving the scene?"

"She wasn't 'leaving the scene,'" I said. "She was being abducted at gun point. Who knows what those guys would have done to her?"

"So you did it to save her? Or because you know every successful job has an inside man? And once they were in the wind, we may never have found them again. Not in time, anyway."

"To save her. It was a calculated risk."

"Calculated, how? You may have had time to peep into the back of the van, but don't tell me you knew it was just a tube of aspirins the guy was holding, and not a remote trigger."

I didn't reply. Because I knew he was right again.

Chapter Sixteen

I wasn't ready to place Melissa in the frame. Not as firmly as my control had her there. Not yet, anyway. But I had to admit, when I made sure the thief didn't take Melissa away, it wasn't because I was certain she was innocent. I still hoped she was, though. And as the meeting I'd just endured had made clear, finding out one way or the other was going to be down to me.

There was nothing to be gained by postponing the inevitable, so as soon as I had the office to myself I pulled out my phone and called Melissa's number. She answered on the eighth ring, just as I was expecting to be dumped into her voicemail.

"How's it going?" I said.

"So, so," she said. "And you?"

"I've had better days. And I've had worse. But what's happened to darken your mood? Any news?"

"No. I'm just frustrated. I'm on my way back from Leytonstone. The surveillance team leader from GCHQ emailed me right after you left Millbank. She thought she had something, but, well, no cigar."

"Just a red herring, then?"

"Not entirely. They'd picked up a suspicious word repetition in a series of emails from a community centre over there. But you know how those tend to go. It didn't pan out. The traffic's like a particularly malicious practical joke. And on top of that..."

"What?"

"Nothing."

"Come on. Tell me."

"I will. Just, not on the phone, you know?"

"Do you want to meet for a drink when you get back into town? We could chew the fat for a while? Set the world to rights?"

"Why not?" she said, naming a little pub she knew on Albermarle Street. "That sounds fun. I've got to close the file on this non-lead, so see you there at six?"

I arrived at the pub a quarter of an hour early, but Melissa was already there. She'd picked a table in the corner and was sitting with one hand on a glass of hard cider and one eye on a TV that was showing 80s music videos with the sound turned off.

"I got you a drink," she said. "Beer. It's called Old Speckled Hen. I hope it's OK."

"It's more than OK," I said, taking a sip. "It's one of my favourites. Thank you."

"That's a relief. I only picked it for the name."

"That can work sometimes."

"You don't think I'm crazy?"

"Not at all."

"Could you tell, if I was? Do you get many basket cases in the Navy?"

"I don't know. I've heard of a few. I've got no idea if the stories are real, though, or just urban legends."

"What about people you've worked with?"

"I work alone, most of the time. The people I spend time with aren't in the Navy. They're the ones who are out to do us harm. Some of those are crazy, of course. But I stop them, anyway. I'm an equal opportunity operative. Why do you ask?"

"It must be very different where you work. Being isolated like that. With us, it's all-for-one, you know? Instinctive interdependence. Whatever you're doing, you've got someone else's back and someone else has got yours. You thrive on that sense of belonging. On being part of something bigger than yourself. You need it to function. Only now, I suddenly don't feel like I belong. I feel like everyone's eyes are on me, but in a bad way. Does that make any sense to you?"

I nodded my head. It made absolute sense. If she was innocent, I could understand how being cast out of the nest would leave her disoriented. But if her hands were dirty, she was laying the perfect foundations to excuse her behaviour, however erratic or suspicious it might become later. I didn't know whether to sympathise with her predicament, or applaud her foresight.

"Fancy another one?" I said, nodding towards her empty glass. "Or would you like to grab a bite to eat somewhere?"

"No," she said. "Thank you, though. I'm not really hungry, to tell the truth. Do you mind if we just go... somewhere else?"

I didn't have a reply for that.

"Oh, no," she said, when the penny dropped. "Wait. I didn't mean... what I did mean is, could we just walk around for a while? Would that be OK?"

"Of course," I said. "As long as we don't have to leave the city. I don't want to be involved with leaves or plants or animals of any kind."

"Absolutely. I love the city, too. It's just - I don't want to be around people right now. People I don't know."

"I'm with you one hundred percent. And I have an idea. Will you wait here a moment, while I make a quick call?"

Melissa nodded.

Although strictly, I should have said *two* calls.

When I returned to the table, Melissa had pushed the empty glasses to one side and was sitting with her coat on, ready to go.

"May I?" I said, taking her by the arm and leading the way to the door.

"Please do," she said. "But are you going to tell me where we're going?"

"No. It's a surprise."

"How far away is it?"

"A mile? Maybe a little over? If we were going straight there."

"We're going somewhere else first?"

"No. But we're not taking the most direct route."

"Why not?"

"Because you said you wanted to walk. And because the guy I spoke to needs forty-five minutes or so to get things lined up for us."

"What things?"

"You'll see."

"Who did you speak to?"

"A friend of mine."

"Who?"

"He's ex-Royal Corps of Signals. We worked together on a job in Gibraltar, once. I did him a couple of favours. He told me to give him a call if there was ever anything he could do for me."

"Where does he work now?"

"You'll find out, soon enough. Don't be so impatient."

We crossed Piccadilly against the lights, continued straight down St James's Street, and swung round to the left onto Pall Mall. The wind was picking up a little so Melissa buttoned her coat as we walked. We kept going at a relaxed pace, neither of us speaking, until we reached the outskirts of Trafalgar Square. Then I saw Melissa stiffen, and wrap her arms across her body.

"Is everything OK?" I said.

"I'm fine," she said. "It's just these pigeons. I hate them."

"Oh. I didn't know that. Why?"

"It's not just pigeons. It's all birds."

"All of them?"

"Yes. Except one kind."

"Dead ones?"

"No. Because then I'd still have to see the nasty, feathery bodies. As far as I'm concerned, the only good bird is an extinct bird."

"I see."

"Now you probably think I'm weird."

"Why would I think that?"

"Oh, I don't know. Maybe because I'm an adult with a concealed 9mm and I'm freaked out by small, harmless creatures."

"Well, I don't think it's weird. I think it's nice."

Melissa didn't respond for a moment. Then she jabbed me with her elbow and nodded towards a couple of teenagers. They were standing next to the vacant fourth plinth, staring at each other, their faces about two inches apart.

"Those kids, over there," she said. "What will they do next? Kiss? Or fight?"

They were gazing earnestly into each other's eyes, mirroring each other's posture, and the boy's head was moving very slowly towards hers, their lips closing inexorably together.

"Kiss," I said.

The girl took a step back and slapped the boy across

the face so hard we could hear it twenty feet away.

"Really," Melissa said. "Shows what you know about nice."

We made it past the front of the National Gallery without any pigeons coming too close to us, crossed St Martin's place and followed round to the left towards Charing Cross Road. The pavement grew noticeably busier the closer we got to Leicester Square tube station, and it became more difficult to keep together as we elbowed our way through the unruly crowds. We kept up our momentum, though, and when we were almost at Oxford Street a guy stepped forward and handed Melissa a flyer.

"Look at this," she said, handing the paper to me.

It was an advert for an Elvis impersonator who was appearing that night in a pub on Wardour Street.

"Do you want to go?" I said.

"Not really," she said. "I just thought it would be funny if it was our guy. The one who saw our fireman."

"You're right," I said. "It would be hilarious. Although, if he is as good at singing as he is at running from the police, it might not be too bad."

We pushed our way through a gaggle of people milling around outside the Dominion Theatre, then continued down Tottenham Court Road until we were level with Goodge Street tube station.

"So where are you taking me?" Melissa said.

"Somewhere I think you'll like," I said, guiding her left into Howland Street.

"How much further is it?"

"Not far. We're nearly there."

"Is it a pub?"

"No."

"A restaurant, then?"

"No. Not even close."

"Then, what? she said, scanning buildings on both sides of the street. "I can't see anything. Is it underground?"

"Absolutely not," I said, leading her across the road and into the narrow entrance to Cleveland Mews. "In fact, quite the opposite."

"Now I'm getting intrigued. If we were in a car, this is the time I'd expect you to say we'd run out of petrol…"

"It looks a little strange, I'll give you that. But we can't go in the main entrance, so we're meeting my friend along here."

We continued for another thirty yards and then stopped in front of an unmarked, grey steel door set into a textured concrete wall. A keypad was mounted on the frame, but I ignored that and knocked twice on the metal surface. Immediately the door swung open and a man in dark blue overalls beckoned us inside.

"Gerard, good to see you," I said, and introduced him to Melissa.

Gerard closed the door behind us and led us across a narrow, grey-painted waiting area to a pair of full height metal turnstiles in the centre of a glass wall. He held a proximity card up to a reader to the side of the right-hand turnstile and gestured for Melissa to go through.

"It's OK," he said. "There are no metal detectors here. They're only at the public entrance."

"What is this place?" Melissa said when I joined her on the other side.

"You'll see, soon enough," I said.

Gerard emerged from the turnstile and lead us to a pair of lifts. He hit the down button, the doors to the right hand car slid open, and we followed him inside.

"These lifts only serve the admin offices," he said, pressing the button for the basement.

We descended one level and followed Gerard out of the left and a long corridor to the left. After twenty-five yards he stopped to open a door in the right-hand wall and hold it for Melissa to go through. This led to another corridor, but this one was curved. We followed round half of the circle and found the entrance to another lift. Gerard hit the only button, but this time it took thirty seconds before the door began to open.

The inside of this elevator car was about three times as tall as a standard one. A rail ran round the outside for passengers to hold on to, and above the door a panel displayed not only the floor information but also the speed. Gerard hit the button for the thirty-fourth floor and the lift started to climb. We picked up speed till four of the seven bars in the triangular pictogram speedometer had turned green.

"We could go faster," Gerard said, seeing me looking at the indicator. "But I don't like to. It messes with my ears."

"That suits me," Melissa said. "I have no ambition to hurtle up in the air like I'm in a Saturn V."

In less than a minute we slowed, then came to a stop. The doors opened and Gerard stood back for us to exit first. We stepped out into a tall, circular space, like we'd emerged from the hub of a wheel.

"Oh, my goodness," Melissa said, striding across to the wall of curving windows. "This view. I can see… everything."

"Do you know where you are now?" I said.

"This was a surprise?" Gerard said.

"It was," Melissa said. "But I've figured it out now. I'd know this place anywhere, from the outside. I've never set foot inside before, though. It's the BT Tower. We're at the top, right?"

"We are," I said. "Do you like it?"

"I do," Melissa said, turning to look back towards the interior of the structure. "But why is it such a mess?"

There was no furniture. Some of the ceiling tiles were missing, and in places pieces of carpet had been removed, too. Wallpaper was hanging off the curved walls, and the doors were missing from a pair of doorways on either side of the lift.

"We're in the restaurant," Gerard said. "The place is being refurbished. They've got a plan to reopen it to the public. Doesn't sound like a good idea to me. But it's not like they asked for my opinion."

"Will it still be a restaurant?" I said.

"Yes," Gerard said. "That's the idea. They're looking for a celebrity chef to take the place on, apparently."

"Where will the kitchens be?" I said. The space seemed much smaller than you would have thought from ground level.

"In there," Gerard said, nodding to the left-hand doorway.

I moved across and looked inside. The room was tiny. It was about six feet by ten, allowing for the rounded walls. And it was piled to the ceiling with junk. I could see chairs. Four different kinds. Tables. Cardboard boxes. Buckets. Packets of paper towels. Wine glasses. About fifty. Two mops. A broom. A stepladder. And thrown in on the top, a fluorescent yellow coat.

"Really?" I said. "What will they be serving? TV dinners?"

Gerard joined me and immediately shook his head.

"Sorry," he said. "It's not this one. It's the one over there."

"Does this place still revolve?" Melissa said, turning

to gaze out over the city once again.

"It does," Gerard said. "That's always been its most famous feature."

"Does it go fast?" she said. "I mean, does anyone get sick from it?"

"No," Gerard said. "It's not like a fairground ride. It turns so slowly you can hardly feel you're moving."

"Are we moving now?" she said.

"Not right now, no," Gerard said. "The motor isn't switched on. But I could go and start it up."

"Really?" she said. "That would be amazing. Could you really do that?"

"Give me five minutes," Gerard said, turning and heading for the lift.

"Wait," she said. "Are you sure about this? You won't get in any trouble?"

"I doubt it," Gerard said, over his shoulder. "And if anyone asks, I'll just say a maniac from Royal Navy Intelligence made me do it."

Chapter Seventeen

Gerard returned at a minute before eleven and escorted us back to the Cleveland Street exit. That got us out of the building, but it didn't solve my other problem. Ever since we'd left the pub I'd been hankering after a curry, and when Melissa jumped into a cab on Tottenham Court Road I didn't suddenly stop being hungry. So I stood and watched her taillights disappear around the corner, and then made my way to a little restaurant I knew in Charlotte Street.

I was pretty sure what I wanted to eat, but when I saw some of the things the other customers had chosen I decided to have a quick look at the menu before I ordered. The selection was fairly standard – the place was known more for quality than innovation – but as my eyes scanned the page I picked up on a couple of things that were new. They were tempting, but before I could catch the waiter's eye to confirm my usual choice - chicken jalfrezi - my phone rang. It was my control. He was the second person I'd called from outside the pub on Albermarle Street, before we left for the Tower. And he had answers to both of the questions I'd asked him.

Melissa had received no emails from GCHQ earlier in the day. And her mobile phone records showed she'd been nowhere near Leytonstone.

I was still wondering what to make of this news when my phone rang again. This time it was Melissa, herself. She told me that Elvis had been caught, and was being held by the police outside St Joseph's Hospital.

"They took him back there?" I said. "Why?"

"They didn't take him back," she said. "They found

him there."

"He'd gone back to work?"

"Not exactly. He was 'on the job' when the bobbies grabbed him, though."

"What do you mean?"

"Well, you've got to understand, the people in the hospital are pretty paranoid by now. As far as they know there's been a fire, an explosion, a radiation leak, and a robbery. They're seeing ghosts in every shadow. Hospital Security's been overwhelmed with calls, day after day. But tonight, when their lines were jammed even worse than usual people started dialing three nines, saying they could hear screaming coming from the basement."

"Which turned out to be what? Elvis rehearsing?"

"Ha. No. It was a woman. He had her in a tiny room at the end of one of the corridors. It was barely big enough for a mattress. And the entrance was completely hidden. The police would never have found it without the racket she was making."

"Was he attacking her?"

"No. She was there voluntarily. Or so she claims. I'm not sure I believe her, though, given that Elvis was fully decked out in sequins and flares."

"You saw that with your own eyes?"

"No. Fortunately not. His clothes had been taken away as evidence by the time I arrived. But I did get a full description."

"Poor bloke. Sounds like his delusion's getting worse."

"On the contrary. It seems he knows exactly what he's doing. He's made it into a second job, apparently. I'm told people pay him to sing at pubs and parties. Then, if he plays his cards right, he brings one of the audience members back to his lair. His underground love den. And my impression? The place sees quite a lot of action."

"And no one knew it was there?"

"No. Not even the caretaker. There are miles of passages down there - literally - and that end of the corridor is a complete warren. And there aren't even any plans or records, any more. There were all destroyed in the war."

"Didn't they make new ones?"

"Of the hospital itself? Yes. And the major parts of the basement. But not the extremities. I guess that's why the staff have such a free rein down there."

I thought about the maintenance guys I'd found smoking in the old equipment room, and could see how what she'd heard could be true.

"So what's happening now?" I said.

"It's make or break time," she said. "I'm about to talk to The King, himself, and I thought you'd like to be in on that if you can get down here in time."

The figure I saw slumped in the back seat of a police car outside the hospital's main entrance looked like a shrunken, deflated version of the guy I'd fished out of the basement smoking room the previous day. The oversized crime scene overalls he was wearing didn't help, but when Melissa opened the passenger door and let me in, I sensed the change in his demeanor was more psychological than physical. Bearing in mind his reaction to the policeman he'd seen coming out of my room, I guessed he was never going to feel at home in one of their squad cars. And if he didn't feel at home, he wasn't going to be any use to us.

"Can you scare up a coat from one of the coppers, do you think?" I said to Melissa.

"Maybe," she said. "Why?"

"For Elvis to wear," I said. "I think the three of us need a cup of tea. There's a twenty-four hour cafe round the corner, but he'll freeze walking there in that outfit."

It took Melissa eight minutes to return with a giant yellow high visibility jacket clutched in front of her. It took us four minutes to reach the cafe. And less than twenty seconds for the sight of us to clear the rest of the nocturnal customers out of the place.

We took the table furthest from the counter, our need for relative privacy trumping my desire to avoid the worst of the cracked, food-encrusted lino-covered benches. The crone who had the pleasure of working the nightshift stood and scowled at us for a few moments, apparently weighing her annoyance at our choice of location against a wish to not aggravate anyone connected to law enforcement. Eventually a solution struck her, and she bellowed across the room to us without moving an inch.

"What can I get you, my darlings?" she said, in a surprisingly gruff voice.

"Three teas, please," Melissa said.

"Be right with you, my lovely," the crone said, batting her way through a dilapidated fly screen and disappearing into their dingy excuse of a kitchen.

"I don't like tea," Elvis said, when she'd gone.

"You want something else?" Melissa said. "You tell her."

Elvis stared at his fingernails for a moment.

"Tea'll be fine," he said.

"Good," Melissa said. "I thought it would be. You can't beat a nice cup of tea. Specially to get a bit of a conversation going."

Elvis dropped his stare back to his nails and remained silent.

"You're not big on hints, then," Melissa said.

"What?" Elvis said. "The tea's not here yet."

Melissa let out a long, slow breath, like she was a

teacher dealing with a class of delinquents.

"You're right," she said. "But let's pretend it is. Let's imagine it's sitting right here in front of us, right now, and that you're going to show your gratitude by telling us all about what you saw on the night of the fire alarm."

"What fire alarm?" he said.

"The one at the hospital. Where you sometimes show up for work."

"When was this?"

"Three days ago."

"I don't know anything about it."

"Yes, you do. You told Commander Trevellyan all about it. Now I want you to tell me."

"Commander Trevellyan? He said he's a lawyer. What's this all about?"

"Well, he also does legal things for the Navy. Sometimes. Anyway, that doesn't matter right now. What's important is you telling me about the night of the fire alarm."

"I can't remember."

"Yes you can."

"I wasn't even there. I didn't see anything. I just made up what I told him cause I thought that's what he wanted to hear."

"Is that true?"

"Yes. I swear."

"David?" Melissa said.

I stood up and started to fasten my coat.

"Where are you going?" she said.

"Back to the restaurant I was at," I said.

"Why?"

"I'm still hungry, and I don't fancy eating here. Would you?"

"Well, no. But what about Elvis?"

"Yes, poor Elvis. When you've got him situated, please let him know how sorry I am."

"For what?"

"His injuries."

"What injuries?"

"The ones he's going to sustain, trying to run away. Again. But then, those hard stone pavements can be very slippery at this time of year. Accidents will happen. I mean, can happen..."

"Wait," Elvis said. "What do you mean? I didn't run anywhere. I didn't get any injuries."

"Not yet, maybe," I said. "But the night's young. There's plenty of time."

Melissa called her contact at the Met to come and collect Elvis as soon as he'd finished babbling. She showed no emotion when she walked with them to the door of the cafe, but when she turned to make her way back to our table I could see she was feeling the same way as me.

"We didn't make any progress at all, did we?" she said, as she slid onto the bench opposite me.

"None to speak of," I said. "But realistically, what were expecting?"

"What I wanted was an ID. What we got was a vague description of two guys dressed as firefighters. He didn't even see the one hit the door to the vault. He just assumed it. Great insight."

"Did you believe what he said?"

"Yes. I think so."

"I did too, and that's the second time I'd heard it. What's interesting, is he does make it sound like it all happened by accident. The way the one guy was yelling at the other, like he hadn't known to stay away from the door."

"True. But there are any number of explanations for

that. We should have known better than to rely on a witness."

"I was hoping he'd have remembered something, like a mark on the fireman's suit or a scratch on his helmet. Some useful detail we could have narrowed the field with."

"That would have been excellent. No such luck, though."

"We shouldn't complain. At least he didn't break into song."

"You're right. But it was a good idea, bringing him here. I bet we wouldn't have got a word out of him in the back of that police car. I wonder though, whether you'd have been so hospitable, if you'd known about the other thing."

"What thing?" I said.

"Remember your boots?" she said. "The original ones, that were stolen?"

"Of course," I said.

"Elvis had them."

"Are you sure?"

"Absolutely."

"I mean, are you sure they're mine?"

"I'm certain. I know the make, size, colour, everything, remember."

"So, seriously? Elvis is the boot thief?"

"I'm afraid so."

"Those poor boots. They didn't deserve that. He wasn't wearing them, was he?"

"No."

"Thank goodness. Now, just tell me one more thing. Please. He didn't have them with him in his sex hovel, did he?"

"No. It's OK. They were in another room, nearby."

"How do you know it was Elvis who took them,

then?"

"He confessed. The police say they might never have found the stash, otherwise."

"He had a whole stash? What else was there?"

"It was amazing, apparently. Piled high, like his own private bank vault. He had all kinds of things. I've seen a preliminary list. Stuff he'd taken from the hospital. Pieces of furniture. Blankets. Crockery. Doctors' coats. Nurses' uniforms. Medical things, like crutches. Bandages. Medicines. Office supplies. Boxes of paper. Old files. A photocopier. Pieces of wood. Rocks. A lawnmower. Things that had fallen off cars, like door mirrors and radio aerials. Pretty much anything you can think of."

"Including my boots."

"Yes. They were there, near the door. Under a hazmat suit he must have somehow pinched from the emergency crew."

Chapter Eighteen

Melissa kicked off the next morning's work by dividing the stack of papers she was holding into three and sharing them out between Jones, herself, and me.

"Do you know how Sir Arthur Conan Doyle defined genius?" she said, as she straightened the piles.

Jones shook his head.

"I have no idea," I said, although I was pretty sure it had nothing to do with paperwork.

"He thought it was an infinite capacity for taking pains," Melissa said. "And boys, I know this isn't going to be fun. These interview summaries aren't light reading. The Met aren't famed for the tightness of their prose style, and from the ones I've seen the fire brigade aren't very original with their answers. I'm sorry about that. But if it helps to look at it this way, what I need from you today is a big dose of genius."

"No problem," Jones said. "Painstaking is my middle name. One thing I'm not sure about, though - what do you expect us to find that's been missed before?"

"Anything that doesn't ring true," Melissa said. "Any contradictions. Discrepancies. Anything we know can't be true. We're running out of options, and if our fresh eyes could just spot something - one single clue - to help us find who caused the original damage to that door, it would be huge."

The whole exercise smacked of desperation to me, whether it was aimed at finding a gem hidden in the reports, or preventing us from pursuing more fruitful avenues elsewhere. At best it seemed like a fool's errand, but I told myself that wasn't my problem. I concentrated on what my control had been at such pains to spell out. My job was to look for signs of guilt. But to focus on the people inside the room. Not outside, in the fire brigade or the police. Specially bearing in mind Melissa's unexplained absence, yesterday.

Jones scooped up his allocation of papers and took them to the far corner of the long rectangle of desks that filled the meeting room Melissa had requisitioned for us. He sat down and started working his way straight through from top to bottom, keeping up a steady pace. He certainly looked conscientious, but I noticed he couldn't keep his gaze from wandering to the window in between pages.

Melissa took a seat at the centre of one of the rectangle's long sides and spread her copies out in front of her, face down, like a child shuffling cards. She picked them up to read, one at a time, apparently at random. Then she started to form a series of piles, some separate, some overlapping. I was curious to understand her method - unless she was just trying to create the appearance of a system - but before I could reach a conclusion her phone rang. She talked for just over two minutes, standing up half way through and nodding as she listened. Then she hung up and turned to look at us, her head tipped to one side and a half curious, half suspicious expression on her face.

"OK, hands up," she said. "Which one of you was it?"

"Which one of us, what?" I said.

"Which one of you prayed for a miracle?" she said. "Because it looks like we might have come across one. From a most unlikely source."

"Excellent," I said. "You can't beat a spot of divine intervention in a case like this. Who was it? And what did they tell you?"

"It was Stan Leckie. Head of Hospital Security. He

just took a call from one of his old snouts. One from way back, when he used to work here. The guy has something that could help us, apparently."

"Can we trust him?"

"Leckie? I think so. We've re-done all the background checks. And he's doing the right thing, passing this on to us. As for the snout, your guess is as good as mine. But for what it's worth, Leckie's sure the guy is who he claims to be. He says his material was always A1 in the past. And the group he was embedded in have the capability to handle something like this. Or did, when Leckie was running this guy."

"Why did he contact Leckie?"

"Leckie recruited him. When Leckie moved on, the guy dropped out of sight. Some snouts are like that. They don't like being passed to a new handler."

"And he's just resurfaced now?"

"Yes."

"Why?"

"Because he found out something too important to ignore. I hope."

"Sounds interesting."

"Who knows? It might come to nothing. But it's better than a poke in the eye. Leckie's putting together a meet, right now. You guys pound through a few more of those forms. I need to dig up some old files. I have a feeling our morning's about to get a whole lot brighter."

It turned out Melissa hadn't contented herself with running background checks. She'd also snagged us a car. By the time we stepped outside thirty minutes later a black Range Rover was already sitting at the kerb, waiting for us, with its engine running. The driver was standing next to it, ready to shake hands. Bright blue eyes scanned us from beneath bushy eyebrows, and between his neatly combed fair hair and pinstriped blue suit, he looked every inch a banker or stockbroker. I wondered if he picked the outfit to match the car, or if he dressed like that out of choice. I also wondered if he'd be open to the idea of stopping at the nearest Starbucks.

"Pleased to meet you all," he said, climbing back in behind the wheel. Melissa took the passenger seat, and Jones and I slid into the back. "My name's Pearson. Nigel. Thanks for getting me out of the office, today."

"We'll get you out whenever you want, if you help us get a result today," Melissa said.

Pearson smiled, and was silent for a moment as he squeezed the Range Rover between two black cabs. From the general direction he was taking, I guessed we were heading for the start of the M1. I felt a surge of nostalgia for the area, involuntarily thinking back to all the times my father took me to the RAF Museum in Hendon when I was a kid. But this was quickly replaced by other memories, less wholesome, of my various visits to the police training college just down the road.

"Do you know much about this place we're heading for?" Melissa said.

"A little," he said. "You?"

"Not much, beyond the address."

"Well, if it was a private party, I wouldn't be fighting you for tickets. In terms of location, it's awful. But then, it's in Luton. What more can you say?"

I'd been to Luton many times as a kid and a teenager, and under normal circumstances it wouldn't be high on my list of places to revisit, either.

"Whereabouts in Luton?" I said.

"A horrible, decrepit part, about four miles north of the city," he said. "An industrial suburb called Frankston. Ever heard of it?"

"I've heard of it. I've never been there, though."

"You've not missed much. The specific place we're going to started life as a workhouse. It would have been grim enough in the 1840s. And it's worse, these days."

"Most of those places have been turned into apartments, by now."

"Right. And if this one hasn't, what does that tell you?"

"What size of place is it?"

Pearson rummaged in his door pocket and pulled out a piece of office paper. He passed it to me, and I saw it was a poor photocopy of a hand drawn building plan.

"Here," he said. "Have a look for yourself."

The main part of the complex looked like a letter E, with three parallel wings stretching back from a broad central block. It was connected to the road by a formal driveway at the front, and an apparently random selection of outbuildings was scattered throughout the rest of the site.

"Such was the civic duty of our Victorian forefathers," Pearson said. "They did a good job though, I suppose, from a constructional point of view. Most of that big main building is still standing. The other odds and sods are mainly gone, though. A stray bomb took out several of them back in '42, and the local vandals, junkies, and care in the community victims have accounted for the rest."

"Which part are we meeting this guy in?" I said to Melissa.

"We'll find out the exact spot when we get there," she said. "Leckie'll be there. He'll show us."

"Leckie's coming with us?"

"Unofficially. I had no choice. His snout wouldn't agree to meet unless he was there. Would you?"

Pearson didn't relax his right foot, but the pitching and rolling of the Range Rover subsided a little once we reached the motorway and the road ahead straightened out. The conversation had more or less died away, too, so I took advantage of the lull in proceedings to reach into my pocket for my phone. I needed to text my control and let him know where I was headed, but instead of the phone my fingers closed around a piece of paper. It was the flyer advertising the Elvis impersonator Melissa had given me on the way to the BT tower. At first I smiled, imagining I was on the way to see his show. Then my expression changed, as I thought about the women he'd lured back the hospital basement. And finally, my brain made another connection with last night.

"Melissa, you know you told me Elvis had a hazmat suit in his stash?" I said. "Where did he get it from?"

"From the emergency team that came to deal with the explosion, I should think," she said. "Why?"

"Something just occurred to me. Remember when we were at the Tower? And Gerard told me the storage room was the kitchen? Did you look inside?"

"No. I was too busy looking out of the window."

"Well, it was piled high with stuff. Just random junk. But the last thing that had been thrown in there was a coat. And it struck me, what would the owner do when they had to go outside without it?"

"Get cold, I expect. I don't see the connection."

"Did you see the place where Elvis kept his stash?"

"No. I just got a list of what was in it. Why?"

"I figured the two places were probably pretty much alike. One with a coat thrown in on top. One with a hazmat suit. And if the first guy was going to get cold without his coat, what was the other guy going to do without his hazmat suit?"

"I don't know. He'd have a problem, I guess."

"There's no mystery," Jones said. "It was a spare. There were five people in the original team. But only four raiders, right? So one suit was left over. Elvis must have found it."

"But where did he find it?" I said.

"Who knows?" Jones said. "He's obviously a kleptomaniac. Who knows how those people work?"

"The original team," I said. "Had they had time to suit up before they were overpowered?"

"No," Melissa said. "They were jumped before that."

"So why would the thieves have taken the fifth suit out of the van?" I said. "Did they abandon anything else?"

"No," Melissa said. "All their other kit was accounted for."

"So why this one spare suit?" I said.

"Maybe they didn't take it out," Jones said. "What makes you think they did? Elvis could have taken it directly from the van."

"When the place was swarming with police?" I said. "We've seen how he reacts to them. I bet he wasn't within a mile of the place till the fuss died down. He must have found it somewhere, later. And why would the thieves have left it to be found? It doesn't match their M.O. at all. Everything else they did was planned and meticulous. This is random and sloppy."

"No one's perfect," Jones said. "And does it really matter how he got it?"

"Probably not," I said. "But I hate loose ends."

"I do, too," Melissa said. "Chances are it's nothing, but it'll easy enough to find out. We'll just go and ask Elvis, himself, when we get back from Luton. Assuming it still matters then. Who knows what this other guy can tell us?"

We left the M1 at Junction Twelve, and I felt a little like a kid reaching the end of a fairground ride. Invigorated, relieved to still be alive, and slightly disappointed the fun had ended, all at the same time. The official status of the vehicle meant Pearson didn't have to worry about the police, but the way he drove would be more than enough to get you shot in several countries I'd visited. He kept up his speed and aggression on the smaller roads as well, and thirty-three minutes after leaving Thames House I looked out of my window and saw the driveway that led to the workhouse. We didn't turn into it, though. There would have been no point. The gap in the heavy stone walls was filled with blocks of solid concrete. There were six of them. Each was about five feet square. They were connected with a double line of rusty metal cables. That made a far more effective barrier than the original wrought iron gates would have done, before they were undoubtedly melted down for munitions during World War II. They were nowhere near as picturesque, though. But then, we were in Luton.

Pearson followed the wall along to the end and then around to the left. Trees had grown wild behind it, but through the branches I was able to catch glimpses of the top floor of the main building. It was made of pale stone. The roof was grey slate, though large sections were missing. The facade was perfectly symmetrical, and the remains of an imposing clock face were still visible in the portico above the broad front entrance. There was a pair of bay windows on either side. Each was made of six individual, ornate casements, and even without the glass the skill of the stonemasons was clearly apparent. Taken all together, the place looked more like the ruins of a fairytale palace than a brutal semi-prison, and it was hard to imagine the degree of institutionalised misery that must have lingered for so many years behind its picturesque walls.

We continued for another hundred and fifty yards, then Pearson slowed to a sane speed, pulled sharply to the left, bounced across the curb, and steered the Range Rover through a ragged gap in the wall. We clearly weren't the only ones to know about this makeshift route, though. I could see other tyre tracks snaking across the rough ground in front of us. One set. Still fresh. They led straight away to our right and disappeared behind a precarious looking mound of bricks and rubble. I turned in my seat and checked the patch of pavement we'd just crossed. It was perfectly clean. I didn't know who'd arrived before us. But whoever it was, they hadn't left.

Pearson followed round to our right, and as soon as we cleared the side of the rubble heap I saw another car. A silver 7-series BMW. It was clean and shiny, and had this year's registration. A car like that would have looked perfectly innocuous on the motorway or in an office car park, but it was as suspicious as hell in that particular location.

The driver's door swung open as we appeared behind the car and a man emerged, slowly swinging his legs around and placing his feet tentatively on the uneven ground. It was Stan Leckie, but he was dressed for the office rather than a demolition site. He paused, nodded to Melissa, then approached Pearson's side of the Range Rover.

"Good, then, you're here," he said, as Pearson hit the button to lower his window. "Let's get on with it. Our boy will probably be a bit spooked, already. Let's not keep him waiting. It'll only make him edgier. Melissa and I will stay in the vehicles till you boys give us the word you're in position."

"OK," Pearson said, handing him plan of the site. "Where's the rendezvous point?"

"Pretty much dead in the centre," Leckie said,

pointing to a spot in the middle of the page. "At the entrance to this charming place. It was the workhouse asylum. You can imagine the kind of things that used to go on in there. In fact, whenever I'm in a sticky spot, I think of it. I tell myself that whatever kind of trouble I'm in, I can't be worse off than the poor sods who ended up in that hell-hole."

"Probably not," Pearson said. "And we'll find the place, no problem."

"I'm ninety-nine percent sure our boy's working alone," Leckie said. "But I'd suggest you do one more sweep of the perimeter anyway, to be on the safe side. Then if you set up where you can see him waiting, we'll get the show on the road."

Chapter Nineteen

We all walked together as far as the BMW, then Pearson, Jones and I continued under cover of the rubble heap.

"Your man's picked a good spot," Pearson said when we out of Leckie's earshot. "It's the easiest place to surveil from multiple vantage points."

"You've used this site before, then?" I said.

"A few times," he said. "The question is, has he?"

"I wouldn't know," I said.

"And the way he spoke to Agent Wainwright," he said. "They've worked together before, have they?"

"Not since I've known them," I said. "But why here? It's hardly a convenient location for you."

Pearson shrugged.

"It just works for us, being out of town," he said. "People feel comfortable with it, for some reason. We've done dead-drops. Snatch jobs. Set ups. Covert meetings, where people don't want to be seen leaving. Or meetings where people don't leave at all. Although we generally use a different part of the site for that."

"The buildings are in better shape than I'd imagined," Jones said. "The main one is, at least."

"It's in amazing shape," Pearson said. "Apart from that section, over there."

He was pointing to the narrow wall at the end of the middle bar of the E. It looked fine from the first floor up, but three holes had been punched in the stonework, four feet from the ground. They were roughly circular, about three feet in diameter. The first was almost dead in the centre, and the other two were equally spaced out between it and the edge of the wall.

"Did someone hit it with a canon?" I said.

"No," he said. "A wrecking ball. Attached to a mobile crane that was here for a while."

"That's a strange way to kick off a demolition job."

"It would be. If demolition was what you had in mind."

"There are other uses for a wrecking ball?"

"Somebody found one."

"What was it?"

"A tongue loosener. Someone took five people. Four men and a woman. They fixed them to the wall, spreadeagled, by their wrists and ankles. Then they started pounding away. One chance to talk. One swing each."

"Five people? There are only three holes."

"The police found two empty sets of shackles hanging from the wall. They'd definitely been used. There was plenty of blood and skin cells on them."

"Creative."

"Psychotic."

"Imagine holding out while three of your friends are crushed by a wrecking ball, a few feet away."

"Maybe there are worse things than the asylum block after all."

"Who did it?"

"I don't know. The police never nailed anyone."

"Any suspects?"

"A few. None panned out, though."

"When did..." I said, when Pearson stopped dead and held up his hand for silence. Then he gestured towards a clump of bushes that was sprouting from the remains of what looked like a greenhouse.

"Sorry," he said, after a moment. "I thought I saw something moving."

"It looks clear to me," I said.

"I think you're right. Anyway, we better not dawdle. Come on. Follow me. And keep your eyes open, just in case."

Realistically, there was no possibility of the three of us conducting an effective sweep of the area. It was too large. There wasn't enough time. And even if you forgot about all the invitingly ruined buildings and outhouses, you would still have a sniper's paradise to deal with given the uneven, overgrown terrain. What we were doing was no better than window dressing. I wasn't happy about it, but it was too early to tell if the shortcomings of the plan were by accident or design.

We reached the corner of the main building without any further alarm, and Pearson led the way to the first of four doors that were evenly distributed along the length of the external wall.

"Ready?" he said, reaching for the handle.

Jones and I nodded, and we followed him inside. The door opened directly into a rectangular room, about thirty feet by sixty. The space was empty and unbroken, except for a line of square pillars that ran along the centre. The floor was strewn with slabs of plaster that had fallen from the ceiling. Large chunks were missing from the walls, too, revealing coarse red bricks beneath. Most of the sections that had remained intact were covered with crude graffiti, and half a dozen spray cans had been discarded along with some candle stubs and a burnt out packing case.

"What was this room used for?" I said.

"No idea," Pearson said, already fifteen feet away from me. He was striding towards the opposite corner, throwing up clouds of grey dust with every step he took. "We're just using it to get to the stairs. Come on. We need some height."

We went up two flights, to the top floor, and Pearson set off into a long, narrow corridor. Doors on either side led to a series of identical square rooms, each with a pair of windows. I guessed they'd been dormitories of some kind, but decided against asking him about them. I just followed him in silence until we reached the last door on the right hand side.

"Keep your head down," he said, and slipped inside, beckoning me to keep up with him. "Take the window on the left. Can you see our boy?"

I took up a position at the corner of the window and peered down to the ground below. I saw a man about forty feet away. He was sitting on a motorcycle. A skeletal, lightweight machine designed for riding off-road. The engine wasn't running and the guy was sitting upright, his hands on his hips. He was slender. Probably about five foot six. I couldn't tell his age or hair colour, because his head was covered by a skull and crossbones bandana. He was wearing a set of blue and white racing-style leather overalls, complete with pretend advertisements, and he had a blue helmet with a mirrored visor tucked under his left arm.

"Got him," I said.

"Confirmed," Jones said, from his position at the other side of the window.

Pearson called Melissa.

"We have visual," he said into the phone. "Proceed when ready."

The guy's bike was facing the side of the site where we'd parked, and he had stopped it in front of a two storey stone building. The doorway and all of its tiny ground floor windows had been bricked up, and the roof was missing completely.

"Is that the asylum?" I said.

Before Pearson could answer I caught movement out

of the corner of my eye. It was Leckie. He was on foot, hands at shoulder height, walking gingerly as if trying to avoid getting too much mud on his shoes. Melissa was three paces behind him. They closed to within three yards of the guy and stopped, their hands still in the air. The guy got down from his bike and hung his helmet on the handlebars. He took a step towards Leckie. And froze as a bullet kicked up a plume of dirt and brick fragments about four inches from his right foot.

Pearson raised his phone and started to shout out a warning, but there was no need. Melissa dived to the side and Leckie sprang forward, knocking the guy to the ground and covering him with his body. Two more bullets struck the spot where he'd been standing. A moment passed in silence, then Leckie rose into a crouch and started to pull the guy along the ground by his collar. He looked completely inert. Melissa joined him and they dragged the guy a couple of yards before he snapped out of his trance, his arms and legs beginning to scrabble desperately over the loose surface.

A bullet took out the motorcycle's rear tyre and it toppled sideways, away from us. The helmet slipped from the handlebars and started to roll across the uneven surface in a crooked arc, until another bullet split it in half. Leckie and Melissa tugged harder, turning to their right, and hauled the half-crawling biker along the face of the asylum building. Another bullet hit the bike's rear light, shattering its red plastic cover. Then they reached the corner of the building, threw the guy around it, and disappeared into cover themselves.

Beside me, I heard Pearson exhale loudly. Jones gasped. Outside, the gun was silent. The sniper had no target. Melissa and Leckie had taken themselves and their contact out of his line of sight.

And, I realised, out of ours.

I didn't hear Pearson's and Jones's footsteps pounding along the upstairs corridor until I was half way down the second flight of stairs. They were moving fast, and coming in my direction. I took the remaining stairs two at a time, but when I reached the bottom I didn't go back into the room we'd passed through before. I headed for the one opposite. It was a similar size. Its floor had a similar covering of debris. Similar graffiti was daubed on the walls. But there was no external door.

None of the windows had any glass left in them, so I crossed to the nearest one and peered out. There was no sign of anyone watching, so I climbed through the empty casement and dropped down between a bush and the wall. I paused, then started towards the far end of the building. The foliage gave me cover for about three quarters of the distance, and I cleared the rest of the ground without attracting any unwelcome attention. That left me at the corner of the west wing, almost directly under the window we'd used for observation.

The motorcycle was still lying on its side, diagonally to my right, with the old asylum building behind it. The bullets that hit it came from the left. That meant I'd either have to go back and find a way to loop the opposite way around the site, or take the direct route and cross the sniper's field of fire. One option was impractical. The other, undesirable. But time was also a consideration - a major one - so I made the decision. I took a deep breath, drew my Beretta, then broke cover.

The ground was deceptively slippery in front of the asylum building, and I almost lost my footing as I rounded the corner on the far side of the abandoned motorcycle. But at least no one shot at me as I crossed the open space, and straight away I could see that Melissa and Leckie were both in one piece. I wasn't so sure about the guy from the bike, though. He was lying on the ground between them, not moving, and as I stepped closer I could see his leathers were soaked with blood from a crescent-shaped gash on his neck.

"This isn't good, David," Melissa said, when I reached her side.

Leckie turned away from me and slammed the palm of his hand into the wall.

"This isn't good at all," she said, and I noticed the right side of her face was splattered with faint droplets of blood.

"What happened?" I said. "I didn't see him get hit."

"He didn't," she said. "A spent round hit the wall and kicked out a fragment of stone, is the best we can figure it. Unbelievable bad luck."

I heard footsteps approaching from behind me and a second later Pearson and Jones appeared around the corner of the building. Pearson had a rifle in one hand, and a metal worker's file in the other.

"We'll never trace the gun, now, if he rammed this down the barrel," he said, brandishing the file. "And its owner's in the wind. Shit. What happened here?"

"Is he dead?" Jones said.

Melissa nodded.

"Did he at least tell you anything?"

Melissa nodded again.

"Two things," she said. "The thing his group is planning will happen in three days' time. And it will be bad enough to bring down the government."

Chapter Twenty

Pearson started by heading back towards the motorway, but changed his mind at the last minute. He wanted us to make our way to London via the chain of towns that straddled the old Midland Railway line, instead. It would take longer, but there would be more people around. He was worried that whoever had taken out Leckie's informer might be looking to add to their tally for the day.

"Face it," he said to Melissa. "We all saw the spread of rounds. There was no way someone was just targeting the stoolie. He was bait. They were after you. Or Leckie. Or both."

Or they were trying to make Melissa look innocent. Or Leckie. Or both.

"And the shooting didn't start until the moment you two appeared," he said. "Coincidence?"

No one else seemed in the mood for debate.

"The snitch was sitting on his bike, in plain sight," he said. "The trigger man knew where he was. He could have taken him at any time. But he waited. Why?"

"You're sure the sniper was there all along?" Melissa said.

Pearson shook his head, very gently, but didn't speak.

"Who else knew about the meeting?" I said.

"Colin Chaston, my boss," Melissa said. "I told him. Pearson knew our destination, but nothing else until we were on the road. You two knew what we were doing, but not where we were going. And of course Leckie knew all about it. I doubt he told anyone, though. He always had the reputation for playing his cards close."

"So I was right," Pearson said.

Melissa ignored him.

"What about the informant's own organisation?" Jones said. "His own people could have been on to him. Followed him, aiming to silence him, and taking the chance to rack up a couple of bonuses at the same time."

"That's possible," Melissa said.

"What do we know about the informer?" I said.

"Not enough," Melissa said. "I'll do some digging."

"We should find out more about the group he was embedded in," I said. "And I'd like to know more about Leckie's history with him."

"I'll find out," Melissa said. "The Deputy DG's called an emergency briefing for first thing tomorrow. I'll try to have something by then."

No one spoke much for a while after that. The afternoon's excitement had left everyone irritable and out of sorts. There wasn't much evidence of the interdependence Melissa had told me about, instinctive or otherwise. I wondered how much truth there was in everything else she'd said. I began to sift her words, starting from when our paths first crossed, and just as we were approaching the vehicle entrance to Thames House something triggered a connection in my head. It was in an unanswered question from earlier. I didn't say anything straight away, though. Because what I what I wanted her to do would definitely be outside the scope of normal behaviour. The more people that knew, the less chance she'd agree. Specially because there was a good chance it would leave us both barking up the wrong tree.

Melissa was less resistant than I'd anticipated, but looking back I suspect that had more to do with taking the path of least resistance than having any expectation of my being right. She couldn't help right away, though. Her boss had asked for a follow-up briefing, and she wanted to ferret out some of the information we'd talked about. Plus it would take her a while to lay her hands on the things we'd need. A couple of hours in all, she reckoned, so we agreed to meet at the hospital at seven o'clock.

My clothes and hair were dirty from the workhouse so I used the time to head home, shower and grab some clean clothes. I found a taxi easily and had the driver drop me half a mile from St Joseph's. I strolled the rest of the way, and had just passed through the arch at the main entrance when I felt my phone buzz in my pocket. It was a text from Melissa:

On my way, but running late... M.

I didn't want to draw attention to myself by leaving and coming back an extra time, so I kept on going and made my way to the hospital cafeteria instead. The tables had been rearranged since my last visit. There were fewer of them near the windows, and none of these were free. I didn't want to sit in the middle of the room, so I bought my coffee to go and carried it down to the garden. All the benches were available, out there. Maybe it was too chilly for people to spend much time outside. Or maybe they thought the place looked less picturesque in the wash of the faux Victorian street lights that had been planted at random intervals in the flower beds. At least it had been cleaned, though. There was no more sign of storm damage, and the plants and bushes looked like they'd recently been trimmed.

I was nursing the final drops of my drink and waiting for Melissa to let me know she'd arrived when the door at the far end of the garden swung open. Three people came through. They were male. In their early twenties. Scruffily dressed. And I was half way to my feet before I realised they weren't the same ones who'd called the police on me after our encounter, last time.

One of the guys lay down on the nearest bench and pulled out a packet of cigarettes, but the other two seemed to be in the middle of an argument. They stayed on their feet, glaring, muttering, and occasionally pushing each other. It was pretty half-hearted stuff, but I kept an eye on them anyway, just in case. The dispute continued for another five minutes without coming to the boil, and just when I thought it was going to peter out altogether I felt my phone buzz:

I'm here! Where are you? M.

Coming... I replied, and stood up to leave.

The guys didn't seem to notice me, even when I moved. I took one final look at them as the door closed behind me, amazed that people could be so unaware of their surroundings, and saw that their attention had been taken by something else. Movement. At the far end, near them. Someone else was entering the garden. It was a man, in the security company's uniform. I reached out for the door handle, remembering how the last security guard had been faced down so easily. But I didn't go back through. There was something about the way this guy moved that made him seem less helpless. He was taller. Broader. More assured. The two lads who'd been arguing stepped back, away from him, and the other one jumped up from the bench and joined them. The guard took a radio from his belt and spoke into it, looking over at the wall to his right. He waited for twenty seconds, still holding the radio to his ear, then clipped it back in place and turned to face the yobs. I could see the smile on his face, and before his fist had even connected with the first lad's jaw I would have bet money this was the part of his job he enjoyed the most.

I didn't want to keep Melissa waiting so I thought it was better not to waste time hanging around to see what he did with the lads' unconscious bodies. It had taken him less than thirty seconds to put them all on the ground, and even walking quickly it took me ten times that long to reach the room in the basement where we'd agreed to meet.

"I washed my hair this morning," she said as I opened the door. "Now it smells of smoke. I'm not happy."

"I hadn't thought about that," I said. "Do you want to move to another room?"

"No," she said, pointing to a large black holdall with her foot. "Not after I've dragged this thing all the way down here."

The bag was about five feet long, two wide, and two tall. There was a logo in the centre of the long side. From one angle it looked like a bird with its wings spread. From the opposite angle, it looked like a fist. A row of letters was printed underneath, but a fold in the fabric made them hard to read.

"They're initials," she said. "LASSKC. London All Style Sport Karate Club."

"I didn't know you were in a karate club," I said.

"I'm not, anymore. When would I ever find the time?"

"Good point. And that explains the fist. But why's there a bird on your bag?"

"It doesn't look like a real bird, so it doesn't bother me. And it's a dove. It represents peace. That's probably why you didn't recognise it."

"That could explain it. Is the hazmat suit in there?"

"Yes. I didn't have anything else big enough to carry it in, and I didn't want to attract attention, lugging it around."

"Good thinking. Thanks for bringing it."

"Are you sure you want to do this?"

"I'm sure I don't. Let's check the video first, and see if I really need to. Did you get hold of a copy?"

Melissa nodded, pulled out her phone, hit a few keys, then handed it to me. The screen was filled with a black and white image of the hospital garden. It was deserted. A timecode across the bottom showed the early hours of the morning, two days ago. Five seconds rolled past, then a figure appeared at the left-hand side of the screen. He was followed by three others. They were pushing a steel trolley. It held four caesium containers, and the men were making no attempt to rush or disguise what they were doing. There was no need. Their faces and any possible identifying features were completely covered by the hazmat suits they were wearing. I wasn't surprised by what I saw. Because even though it had been shot from a different angle, it matched exactly what I remembered watching through the window on my way back from the cafe that night.

I watched until the bulky figures had disappeared from view, then returned the phone to Melissa.

"Nothing new there," she said.

"No," I said. "Unfortunately."

"So what's the verdict?"

"I need to go in."

"You're certain? Because I don't think it's a very good idea."

"I'm not certain, no. But I think I should."

"OK," she said, leaning down to unzip the karate bag. "Let's get it over with, then. Have you ever used one of these before?"

"Not a civilian one," I said, taking off my coat and hanging it on a pipe that snaked out from one of the old ventilation machines. "But I've done the standard drills in NBC suits a couple of times. They can't be too different."

"I hope not. And there are a couple of problems you should know about. There's only seven minutes of oxygen left, according to the gauge on the tank. And the radio's missing."

"That shouldn't matter. Seven minutes will be long enough."

"Are you sure? Because you don't want to be cutting it fine, in there. You can't just look at your watch. And with no radio I can't warn you when you're getting close."

"Don't worry. I'm not going to linger, in there."

"And what if you have a problem? You won't be able to call for help."

"It wouldn't make any difference. We only have one suit. It's not like you could come in after me."

"I don't like it. It's dangerous."

"Nonsense," I said, slipping off my boots. "It'll be a walk in the park."

The hazmat suit was surprisingly easy to move in, because it was much looser than the military versions I'd had experience with before. It was harder to see out of, though, because the visor was smaller and further from your face. It looked comical rather than menacing, because it was bright yellow rather than matte black. But one thing was very similar. The heat you generated as soon as it was on. I knew that even seven minutes was going to feel like a very long time.

Melissa had given me the security code for the door to the caesium vault, but I had trouble entering the digits because the clumsy gauntlets turned my fingers into bratwursts. Eventually, after three tries, the tiny indicator light switched from red to green and the door swung open. I lumbered through and waited for it to close automatically behind me. For a moment I stood alone, in the dark. Then, one after another, four banks of fluorescent ceiling lights flickered into life and gave me the first glimpse of my new environment.

Maybe my expectations had been shaped by being in a hospital, where things are supposed to sterile. Or maybe all the talk of exotic chemicals had led me to imagine the kind of pristine laboratories you see on TV. But whatever the reason, I was surprised by what I saw. The room was square, maybe fifty feet by fifty. I was standing in front of the entrance, at the centre of one wall. Another heavy steel door stood out from the rough whitewashed brickwork directly opposite me. There obviously weren't any windows, but the wall space was busy all the same with safety notices, radiation monitors, fire extinguishers, two large Swiss Railway style clocks, and a bank of round nozzles for supplying oxygen via flexible tubes to the sort of hazmat suits that can be used for extended periods of time. There was also a selection of posters. Two on each wall. But these weren't framed like the CEO's had been.

The rest of the space was divided into four zones, each with an apparently different purpose. Immediately to my right was a work area - two pairs of desks, cluttered with papers and computers and all the other standard office paraphernalia. Diagonally to my right, opposite the desks, was a place to relax - four easy chairs, evenly arranged around the sides of a threadbare rug. Their tweed covers were worn and stained, and a chipped coffee table sat between them. It was complete with unruly piles of newspapers and two dirty mugs. A low cupboard in the corner was home to a kettle, a biscuit tin, and a giant whisky bottle half full of pound coins. The redundant generator Melissa had mentioned completely filled the far left hand corner. Nothing seemed to be attached to it anymore, and as if it were in disgrace for no longer supplying power, it was surrounded by the bars of a metal cage. The final area was fenced off in the same way. Its central section was designed to slide to one side, but it was locked in place. I didn't have the key, but that wasn't a problem. I didn't need to open it. I could see what was inside. There was a metal table, which was bolted to the floor. A clipboard, hanging from a nail on the wall. And one other thing. A metal canister. It was silver. Shiny. Eighteen inches high.

And marked with the unmistakable, universal symbol for radiation.

Chapter Twenty-One

I picked the same chair in the meeting room in Thames House the next morning, but the leather was noticeably cooler than the last time I'd sat in it. Melissa was at my side, once again, and her boss - Colin Chaston - was opposite us. Arthur Hardwicke – the Deputy DG – was back in his place at the head of the table, but on this occasion his attention seemed to be focused entirely on a paper clip. He'd pried one end open so that it stuck straight out, and was rolling it up and down between his thumb and index finger, causing the rest of the clip to spin like a tiny propeller. I watched the thin strand of metal relentlessly twirling round, and realised it mimicked the thoughts that had been plaguing me since last night. I was back to trying to solve the problem rather than assign blame. But old habits die hard. And with so much at stake, what else are you supposed to do?

"So we're dealing with two supposedly impossible things," the Deputy DG said, without interrupting the even rotation of the clip. "A canister in a room where there should be no canisters. And caesium in a canister, when all the caesium in the country is apparently accounted for elsewhere. There definitely was caesium in the canister?"

"Yes, sir," Melissa said. "The lab's confirmed it."

"Can we assume it was connected to the current threat against the government?" he said.

"I never like to assume anything," she said. "But that does seem reasonable."

"What have you done about it?"

"The container was removed for inspection, and the caesium is now under guard at an army facility. A replica was put in its place in the vault, complete with an invisible tracking device, and a wireless surveillance camera has been installed which is independent of the hospital's joke of a system."

"Those are good moves," Chaston said. "But the room was checked on the night of the robbery. It was definitely empty. Photos were taken. I've seen them. There were no canisters. So how could there be one last night?"

"Someone put it there," Melissa said.

"When?"

"Sometime after the photos were taken."

"That's not helpful."

"That's as specific as we can be, right now."

"Why was it put there?"

"A couple of reasons, I guess. One - can you think of a better place to store radioactive material than a specially designed and secured vault? And two - it's the last place anyone would think to look."

"But you thought to look."

"To be fair, Commander Trevellyan did. I thought he was insane, at the time. It never would have occurred to me."

"So what happened? Some unidentified group had stolen some caesium, needed somewhere to store it, heard about our break in, and figured the room at St Joseph's would be free? That's ridiculous."

Melissa shrugged.

"It is ridiculous," I said. "And it's not what happened."

"Where did the canister come from, then?" Chaston said.

"St Joseph's, itself. It was stolen from the hospital."

"No. Four canisters were stolen, and they were all recovered."

"That's what you were meant to think."

"It's true. We have CCTV footage. Scientists' reports. And hospital documentation. All the material was recovered. It's a proven fact, Commander."

"What if there were two thefts? One covering the other."

"What does that mean?"

"Let me show you."

I waited until Arthur Hardwicke was watching, then pulled two pound coins out of my pocket and place them on the table.

"See these coins?" I said. "They're my containers of caesium. They're safe in my vault. Now, Melissa, could you pass me a piece of paper, please?"

Melissa looked dubious, but she did as I asked.

"This is actually an official hospital document," I said. "It confirms the total number of coins. It says there are two. OK so far?"

Everyone nodded.

"Oh no," I said, sliding the two coins away with my right hand. "Look - the caesium is being stolen. And the CCTV camera in the hospital garden – the one in the garden, notice, not the one outside the vault door - is recording the fact that both coins have been taken."

I slid the coins a little further, and covered them with my right hand.

"Now where could they be?" I said. "No one knows. The thieves have made a clean getaway. But wait. The Security Service intervenes, and brings them both back."

I lifted my right hand and slid the coins back to where they'd started.

"Here they are, safe and sound," I said, picking up the piece of paper again. "Let's just check with the records. Yes - both the coins accounted for."

I picked one of them up and bit it gently with my front teeth.

"Now the scientific analysis has been done," I said. "And they haven't been tampered with. So, we definitely got back everything that was stolen."

I slid them across the table to Chaston.

"And from now on, we'll keep them at our back-up site," I said.

Chaston looked at me and scowled.

"What does that prove?" he said.

"That you were looking in the wrong place," I said, lifting my left hand and revealing a third coin. "What about this one?"

"Where did it come from?" he said.

"I stole it a while ago and kept it with the others. But then, a fireman accidentally took a chunk out of my door with his axe. I knew there'd be an inspection, and I couldn't risk being caught with the extra when the technicians showed up to do the inventory. So I needed a diversion. And quickly."

"OK, stop. You're theory doesn't hold water. The third coin couldn't have stayed there the whole time because we know the raiders completely cleared out the vault. I already told you, we have photos."

"I know. But there's something you didn't see. While everyone was distracted by the four guys on the tape who carried off the exact amount that was supposed to be there, I put my fifth guy to work. He took the other suit and used it to hide the balance of the caesium - the stuff I'd stolen some time before - until the vault had been checked and photographed. Then he put it back."

Chaston was leaning forward now, and I could see he was chewing on his lower lip.

"How much of this is fact?" he said. "And how much

is guesswork?"

"It's mainly guesswork," I said. "But can you think of a more likely explanation?"

"Not off the top of my head."

"I think a more important question is, how did they do it?" Melissa said. "The earlier theft. Assuming there was one."

"Well, nothing was physically taken at that time," I said. "The theft was basically done on paper. They changed the amount of caesium people expected to be there, not the amount that was actually there. So, the key must be the way the records are kept."

"OK. So, if someone changed the records, we should be able to trace that."

"I would hope so. I've had experience with inventory falsification before, and what usually happens is that fraudulent entries are hidden behind real events. You told me St Joseph's is some kind of hub for other hospitals, where they concentrate the contaminated waste, or am I making that up?"

"No. That's right. I told you that."

"Which means the most vulnerable moment would probably be when the deliveries were being made. My guess would be, someone didn't record everything that came in."

"How often?"

"I don't know. It could have happened once, with a whole batch. Or it could have happened over and over, with a tiny bit skimmed off each time. Although that way, they'd need someone to suit up and transfer it into their extra container, which might complicate things. It would depend on who was cooking the books for them, I suppose, because they'd want as few people involved as possible."

"Do you believe the first attack on the vault was unconnected, then, Commander?" Hardwicke said.

"No sir," I said. "I don't believe it was some kind of precursor, as we originally thought. It was the catalyst. It made the second attack necessary. But this in turn was not designed to remove any caesium. It was undertaken to cover up the fact there was too much."

"And this excess quantity was acquired through some kind of false accounting?"

"Yes sir."

"Of which you've had previous experience in unraveling?"

"Some, sir."

"Good. In that case, I'd like you to look at how this strange form of theft was carried out. And more importantly, by whom."

"Of course, sir."

"Now Trevellyan, given the other news we uncovered yesterday, and the imminence and scale of the threat, one might expect this task to carry a lower priority. One would be mistaken. You understand why, I take it?"

"I do, sir. The way in which the second attack was launched reveals not just a knowledge of hospital practice. It requires knowledge of MI5 procedures, as well."

"Good man. But wait. There's more. If your theory is correct, it completely negates our assumption that we have tabs on all the caesium in the country. More could have been stolen through the same method. It could be in terrorists' hands already. They could be strapping it to a bomb as we speak. So. It's imperative that we find out who did what, when, and with how much. Is that clear?"

"Yes, sir."

"Good. Wainwright will help you. Now. Let's return to the other matter. The threat. This informant stated that the result of the planned attack would be to bring down the government. Is that correct?"

"Yes sir," Melissa said.

"I find that rather strange. To bring down the government. How could they hope to achieve that? Look at 9/11. The London Tube bombs. The Falkland Islands, and so on. Politicians are fairly adept at using such things to gain popularity, not lose it. Why would it be different this time?"

No one spoke for over a minute, and in the silence all eyes were drawn to Hardwicke's relentlessly spinning paperclip.

"What if the government was known to be aware of a threat?" Jones said, eventually. "But did nothing to avoid it. Or responded in such an incompetent way they lost the public's sympathy?"

"But we haven't received any threats," Melissa said.

"No," Hardwicke said. "Not yet. But there's still time."

"Time?" Jones said. "Let's approach things from that angle, instead. The timescale. Three days, yes?"

"That's what the informer told me yesterday," Melissa said.

"So, two days now," Jones said. "What's happening over the next two days?"

"Oh," Chaston said. "Wait a minute. Melissa, let me ask you something. Is there any way the informer could have said 'close down,' rather than, 'bring down?'"

"No," Melissa said. "Definitely not. I heard him say 'bring down.'"

"But what kind of state was he in?" Chaston said. "He was in the process of betraying his comrades, wasn't he?"

"He was," Melissa said. "And he'd just been shot at, so you could say he was under a fair bit of stress."

"He hadn't only been shot at," Chaston said. "In fact, he was bleeding to death. And what about his language skills? Was he a native English speaker?"

"I don't know," Melissa said. "I don't know his full background. But it sounded like English might not have been his first language. I couldn't be sure."

"Where are you going with this?" Hardwicke said.

"Well, sir, if you take two days and add it to 'close down' the government, do you know what you get?" Chaston said.

Hardwicke stopped the paperclip's motion dead.

"The State Opening of Parliament," Chaston said. "The beginning of the new Parliamentary year. All the MPs. The Lords. The bishops. The most senior judges. Not to mention Her Majesty. All together, in the same place, an iconic location, up to their necks in pomp and ceremony. Can't you just hear the terrorists drooling?"

Chapter Twenty-Two

The Deputy DG had said he wanted Melissa and me to get to the bottom of how the caesium had been stolen as a matter of urgency. He'd made that very clear, so I expected us to head straight over to the hospital when the meeting finally wrapped up and start digging. But Melissa had other ideas. She thought she could turn more up from the office, via the computer and the phone. And this time, she didn't invite me to sit with her.

There was nothing inherently suspicious about that. Plowing two furrows in parallel can be an effective strategy. But when someone's behaviour unexpectedly changes, it makes me wary. And when I added that to her unexplained absence after our last meeting at Thames House, my sixth sense went into overdrive. So I may have agreed to go to St Joseph's right away on my own and start the groundwork, but I didn't actually leave the building. I set myself up in an empty meeting room diagonally opposite the office Melissa shared with Jones. I jammed the door open a tiny crack, just wide enough that I could see out but no one could see in. And I settled down to watch.

Jones came into the corridor three times in the next hour. Twice he returned. Once with coffee. Once with an armful of red folders. And while he was gone the final time, Melissa appeared. She was wearing a coat, but didn't turn right, towards the exit. She went further into the building and then through an unmarked door, which I knew led to a set of stairs. If she went down, she'd end up in the basement. And in the basement, she'd have access to any of the vehicles in the car pool.

I hailed a cab directly outside, on Millbank, and had the driver loop round into Thorney Street and stop where I could see the exit from Thames House's garage. A pair of Fords pulled out almost immediately, followed by a Jaguar, but all three were driven by men. An unmarked van was the next to leave. I couldn't see who was inside it, but my gut told me to ignore it. I was beginning to wonder if I'd made the right choice – and the cab driver was becoming increasingly anxious, but for a different reason – when a bottle green Land Rover Discovery cautiously nosed out into the street ahead of us. It sped up once it reached the top of the ramp, but I had enough time to confirm it was Melissa behind the wheel.

We followed as she turned right onto Horseferry Road, then left onto Millbank and along towards the Houses of Parliament. The traffic was light so we had no trouble keeping up as she crossed into Whitehall, and only fell four cars back as she skirted Nelson's column and started up the east side of Trafalgar Square. My driver was taken by surprise, though, when she lurched without warning into the mouth of William IV Street and came to a sudden stop. I told him to keep going for another hundred yards, and then made my back down the other side of Charing Cross Road on foot.

A gaggle of people had formed outside the box office for the Garrick Theatre, so I joined in the middle of them and kept an eye on the Land Rover. Melissa was still in the driver's seat. She was sitting completely still, looking to her right, back the way she'd come. I had no idea what she was watching for, though. She could have been checking for a tail. Observing a suspect. Waiting for a contact. Or just getting away from the office for a nervous breakdown. Nothing in the pattern of people or vehicles in the vicinity gave me any clue. I was still none the wiser fifteen minutes later when she climbed down from the vehicle. She made a show of locking the door, but I knew she was really scanning for anyone paying her too much attention. Then she walked across to a broad glass cylinder that sprouted from the pavement – the modern entrance to the ancient crypt of St Martin-in-the-Fields church – and disappeared through the door.

I waited two minutes, then followed. There was no sign of Melissa near the bottom of the spiral staircase, or in the church's gift shop. That left two options: the bathroom; or the cafe, which filled the crypt itself. There could be a perfectly innocent explanation for visiting either place. And both would be ideal locations for a covert rendezvous.

It would have been impossible for me to go into either area without being seen, so I made my way over to a woman who was taking photographs of a set of brass plaques that were leaning against the base of the left hand wall.

"Excuse me," I said. "I'm sorry to bother you, but I've got a real problem. I was wondering if you could help me?"

"I can't spare any money," she said. "Sorry."

"Money? No. It's more awkward that. I'm here with my girlfriend. She loves this place – the vaulted ceiling, the golden light, all those kind of things, and..."

"I don't see any girlfriend."

"Well, no. She's hiding in the bathroom. Because what happened is, when we arrived just now, she thought she saw her ex husband go into the cafe. He's – well, bad news. There've been some stalking issues. The police have been involved. There've been court orders. I won't bore you with the details. But the thing is, I need to know if he's in there. If he is, we'll just leave. Avoid any trouble. But I can't go and look myself. He'd see me. And obviously Marie can't."

"So what do you want me to do?"

"Well, I was thinking, if I show you his picture, would you mind just popping your head round the door, and seeing if you recognise him?"

"That's a little weird. But I suppose I could."

"Thank you," I said, pulling my phone out my pocket and opening the photograph folder. "I really appreciate it. Now, let's try and find a recent one."

I fiddled with the phone for another thirty seconds, then threw up my hands.

"Oh, this is ridiculous," I said. "Of course. After the last incident, Marie made me delete them all. There are none left. Not even old ones. This isn't going to work."

"Oh well," the woman said. "Sorry I can't help."

"No, wait. Here's an idea. How about this? How about I give you my phone, and you take a couple of pictures inside the crypt? Just a few random shots. Tourists are always taking photos in there."

"No way. I can't do that. It's too weird."

"Why not? Please. You've already been taking pictures. You're obviously good at it. It'll only take a minute. And if I can't convince Marie that John's not here, she might never come out of the bathroom. We could be here for days."

"Well, OK. I'll take two pictures for you. I'll give it thirty seconds, max."

"That's great. Thank you. I really appreciate it. I'll wait here in case Marie panics and tries to make a run for it."

In the end, the woman was in the cafe for three minutes. She took seven pictures. She told me she thought the single men in two of them looked dangerous. But it was the shot of a couple sitting at a high table against a pillar at the far side of the room that interested me. One of the people was Melissa. The other was a woman I'd never seen before. She was dressed more smartly and was older, maybe in her fifties. And even though it was a still photo, you could see they were arguing.

Melissa was the first of the pair to leave. She paused in the doorway of the entrance cylinder and scanned the area, then walked a little stiffly back to the Land Rover. She started the engine, but didn't pull away. She just sat until the other woman appeared, five minutes later, and watched as she lit a cigarette then turned left and headed towards The Strand.

It was interesting that Melissa waited, I thought. And also inconvenient. Because it meant I couldn't follow her lunch companion.

I had to be content with emailing the picture of the two women to my control in the hope that the stranger could be identified, and was weighing up whether to walk to St Joseph's or take a cab when my phone rang. It was Melissa.

"How's the rest of your morning been?" she said. "Find anything out?"

"Nothing concrete," I said. "I thought I might be onto something, but I hit a block in the road. How about you?"

"Up and down. I've come up with something that might help us, though. The name of a woman at the hospital I think we should talk to. I'm on my way over, now. Where should I meet you?"

"I'm not actually at the hospital yet."

"You're not? Where are you, then?"

"Well, what you said about working on the background got me thinking. About the detail of some of those old fraud cases I claimed to know all about. I realised I was little rusty. I thought it might be an idea to brush up a little before diving in the deep end."

"That's smart. You're not still at Thames House, are you?"

"No. I needed some old notes I'd made."

"So you're at Tottenham Court Road?"

I had to think before I replied. There are entry and exit logs at all Navy buildings. They'd show I hadn't set foot in the place, and if she was getting access to information about me in the same way I was about her, she'd know if I lied about being there.

"No," I said. "I'm at home. The notes I'm taking about aren't exactly official copies, if you know what I mean."

"I do know," she said. "And that's no problem. I'll swing by and pick you up. What's your address?"

"What do you mean, 'swing by?'"

"Didn't I tell you? I've got my hands on a vehicle."

"You didn't. What do you need one for?"

"Well, I figured if we're going to question this woman, we'll need some privacy. I'd hoped we could steal a room at the local nick for half an hour or so, but they knocked me back. I don't want to drag her all the way to Millbank, so I had an inspiration. Borrow a surveillance vehicle. We have ones with built-in cameras and recorders."

Melissa said she could be outside my building in ten minutes, which made me realise two things. I'd have to hurry, to get there before her. And either I was barking up the wrong tree, or she was better at covering her tracks than I'd given her credit for.

Chapter Twenty-Three

Melissa guided the Land Rover into a service bay on Silk Street - the closest point to my apartment in the Barbican you can easily reach by car - and slid across into the passenger seat.

"I think you better drive, David," she said, as I climbed on board. "No offense, but if you walk up to a strange woman in the middle of the street and ask her to get in a car with you, she's more likely to call the police or run away screaming."

"Thanks for the vote of confidence," I said.

"Sorry. Look, I know my attitude's not where it should be. I know I shouldn't feel like this. I know I sound like a child, but it's just not fair. Look at what the others were assigned to. Security of the parliament buildings. Liaison with the Royal Protection Duty. I feel like I'm being sidelined. I don't deserve it, and I don't like it."

"I know exactly how you feel."

"And there's researching the group Leckie's informer belonged to. I stayed up half the night pulling all that material together, and now I have to hand it over and deal with yesterday's news."

"What did you find out about them?"

"They're based in Yemen, and mostly operate in the Middle East. Their organisation is small, but very professional. In Leckie's day they had a threat assessment of alpha, but this needs to be updated. Although it doesn't sound like it's diminished, any."

"What are they called?"

"al-Aqsaba'a."

"I've never heard of them."

"That's because of how they work. They don't typically go in for big, eye catching stunts. Another 9/11 wouldn't be their style. They've always been much more subtle operators. They aim to get what they want indirectly, by influencing and pressurising others - governments, businesses, charities and so on."

After this morning I was making a renewed effort to focus on my control's instructions and concentrate on Melissa's loyalty, and not to interfere with the case.

"What?" Melissa said, when I didn't answer.

"Blowing up the State Opening of Parliament?" I said, relapsing once again. "Maybe killing the Queen? The PM? The Cabinet? If it's true, it's a major change of direction for a group that's supposed to be publicity-shy."

"It's like I told you - the threat assessment needs updating. That means they could have changed, not gone away."

"Have they done anything in the UK before?"

"Yes. A few things. Several assassinations. Particularly creative, yet brutal, I'm told. And a strong line in blackmail. That's why Leckie was involved, originally."

"Did he have any success against them?"

"He did. His last case was a good example. They were planning to kill the infant son of an Arab diplomat as punishment for their government having too close ties with the Great Satan. Leckie stopped them and saved the kid."

"And after that he was kicked out for brutality?"

"That's right."

"Was the same informant involved?"

"Yes."

I tried to go quiet again.

"Oh, come on," she said. "What?"

"This has all the hallmarks of a set up. This group caused Leckie's downfall, in his mind? And remember what he said about the using the caesium theft as a smokescreen for settling scores? It gives you another explanation for why his old mate suddenly resurfaced at such a convenient moment."

"Revenge as a motive? Of course I've considered it. But someone shot that informant, yesterday, and it wasn't Leckie cause he was standing right next to me, and we both nearly caught bullets, too. So, one way or another, something's going on."

"How does it relate to this woman we're going to see, now?"

"I don't know. Maybe it doesn't. But the DDG wants us to look into the caesium theft you say that was done on paper, and of all the people in the hospital, she's the most likely candidate to start spilling the beans."

"Why?"

"Several reasons. But mostly because she's a loner, and has a terrible HR record. That suggests she has no loyalty to either the place or her co-workers. So even if her hands are clean, hopefully her tongue will be loose enough to dish the dirt on enough others to give us some good leads."

"What do we know about her?"

"Well, her name's Amany Shakran. She's twenty-nine years old. Born in Cairo. Trained as a teacher in Egypt. Moved to London six years ago after marrying a UK citizen. Couldn't get work as a teacher cause her qualifications aren't recognised here, so worked a variety of temporary office jobs before settling at St Joseph's four years ago."

"That could explain her bad HR record, if she never really wanted to work there. I'd be pretty resentful, if I couldn't do what I was trained for because of some bureaucratic nonsense."

"It's possible. And it could also be personal. She got divorced three years ago. I don't know the circumstances, but you know what divorce can do to people. It brings out their true colours, I always think."

"How will we recognise her? Do you know what she looks like?"

Melissa rummaged in her purse, pulled out a grainy eight by ten photograph, and handed it to me.

"It's copied from her immigration file, so it's a little out of date," she said.

I studied the picture for a moment, and allowing for six years of aging, I was sure enough.

"We know this woman," I said. "She was the younger one who was arguing in the canteen just before you showed me the axe marks in the door."

Melissa took the photograph back.

"I thought it was," she said. "I wasn't certain, though, so I wanted to see if it hit you the same way."

"It did," I said. "And If she shows the same spirit she did that day, our afternoon could be quite fun after all."

We arrived at St Joseph's fifteen minutes before Amany Shakran's shift was due to end, so I stopped the Land Rover on a double yellow with a good view of the hospital entrance.

"What if she comes out a different way?" I said. "Do you want to divide and conquer?"

"No," Melissa said. "I don't think so. We're more effective if we stick together, and I'm pretty sure this is the way she'll come. It's the nearest exit to the block she works in. The tube stop she needs to get home is this way. So's the bus stop. And most of the local shops."

"Look," I said. "Heading for the gate. Is that her

now?"

"It is," Melissa said, flicking a switch beneath the glove box to active the vehicle's built-in surveillance camera, then reaching for the door release. "First out of the trap, obviously. It doesn't seem like her attitude's improved any."

The woman we'd spotted was about five foot ten tall. She was wearing flats, suit trousers, and a tightly buttoned wool overcoat, all in black. Her hair was pulled back from her face. She showed no signs of wearing make-up. She was scowling, and her arms were pinned tightly to her sides as she strode briskly out from under the hospital's signature archway. Melissa stood at the side of our Land Rover and waited until she was sure the woman was heading our way. Then, when they were about six feet apart, Melissa stepped into the middle of the pavement and blocked her path. I saw her flash some kind of ID. The other woman stiffened. Worry replaced the hostility that had temporarily flickered across her face, but she didn't attempt to run. Melissa took hold of her arm, just in case, and ushered her back a few steps. Then she opened the back door and guided her into the rear of the vehicle.

"Am I under arrest?" the woman said, as I pulled away from the kerb.

"No," Melissa said. "We're not here to arrest you. We'd just like to talk to you. We think you might be able to help us make sense of something that happened recently in the hospital. In the department where you work."

"Who's that?" the woman said, pointing at me.

"His name is David Trevellyan," Melissa said. "He's my colleague. Another officer. He's here to help. David, this is Amany Shakran."

I adjusted the rear view mirror so that the woman knew I could see her, but I wasn't ready to say anything yet.

"Now, Amany, I want you listen very carefully,"

Melissa said. "You're not in any trouble. And we're not looking to get you in any trouble. In fact, if you can help us with our problem, we'll make sure you stay out of trouble, even if it turns out other people you know have done things that are wrong. Do you understand me?"

The woman didn't reply.

"OK," Melissa said. "Maybe that was the wrong question to ask, because I know you're an intelligent, educated woman. In fact, I know all about you. Your early life in Egypt. Getting married. Moving to the UK. Having to work at the hospital, instead of in a school. And I also know the people you work with don't like you very much. Do they?"

The woman still didn't speak, but I saw her shake her head very slightly.

"Now, I'm sure that's very unfair," Melissa said. "But here's the situation. Laws have been broken. Serious ones. Pretty soon hard-core investigators are going to be crawling all over your office. And when that happens, do you think your co-workers are going to stand up for you?"

"Ha," the woman said, after a moment. "Those sons of donkeys would stab me in the back sooner than look at me."

"That's pretty much what I thought. I've had to work with people like that more times than you'd believe, so I know exactly what you're going through. It's a horrible experience. But if you help us with this one thing, we can make sure that when the time comes, those people get what they deserve. And, more importantly, we can stop them putting the blame on you instead."

"What kind of help do you need? I am just a clerk. What can I do?"

"I need some information. Just so I can understand how something works in the hospital. No one will ever know it came from you."

"What can I tell you? I'm a teacher, not a medical person. It's because of your stupid Department of Education that I am where I am, surrounded with cruel, ignorant rodents. You should save your time with me, and go interrogate someone else."

"This isn't an interrogation. It's just a friendly chat. And it's your job I'm interested in. Part of it, anyway. I just need to understand how one thing works. Then, I'll be able to see how something else was able to happen. Something you absolutely won't get in trouble for."

"I can try, if that will help keep my name out of the mud. Which thing?"

"You don't know what I'm going to ask you about? You don't have any idea?"

"No. My job is very boring. I can't imagine how talking about it can help anyone. But I'm willing to try, if you tell me what you want to know."

"Well, I'm interested to know what happens when the containers of special waste arrive from the other hospitals. You helped keep the records, didn't you?"

"I did. But that doesn't happen any more. Not since some of it was stolen. Now it all goes to another hospital. Someone there does all the logging in and out."

"I know that. But can you tell me how you used to do it, when the waste still came here?"

"It was easy, to tell you the truth. A trained monkey could have done it. On the morning of the transfer, I got an e-mail, which was also copied to my boss. It told us the number of canisters that were coming, what was in them, and gave a code number for each one. Then, when the truck arrived, I went outside with a barcode reader. I scanned the codes, and if they matched the e-mail, everything was okay."

"So all the containers had barcodes on them?"

"Yes. The code identified the container, and also what was inside it. The system was very good. It meant no one could send too few containers. And they couldn't lie about what was inside."

"That's good."

"Yes. It was very well thought out. A copy of the e-mail went to my boss. The barcode reader automatically copied its results to him, too, so no one could hide anything. Once the containers were safely inside, the technicians would check them, as well. If anything was wrong, they would flag it up. And there were outside technicians who we could call in if we were worried about anything."

"That sounds pretty thorough. But tell me something. What if someone wanted to sneak an extra container into the vault. How could they do that?"

"They couldn't. It would be impossible. The delivery scan wouldn't match the e-mail. The system would pick that up automatically, even if I didn't notice there were the wrong number."

"But what if you accidentally forgot to scan one of the containers? Couldn't it be missed?"

"No. Once again, the scan would not match the e-mail. And the e-mail is known about by the original hospital, and my boss. You see, that's the strength of the system. At no time does it depend on only one person. If something was done wrong, by accident or on purpose, two other people would see. As well as the computer. It's as they told us on the training. Impossible to fiddle."

"It does sound like a strong system, Amany," Melissa said, shooting me a disappointed glance in the mirror. "Thank you for explaining it to us."

Chapter Twenty-Four

"It does sound pretty watertight," I said. "Do you mind if I just ask one thing, though?"

The woman shook her head.

"You said you scan the barcodes," I said. "That sounds complicated. How do you do it?"

"Complicated?" she said. "It's the easiest thing in the world. You take the scanner and point it at the barcode. That's all there is to do. And you can tell you're pointing it in the right place, because it shines a red light."

"So the scanners are portable?"

"Of course. You would need a crazy long wire, otherwise."

"And what powers them? Batteries?"

"They are rechargeable. You never have to change the batteries."

"What if you forget to plug then in? What if the batteries go flat?"

"They last for weeks. And we have spare ones. And the truck brings a spare one of its own, which is charged up by the engine. We've never had a problem, and I doubt there could be one."

"What if they break down?"

"Then we'd use a spare one. We have several, like I said. But I can't ever remember that happening."

"OK. Forget about the handsets for a minute. What if the system went wrong? The computer system itself, I mean. The place where the scanners send the information to be matched with the e-mail?"

"It is very well designed. It never goes wrong."

"Never? It never throws a fit? Melissa, have you ever heard of a computer system like that?"

"No," Melissa said. "I've never heard of a computer that's not constantly falling over, in fact."

The woman stayed silent, but turned her head to look out the opposite window.

"Seriously," I said. "You're saying this system never crashes?"

"I don't recall that ever happening," the woman said.

"Okay. Let's just go with the idea that this thing is bullet proof. We'll take your word for it. But let me ask you something else. There must have been an emergency procedure for you to follow, just in case there ever was a crash?"

"The hospital is very thorough. There are processes and procedures and roadmaps and guidelines for more or less everything."

"Including what to do if the barcode scanner system wasn't working?"

The woman said nothing.

"Amany?" Melissa said. "What's your answer? This is all part of keeping you out of trouble, you know. Don't dry up on us now, or you'll only be hurting yourself."

"OK then, yes," she said. "There was a procedure. But it was just for emergencies."

"About this procedure," Melissa said. "How did it work? What did you have to do?"

"It was easy," she said. "The barcodes have little numbers underneath them. You just had to write them down and then key them in to a special form on the intranet. But like I told you, the scanners never went down so that's not important."

"There's something we should, perhaps, have explained at the start," I said. We're not the regular police.

We have access to things that most people can't get their hands on. For example, we could get a copy of the maintenance file for every system in that hospital as easily as you could buy a morning paper. Do you follow me?"

"Yes," she said. "I do. And I bet you could get my attendance record, too. And if you did, and you checked, you would find no scanner breakdowns for any days I was working."

"I'm sure you're right. But here's my real question. How many times would the records show you'd entered the details manually, anyway, even though the system was working?"

"The system never broke down. The backup method was only for emergencies."

"How many times?"

"It wasn't necessary. The scanner has always worked."

"Amany," Melissa said. "We can only help you if you tell us the truth. If you keep lying to us, I'm sorry, but the deal's off."

She said nothing.

I pulled over to the side of the road, took out my phone, and held it up so the woman could see it.

"I'm going to call one of my people," I said. "I'm going to have them compare the maintenance log for the scanners with the method of entry for the information. And when I do, how many times will it say you used the backup?"

She didn't answer.

"Do you know why I picked this exact spot to stop?" I said.

She shrugged.

"Because of that junction," I said, pointing towards the roundabout that was a couple of hundred yards ahead.

"If I go left, there's a police station within a quarter of a mile. If I go right, we can be back at your house inside twenty minutes."

I saw a scowl begin to spread across her face.

"Keep lying, and I'll turn left," I said. "Start telling the truth, and I'll turn right."

"Two," she said, after another few seconds. "Turn right. The answer's two. I used the backup system two times, even though scanners were working."

"Thank you," I said, pulling back out into the traffic but joining the queue in the centre lane. "Now, tell me who asked you to do it."

She didn't respond.

"We're moving again," I said. "We'll be at the roundabout in a moment. The way things are going, I'm turning left. To the police station. Is that where you want to go?"

"No one asked me to do it," she said. "I was just curious. I did it as an experiment. To see how it would work. I know that was wrong. I apologise. But I didn't think it would do any harm. I never thought anyone would find out."

I pulled into the left hand lane.

"No," she said. "Wait. Please. I am confused. I need more time. English is not my first language. I do not understand what you're asking me."

"Keep going straight please, David," Melissa said. "I think I know what's going on here. Amany, I understand that in life, people sometimes do things they're ashamed of. Things they never want their families to hear about. But here's the problem. We are going to find out why you did what you did with those records. And if you tell us now, while there's time for us to make sure no one else gets hurt, we can keep your secret hidden. No one in Egypt will ever know. But if you don't..."

The woman's left hand started to shake, and I saw her draw it onto her lap and hold it still with her right.

"It was a man who asked you to, wasn't it?" Melissa said.

The woman gave a tiny, almost imperceptible nod.

"Were you involved with him?" Melissa said.

The woman said nothing.

"I think you were," Melissa said. "You might as well come clean. You'll feel better if you admit it. Trust me."

"How did you know?" she said.

"A sudden divorce. Falling out with co-workers. Public fights in the hospital canteen. I know the signs."

"It's so shameful. I don't know how to explain."

Melissa gave her a second to catch her breath.

"My husband, Mark, and I," she said, when her breathing was almost back under control. "We were having terrible problems. He's an artist. He doesn't earn much, but he thought we'd be OK, with me as a teacher. Only I wasn't allowed to teach."

"That wasn't your fault," Melissa said.

"I know. But he was still mad with me. He thought I could get a better job if I tried harder. He said I was lazy. That I was a liar. That I was disrespectful to him. His temper was so awful, any little thing would set him off and he'd scream at me, right in my face, for hours and hours. He'd use such horrible language. And he was so much bigger than me. I was terrified. I had no friends. My mother, my sisters, they were on a different continent..."

"And then you met someone? Who was nice to you?"

"Yes. Stewart."

"Stewart?"

"Stewart Sole. My boss. The first man from Scotland I ever met. It's funny. At first I could hardly understand what he said, and soon he was the only person I could talk to."

"And Stewart asked you to enter some numbers manually one day, when a delivery came? To act as if the scanners weren't working?"

"Yes. He came to me, that morning. I could tell something was wrong. At first he didn't want to tell me what, but I pressed him. He said he was in trouble. He'd made a mistake, something to do with the delivery, and he was going to get fired. I was scared. I needed him. I couldn't stand the thought of not seeing him every day. I told him I'd do anything I could to help him."

"The numbers he gave you. They didn't match what was on the containers?"

"I honestly don't know. I thought it would be better if I didn't look. But..."

"But?"

"They can't have been the same, can they? Or what difference would it have made, me entering them?"

"Good point."

"The same thing happened once more, but they were the only times I ever did anything against the rules, you must believe me. And it was only to save Stewart. He's a good man, and all he'd done was make a couple of honest mistakes."

"I understand. And I believe you. But there's one other thing I need to know. When did this happen?"

The woman reeled off two dates, both in mid August.

"You're sure?" Melissa said.

"I'm certain," she said. "It's been heavy on my conscience ever since. I'll never forget them."

"And which hospital did the deliveries come from?"

"I can't remember. But there was only one delivery on each of the days. It should be easy enough to find out. I can check for you first thing in the morning."

"Thank you. Please do."

Neither woman spoke for the next couple of minutes, and I pulled over to the side of the road without waiting to be asked.

"I have told you truthfully," the woman said. "I have told you things I have never spoken of before, to anyone. Please. Will you keep your promise not to let word spread back to Egypt?"

"Are you still seeing Stewart?" Melissa said.

The woman looked away.

"I'll take that as a yes," Melissa said. "He's married, isn't he?"

The woman didn't speak any words, but a short, strangled moan told us what we needed to know.

"OK," Melissa said. "Here's where we stand. We need to talk to Stewart. We need to talk to him today. And it's vitally important that he doesn't know we're coming. So, if you keep your mouth shut, and promise not to warn him, your secret won't leave these shores. Understand?"

The woman nodded.

"Good," Melissa said. "Where will we find him?"

"In the office," the woman said.

"Which office?"

"It's in the same block as mine. One floor down. The far end of the corridor."

"Good. We'll find it. Now, I need you to give me your mobile phone."

"Why?"

"Amany, I like you. I want to be able to help you, and keep this under my hat. But in my experience, mobile phones are too much of a temptation for people to resist. So I want you to give me yours. Just for today. I'll leave it in the office for you to collect in the morning."

The woman reached into her bag, pulled out an old Nokia, and handed it to Melissa.

"Thank you," Melissa said. "Can you find your way home from here? We have an appointment at the hospital."

The woman nodded.

"OK," Melissa said. "Thank you, once more, for your help. I know it wasn't easy, telling us those things. But remember - there's to be no communication with Stewart whatsoever. No phone calls. No texts. No emails. No IMs. No Facebook. No Twitter. Nothing. Otherwise your whole confession was a waste of time."

Chapter Twenty-Five

I pulled an illegal U-turn, and watched the woman's forlorn, stationary figure grow smaller in the rear view mirror. Then Melissa squeezed through the gap between the front seats, slid into place beside me, and switched off the camera before calling Chaston and reporting what Amany had told us about a second batch of caesium.

"She was played from minute one," she said, when she hung up. "Poor girl. I feel sorry for her."

"It was nice of you not to tell her," I said. "Not to tarnish her white knight."

"She knows. She just hasn't admitted it to herself, yet. This guy Sole is clearly an operator. I can't wait to have a chat with him."

"If he needed Amany to falsify the delivery receipt at St Joseph's, the email from the dispatching hospital must have been nobbled as well. We need to know who else was involved at that end."

"I think she might have given us the answer to that, too."

"How?"

"Remember how adamant she was about the date? Of both occasions? August?"

"Yes. So?"

"What happens in August?"

"Lots of things."

"OK. What doesn't happen in August?"

I didn't answer.

"Kids don't go to school," she said. "August is in the middle of the school holidays. So I bet that's the flaw in the whole triangular caesium monitoring system, right there. I bet that when the manager at one hospital is on holiday, the one from the other covers for him. That brings it down to two points of failure. And if one is shagging the other..."

"I bet you're right," I said. "And that explains the timing, too. They stole the stuff when they had the opportunity to take it, and stored it - in the place they'd stolen it from - until they needed it. Why else keep it hanging around for so long?"

I parked in almost exactly the same spot where we'd waited for Amany. Melissa flashed some ID at a traffic warden who had immediately tried to pounce on us. I glared a warning at two kids who were looking greedily at the Land Rover's alloys, and we made our way to the St Joseph's admin block as quickly as we could without actually running.

There were two desks in Stewart Sole's cramped corner office. The messier one was occupied, but as soon as its owner opened his mouth it was clear he wasn't the guy we were looking for. Instead of being Scottish, he had a heavy French accent.

"I am very sorry, but Mr Sole has left for the afternoon," he said. "Is there anything I can do to help you?"

I glanced at Melissa, and saw the expression on her face growing harder.

"No thank you," I said. "It was just a social call. We're old friends, and happened to be in the area. You can't remember what time Stewart left, can you? That might give us an idea which watering hole to look for him in."

"Oh, no, I didn't mean Mr Sole has finished with his work for today," he said. "He was called to a meeting, and didn't expect to come back. I'm sorry if my words were misleading."

"Not at all," I said. "What time did he leave,

approximately?"

"Immediately after lunch. He came in, sat down, and straight away his telephone was ringing. He left the second he hung up. Not later than five after one."

I looked at Melissa again. Her expression was softening. Amany was with us at 1.05. She hadn't gone back on her word.

"Thanks again," I said. "I really appreciate you helping us out like this, after we dropped in unannounced. He didn't mention where his meeting was going to be, by any chance?"

"No," he said. "He just jumped up and was through the door, as if being pulled on a rope by the person from the phone."

"So he could have been going to another part of the hospital?"

"I do not think that is likely, because he paused only to put on his coat. I do not think this would have been necessary if his plan was not to leave the building."

"No, I guess not. Well, thank you anyway. Have a good afternoon. We'll maybe see you another time."

Melissa took the car keys as we made our way back out of the hospital, and took a moment to adjust the driver's seat before pulling away.

"This is a problem," she said. "The trail goes cold without Sole. What do you think? Is it just a coincidence that he suddenly goes walkabout the afternoon we come calling?"

"I don't know," I said. "We don't know how often he does things like this."

"True. He might walk back in tomorrow, pleased as Punch. Or he might never be seen again."

"And he's obviously involved with some pretty

dodgy people, so whatever's happening may not have anything to do with us, anyway."

"Let's come back, first thing in the morning, and see if we can pick him up on his way in."

"Sounds like a plan."

"In the meantime, let's drop this tractor off back at my office. Then we could maybe grab a late bite of lunch."

"Count me in."

Melissa suggested we should eat at the Mint hotel, since it was almost next door to Thames House. Neither of us spoke much as we wound our back through the city traffic, and she dropped me outside while she went to sign the car back into the pool. I found a table in an alcove under a set of stairs, and was still getting to grips with the menu when she slid into the seat next to mine.

"David, are you really hungry?" she said.

"I could eat," I said. "But if I didn't, I wouldn't starve. Why?"

"It's just, I'm uneasy about doing nothing. I don't want to wait till the morning to go after Sole. It feels like too much of a risk. So, I was thinking, how would you feel about heading over to his house and seeing if we can pick him up there?"

"Now?"

"We could be there when he gets back from this mysterious meeting he was summoned to."

"How will we find out where he lives?"

Melissa pulled a folded piece of paper from the inside pocket of her jacket, set it on the table, and pushed it towards me.

"I took a minute when I was back at the office," she said.

I picked up the note and unfolded it. An address in

south London was written in smooth, flowing handwriting.

"Morden?" I said. "That's not too far. OK. Let's give it a try."

"Thanks," she said. "It might not lead to anything - he might not even come home tonight - but trying will make me feel a lot better."

"It would be interesting to see what his place is like, too. It could give us an idea of how discrete this guy is, since his hands are apparently in the till."

"It should."

"How are we going to get there? Tube?"

"I have a confession. I didn't turn the Land Rover back in, after all. It's parked outside. I was hoping you'd say, yes."

The drive to Sole's house took forty-four minutes, allowing for a set of road works on the Balham High Road, a stop at Pret a Manger to pick up sandwiches, and another at a petrol station to refill the Land Rover's tank.

"This guy must have excellent self control," Melissa said, as she guided the Land Rover expertly into a narrow space diagonally opposite a modest semi, a quarter of a mile from Morden station. "Unless he's got a couple of Rolls Royces in a lock-up round the corner."

"Either that, or someone's controlling him with something other than money," I said.

"Could be either. We need to find out which. Let's see if he's in first, shall we?"

"I'll go, if you like."

"No. You better stay put. What if he is there? We don't want him taking to his heels."

"Why do you keep saying things like that?"

"Oh, I don't know. What happened with Tim Jones, the first time you met him, maybe. Or the kids in the hospital garden. Or the city boys, outside the Frog and Turtle."

"I was very restrained, with all of those."

"You're like the iron fist in the velvet glove, aren't you?"

I allowed myself a hint of a smile.

"Only sometimes, it seems like you forget to bring the glove."

I watched Melissa saunter across the road and pick her way along the path through Sole's narrow front garden, and had to agree she could make herself look pretty non-threatening. I couldn't help wondering what would happen if he opened the door and showed any of the smarminess he's apparently employed on Amany, though.

Melissa rang the doorbell, then stepped back and started to subtly peek through the two downstairs windows. She waited a couple of minutes, then rang again. There must have been no answer, because she moved to her right and tried the gate that blocked the passage between Sole's house and the next pair of semis. I could see that the handle wouldn't turn. She glanced around behind her, then put her right foot up on the wall, pushed herself up, pivoted around, and disappeared feet first from view.

She was out of sight for just over three minutes, then the gate opened and she strolled back out, moving calmly as if she owned the place. Two minutes after that she was behind the wheel, next to me.

"It's a very modest place," she said. "There's no sign of a sudden influx of ill-gotten cash."

"Maybe they don't live there anymore," I said. "Maybe they've rented the place out."

"It's possible. We'll just have to see when someone gets home. At least we know the place is occupied. There were dirty breakfast things still on the kitchen table."

Over the next four hours and ten minutes we talked about many things. We started with the first records we'd bought. Then the first concerts we'd been to. The first person we'd kissed. Our favourite books. And movies. And paintings. And buildings. And countries. For two hundred and fifty minutes we sounded like normal members of society, with no place in our conversation for violence or deception or death. The only subject Melissa stayed resolutely away from was her family. And before I could change that, her phone rang.

"They say dead men tell no tales," she said, looking several shades paler. "What do you think? And what about dead men's houses? Or dead men's dead mistresses?"

"Sole's dead?" I said.

"Yes. He is. And so's Amany Shakram. That was the desk sergeant at the police station round the corner from St Joseph's. The guy knew I still have an eye on the place, so when two hospital employees turned up dead tonight, he had the nouse to call me."

"Were they murdered?"

"Oh, yes. It sounds like they were very much murdered."

"Where?"

"Woolwich. In a half-abandoned council estate about thirty-five minutes from here."

"OK. So what would you rather do? Head to the murder scene? Or see what we can turn up inside the house?"

"It's six of one, half a dozen of the other."

"I agree. But if I had to pick one, I'd go for the murder scene. Recent violence is much more fertile ground than somewhere someone's had years to hide and conceal everything. And judging by the outside, at least, this guy was pretty careful not to give anything away."

"That works for me," she said, reaching out and turning the key.

Chapter Twenty-Six

Melissa drove much more aggressively on our way out of Morden than she had done on our way in. The chunky SUV wasn't exactly nimble, but what it lacked in precision she made up for with power as she zigzagged through Colliers Wood and Tooting and Streatham, before turning right onto the A205 and blazing west through Dulwich and Forest Hill and Catford. She slowed right down when she turned left, heading north again, and then my heart sank when I realised what was happening. We were nearly at our destination. Melissa was looking for somewhere to park. I just hoped she had plenty of taxi money with her, because one look out of the window was enough to tell you the Land Rover wasn't likely to be there when we came back for it.

"What just happened?" I said, as Melissa pulled the Land Rover into a layby next to a burnt out bus shelter. "Did you drive so fast that we went back in time, and somehow ended up in Soviet era East Germany? What is this place?"

"Welcome to the Queen's Grove Estate," she said, opening her door. "Some say it's the closest you can get to hell without being dead."

"It looks like they're right," I said, following her out on to the pavement.

"Last year, two guys were stabbed to death here on a Friday night. Their bodies were left lying in one of the gardens - and I say gardens in the loosest sense of the word - for a whole weekend before anyone bothered to call the police."

"Charming. And this is where Sole ended up? Amany, too?"

"Yes. That's what I'm told."

"Where, exactly? This place is huge."

"I have the name of the block."

"Well, good luck finding it," I said, pointing to what used to be a map of the estate. It was still standing, attached to a pair of stout metal girders, but its surface was entirely obliterated with dozens of layers of paint.

"We should be able to find it," she said. "Half the place has been demolished already."

"Why only half?"

"You might not believe it, but a handful of the residents have refused to leave. They can't knock down any more till they get them to move out."

"Why won't they go?"

"These are people who've been here for years. Since it was built. It's their home. They like it."

"But just look at the place," I said, scanning the acres of stained concrete and smashed glass.

"They think there wasn't a problem with the buildings," she said. "The problem was with the people. The ones who chose to use the walkways for muggings or selling drugs. To piss in the stairwells. Or to set fire to the lifts, just for fun."

"I can see how that wouldn't add to the sense of community," I said, thinking about the friends who'd died, alone and away from home, protecting people who did things like this. "Maybe we could have a nose around, later. I wouldn't mind meeting some of these muggers and drug dealers and incontinents. I could pass on the regards from some of my absent friends."

"Don't start with that, again," she said. "Let's see what we need to see, then just get out of here."

I followed her through a kind of rectangular courtyard, boxed in on all sides by the decaying husks of square, soulless excuses for buildings. We passed through a gap in the far corner where the whole sidewall of one of the blocks was missing, and found ourselves at the entrance to another, identical courtyard.

"How many of these are there?" I said.

"I don't know," she said. "Thirty? Forty?"

"Heaven help us. We'll be here all night."

"No, we won't. Look, back there."

Melissa had turned round, and was pointing to the empty space where a window had been, ten floors above us. It was glowing with harsh, white light while all the others around it were dark and derelict.

We made our way to the nearest entrance and pulled aside the remnants of the twisted metal screen that was supposed to have kept the place secure.

"Take a deep breath," Melissa said, and disappeared inside.

I followed her, and we started up the filthy concrete stairs. Even with both hands clamped over my mouth and nose, it was impossible to escape the stench. We climbed steadily, and after seven flights I began to make out the sound of voices above us.

"Oy!" a male voice said, after we'd reached the ninth landing and started on the final set of steps. "Where do you think you're going?"

We kept on climbing, and in another moment I saw a nineteen or twenty-year-old in a police constable's uniform blocking our path. Melissa and didn't say anything, but she showed him her ID and he stepped back without question.

The landing stretched away into the darkness. One side was open to the elements. The other was harsh, textured concrete, interrupted by random panels of black tiles which extended up from the floor, and a regular series of doorways. Only now, the openings were covered by more metal grills. All of them, except for the one closest to us. I took a reluctant step towards it.

"You might not want to go in there, sir," the young constable said.

I stepped past him, looked inside, and saw a large rectangular space. It would probably have been the living room, when the flat was habitable. It was a decent size, and it looked like the wide window would have made the place pleasantly bright to live in. But it was far from pleasant now. Strips of garish, almost psychedelic wallpaper were hanging from the walls. Clods of paint were dangling from the ceiling. The floor was covered with broken glass and mouse droppings. It stank even worse than the stairwell, and the two men who were already in the room had breathing masks over their faces. They were police technicians. Both were wearing white overalls. One was standing between a pair of tripod-mounted floodlights, and the other was crouching down, fiddling with the portable generator that powered them.

"Evening," the standing technician said. "You took your time. We need to get wrapped up. Where's your stuff?"

"What stuff?" Melissa said. "Oh, I see. No. We're not with the coroner. It looks like you'll have to hang on a little longer, for them. Have you been here for a while? Can you tell us what happened?"

Two bodies were lying in the middle of the floor. A man - presumably Stewart Sole - and Amany Shakran. Both were naked. Both had their wrists and ankles bound with plastic ties. Sole's hands were behind his back. Amany's were in front of her abdomen, which was grossly swollen and distended. It hadn't been that way, earlier when we'd spoken to her. A double ring of continuous, deep, jagged, cuts ran round her belly, like a dark belt. Blood had seeped out from the wounds and stained the floor on either side of her, stranding a swarm of wriggling insects in a slowly congealing slick. They looked like some kind of huge ants, and more were caught in the bigger, darker puddles that surrounded the victims' heads.

Both of them had been shot, twice. I could see where the bullets had entered, but there were no visible exit wounds. It looked like someone who knew what they were doing had been to work with a .22. There was no sign of any shell casings, either. But four other items were on the floor, lined up tidily next to Amany's body. Two pale-blue twenty-litre NATO jerrycans. A galvanised steel funnel. And a length of red, sticky barbed wire, about five feet long.

"I think it's pretty obvious, don't you?" he said. "An interrogation? A punishment? An execution? Take your pick."

"What makes someone do this?" Melissa said.

The technician just shrugged.

"I mean, what makes a person capable of doing this?" Melissa said. "Are they uniquely twisted? Or is it something in their blood?"

Chapter Twenty-Seven

When Melissa told me another progress meeting had been scheduled for the following morning, I started to worry. I could see an abyss opening up at our feet, and another fruitless NATO exercise – No Action Talk Only, as one of my old instructors used to say – lying in wait for us in its rocky depths. But when I reached Thames House and made my way upstairs to our usual meeting room, I found my concern was premature. Only Melissa and Jones were there. The others were spread out across London, following through with their various actions from our previous session. The meeting was being replaced with a conference call, apparently. Which would have been doubly fine if they'd thought to tell us before we'd done battle with the morning's traffic.

Melissa reached across and pulled the spider phone to our side of the table so she wouldn't have to raise her voice when she spoke, but for the first twenty minutes she needn't have bothered. The others had been busy, and had plenty to say about the gaps they'd found in the security arrangements at the Houses of Parliament. The revised precautions they were implementing. The discussions they were having with the Queen's protection detail, and the difficulty of persuading her bodyguards to change their existing procedures.

The only area where limited progress had been made was in investigating the group that Leckie's informer had penetrated. None of the existing network of informers could throw any light on them, and GCHQ had been unable to uncover anything on any phone networks, email, or internet interactions that Melissa hadn't already found out. So when she did finally get the chance to report, the satisfaction of having uncovered how the caesium was stolen was outweighed by the disappointment that the only two people definitely known to be involved had been killed.

"This is very worrying," Hardwicke said when Melissa had relayed the last of her information, speaking for the first time and nearly deafening everyone with a blast of background traffic noise as he took his phone off mute. "The fact that another batch of caesium is in the wrong hands is extremely serious. But panic will serve no one's interests - other than the wrongdoers. Chaston?"

"Here, sir," Melissa's boss said.

"If the bath is overflowing, what's the first thing you do?"

"Turn off the tap."

"Correct. So, now that we know the procedure has been compromised, there are to be no further transfers of hospital waste until further notice. Take care of that, will you?"

"Sir."

"We're making good progress on most fronts, but there is zero room for complacency. The existing precautions are good. We're making them better. But in a day's time, they'll be tested. We need to pass that test. And our efforts to penetrate the suspect group - they need to be redoubled. Also, I want to know why GCHQ hasn't turned anything up about the additional material we now know to be out there."

"I'll chase them up, sir," Chaston said.

"Good. Wainwright?"

"Sir?" Melissa said.

"Our deceased friends from the hospital? Good work uncovering them. Now, stay on that tack. It's clear that Sole recruited Shakram, but who recruited Sole? Did it happen before he worked at the hospital, or once he was there? Who was his contact? How did he get his instructions? I want the link back to al-Aqsaba'a nailed down and clearly understood."

"Yes, sir," Melissa said. "And sir? Another thing occurs to me, coming out of what we found."

"I see. What is it?"

"Well, they stole two separate batches of caesium. After the business with the fire, they stored it in two separate places. Or maybe it was always kept separate. But my question is, does this mean they're aiming for twice the damage? Or are they going after two separate targets?"

Or was someone trying to divide our efforts to stop them?

No one spoke for over a minute. Even the traffic noise from Hardwicke's location seemed to reduce in volume while Melissa's suggestion hung in the air, waiting for someone to acknowledge it.

"We should consider that a viable possibility," Hardwicke said, finally. "Everyone is to factor it into their activities. Any other thoughts?"

No one responded.

"Right," the DG said. "Next call - same time tomorrow. Same number. In the meantime - good luck."

Melissa reached out to hit the disconnect button then shoved the spider phone away from us, across the table

"What do you think?" she said.

"We're in good shape," Jones said. "I've already started pulling records. By lunchtime we'll know all there is to know about Stewart Sole. Family background. Bank records. Financial profile. Employment history. Everything. Have no fear. Whatever the DDG asks for, we'll have it."

"Thanks, Tim," she said. "Good initiative. David, what's your take?"

I didn't answer straight away. Not because I didn't

have an opinion. But because I was at a crossroads. I was convinced we were facing a serious threat. Caesium was missing, people had been killed, and more were going to be if the right steps weren't taken in the next twenty-four hours. The snag was, as far as I could see, Melissa and her colleagues were on the wrong track. So, I could either do what my control wanted me to - stand back, wait for the carnage, and see whether either of the people in the room with me had a hand in it. Or I could try and stop the train from crashing, and worry about handing out blame when everyone was safe.

In the end, it wasn't too hard a choice.

"I admire your brown-nosing instincts, Tim," I said. "You'll go far. But for now, Melissa, you need to call your boss. Tell him Hardwicke's barking up the wrong tree. There's a threat, but not to the opening of Parliament."

"You can't be serious," she said. "They've found a dozen ways the place is vulnerable. And the problem with the fire sprinklers? If al-Aqsaba'a could feed in dissolved caesium and trigger the system? There'd be nowhere to hide. Everyone in the building - the Queen, the MPs, the Lords, everyone - would be fatally contaminated."

"How much caesium would that take?"

"I don't know. Why?"

"Because this is where they've gone wrong. They were looking for a target on a scale which matched all the caesium stored at St Joseph's, because that's what they thought al-Aqsaba'a was trying to steal. Now we know they were never after that much. So, if the weapon is different, it follows the target is different."

"Not necessarily. What if there's a way to control where the radioactive water comes out? The system's bound to be broken down into discreet circuits. Then they could target the Queen directly. Or the PM. Or whoever they like."

"That's..."

"And we don't know that they want to kill everyone, anyway. Maybe the chaos that any degree of radioactivity would cause would be enough for them."

"Melissa, no. You could come up with any number of possibilities, but the logic doesn't hold up. You're starting with an answer, and working back to a question. Things don't work that way."

"Have you got a more plausible suggestion?"

"No. That's why we need everyone to stop chasing after something that isn't there, and help find the real target."

"Don't forget what Leckie's guy told us."

"I'm not. But all you can really take from him is the timescale. The rest - to bring down or close down the government - that's too ambiguous. We've got to start again, and this time not lose sight of the facts."

"What facts?"

"That the original plan called for two small amounts of caesium, and that al-Aqsaba'a's M.O. to date involves focused, high value objectives. Not huge public spectacles which depend on weapons they don't even have."

"No. I'm sorry, David. None of this is convincing me. They could have been planning to add the two lots of caesium together. They could have been moving both lots to the same place, and got disturbed half way through. They could prefer storing them separately, keeping their eggs in separate baskets. And by now, they could have a completely different means of attack lined up."

"You're grasping at straws. This makes no sense."

"And nor does throwing the baby out with the bath water."

I didn't respond for a moment. Her reluctance was making me uneasy. Could she really not grasp what I was saying? Or did she have another motive for not warning her people they were on the verge of a huge mistake?

"OK," she said, after a few moments. "Look. I am prepared to expand the parameters of what we're doing. A little. Assuming you're both prepared to put in a few extra hours?"

"Absolutely," Jones said, nodding his head. "Count me in. Whatever you need. We should be sure about this."

"Good," she said. "But I'm not calling Chaston. Not yet, anyway."

"Why not?" I said.

"Tim, could we have the room for a second?" she said.

"No problem," Jones said, getting to his feet and heading for the door. "I need the bathroom anyway."

"Look, I didn't want to discuss this in front of him," Melissa said, once Jones was safely out of the room. "But think how this would look. I'm already under the microscope. My loyalty's being questioned, as it is. What would happen if I started arguing for us to pull away from the one plausible target we have? One that everyone else, from the Deputy DG down, has bought into? They'd think it was sabotage."

"But they'd be wrong," I said. "Are you ready to see people die to save your own career?"

"No. Of course not. And I will make the call. But only when we have something tangible to point to as a reason. Some solid proof."

"Good. So let's get on with finding some."

"We will. We'll look into Stewart Sole as ordered, obviously. If we're really lucky, that might even throw up something we can use. But assuming it doesn't, we need a second string to our bow."

"al-Aqsaba'a, itself. That's where we should be

looking."

"Chaston has a team already doing that. There's no point in duplicating effort. We should look somewhere else."

"I don't agree. Chaston's people are looking to tie al-Aqsaba'a to a scheme that in all likelihood doesn't exist. They're chasing shadows. We should go after them too, but from a new angle."

"How?"

"Let me ask you something. Leckie. Can he be trusted?"

Melissa didn't answer straight away.

"Why do you ask me that?" she said, after a moment.

"I'm just being methodical," I said. "It was Leckie's snout who came to us, and first threw suspicion on al-Aqsaba'a. Leckie's had successes against them in the past. Sole and Shakram worked at the same hospital as Leckie. And that's where the thefts took place. I think we're due another conversation with the man."

"I guess so. I can see where you're going, I suppose."

"But my question is, what kind of conversation? And that hinges on whether we can trust him. What's your view?"

"I'd say we can, and we can't. He feels badly treated by Box, and the hospital's his livelihood now. So if he's screwed something up, I don't see him putting his head in noose to help us. But if you're asking me if he's bent, you already know the answer."

"I do?"

"Yes. He was kicked out, right? That means he did something wrong. Being over zealous with his interrogation methods, or whatever it was. I doubt we'll ever hear the full story. But the point is, if there was even the faintest whiff of treachery, he wouldn't have walked away. The rank he was at, he'd have swallowed his gun. On his own. Or with help. Either way, same result."

I thought about the job I'd recently been assigned in Chicago, where I'd been sent after a Navy Intelligence agent who'd crossed the line. There was no possibility of that guy resigning and walking into a cushy job somewhere else. It made sense that things would be the same for the Security Service.

"How soon can we...?" I said, as her phone started to ring.

"It's my boss," she said, showing me the screen. "You don't think Jones...?"

"One way to find out," I said.

Melissa hit the answer button, and talked for just over a minute.

"I guess he didn't," she said, when she'd hung up. "Chaston wants me to cover a meeting for him, this afternoon. Here. He can't get back in time. Do you want to hang around till I'm done?"

"Not especially," I said.

"Then there's something you can do to help. Do you know the one thing Leckie loves more than golf?"

"No."

"Champagne. The good stuff. Could you pick some up, somewhere?"

"I should think so."

"Good," she said, tearing a page from her pad and starting to scribble. "Here's my address. I'll have him meet us there, since we're flying under the radar for the time being. Will six o'clock work for you?"

Chapter Twenty-Eight

The cab driver dropped me on Piccadilly, but I used the side door to Fortnum's in order to avoid the crowds of inert shoppers, rendered immobile by the bewildering selection of tea and confectionary. My original plan was to just pick up one bottle of champagne, but on the spur of the moment I grabbed a second. My shopping urges weren't completely uncontrolled, though. I did manage to resist the edible baked tarantulas from Cambodia.

I worked my way through to the restaurant and left via the exit on the corner of Jermyn Street. An elderly couple was just clambering out of a cab, so I waited for them to get steady on their feet and then jumped into the back and asked for the Museum of London. It's right at the corner of the Barbican Centre, and out of habit I never let strangers know my full address.

The traffic was heavier than I'd hoped, and I had to swim against the tide of pedestrians that was already building up along both sides of Aldersgate Street. I had to wait at the lights, as well, before finally turning into Beech Street and heading for the main entrance to Cromwell Tower. The plaza in front of the double doors was broad, but for some reason a couple of guys were walking straight towards me. It was as if they were deliberately maintaining a collision course. They would be in their early twenties, I'd guess. They were tall - six foot four or five - and walked with the awkward, lumbering gait that people end up with when they spend too many hours building pointless muscle in the gym. Their clothes were unremarkable - cheap trainers, ill-fitting jeans and black leather jackets. One was carrying a football. And both of them had baseball caps - one the Baltimore Orioles, one the Toronto Blue Jays. I wondered what Melissa would think of two teams that were named after birds.

We closed to within twenty feet of each other, and the guy with the ball dropped it on the ground. He watched it bounce, then volleyed it expertly at the wall of the Tower. It hit the concrete just at the side of a notice beneath a City of London crest that read -

NO BALL GAMES ALLOWED. BY ORDER.

Their attitude reminded me of the yobs Melissa and I had encountered in the garden at St Joseph's, four days ago, and I wondered how many more idiots there were like them spread throughout London. I also wondered about taking a minute and encouraging them to show a little respect for the environment. Specially the environment around my home. But given the upcoming meeting with Melissa and Leckie, I decided to give them a pass. Some things in life are more important than others, and I didn't want to get embroiled in anything that could make me late.

The two guys looked at each other. It was like they were surprised I hadn't reacted to them. Or maybe disappointed. I kept an eye on them, and continued on my way to the entrance. The guys split up when they were about ten feet away from me. The one who'd kicked the ball peeled off to his right, to collect it. The other continued straight towards me. He picked up speed, and started to lunge sideways when he was about a foot away, aiming to barge me with his shoulder. I tracked his movement and spun around sideways at the last moment, pulling my body out of harm's way. Deprived of his anticipated impact the guy was left staggering and off balance, so without thinking

I stepped across to finish the job gravity had started. I stamped down hard, crashing the edge of my right foot into the side of his knee. The joint gave way and he dropped onto all fours, howling with pain. Then I smashed the ball of my foot into the side of his head, and he went down the rest of the way, finally silent.

I spun round, needing to locate his friend. I spotted him fifteen feet away. His right leg was raised, his foot was up almost at chest height, and I was conscious of a white blur closing the space between us. It was the football, rising sharply and blazing towards my head. I had to jump sideways to avoid taking it full in the face, and quickly tighten my grip to avoid one of the bottles slipping out of my left hand. The guy took one step in my direction and then stopped, looking a little confused.

"You nearly made me drop my champagne," I said. "Then we'd have had a real problem on our hands."

The guy started moving towards me again, closing to within six feet.

"You're the one with the problem," he said.

"No," I said, raising the bottles to chest level and holding them out in front of me. "I don't think so. See? They both survived."

"Not for long. I'm going to break them. Then I'm going to break you."

"Actually, breaking them would be quite difficult," I said, lowering the bottles again. "They don't just use any old glass, you know. It has to be extra strong. Able to withstand up to ninety pounds of pressure per square inch, due to all those busy little bubbles inside. So why don't you save yourself the trouble? Turn around now. Walk away. I'll even let you collect your football before you go."

He didn't respond.

"OK," I said. "How's this for an idea? I'm going to

give you a choice. Option one – turn around and walk away, unharmed. Or option two - we conduct an experiment to see which is stronger: The glass in the bottle, or the bone in your skull."

The guy shifted his feet slightly, and his mouth gaped open about a quarter of an inch, but he didn't speak.

"It's your choice," I said. "But you've got to make it now."

He still showed no sign of reacting.

"You're running out of time," I said. "And the longer you stand there, the more I'm favouring option two."

I heard a groaning sound, behind me, and realised the first guy was starting to come round.

"Maybe we should ask your friend?" I said, stepping back so I could both see of them at once.

The first guy grunted and pulled himself back onto all fours, so I gave him another tap on the head.

"Or not," I said, as he fell sideways and rolled onto his back.

That was enough to break the second guy's trance. He roared with fury and lurched forward, trying to rush me. I started to swing the champagne bottle in my right hand but I could see he was watching for it, just as I'd hoped, so I ducked down, set the other bottle on the ground, then straightened up and brought my left arm around, driving my fist into the side of his head.

The blow sent him reeling, but he didn't go down.

"You didn't think I'd really use the champagne, did you?" I said, placing the second bottle next to its twin. "It's Dom Perignon. I've used it for a few interesting things over the years, but never as a weapon. That would be sacrilege."

We stood ten feet apart for a moment, staring at each other. Then the guy charged at me again, swinging his fists this time, trying to bludgeon me.

"Why are you doing this?" I said, pulling back at an angle and jabbing him in the kidneys as he lumbered past me. "When I've offered you the chance to walk away?"

He stopped, turned, and came at me again.

"Give it up," I said, sticking out a foot this time and tripping him. "Show some common sense."

He struggled back to his feet and dived at me, arms out in front like a swimmer starting a race. Only he wasn't aiming for clear water. He was going for my throat, so I ducked down low and when his thighs slammed into me, I instantly straightened my legs and sent him somersaulting over my shoulder.

"Looks like there was a third option," I said, watching to make sure that this time he didn't get up again. "Who would have guessed?"

The two guys had both ended up on their backs with their arms spread wide, about two yards apart, like they'd been crucified lying down. I couldn't see what had happened to their football. The only movement I did detect was an old lady walking very slowly away from the entrance to the building. She was less than five feet tall, and looked at least ninety. We could have been neighbours, I suppose, but I didn't recognise her. She stopped moving when she realised I'd seen her, then shuffled round and made her way towards me.

"Did you kill them?" she said, stopping next to the football guy's head.

"No," I said. "They'll be fine. Nothing more than a couple of bruises."

"That's a shame," she said, poking the guy's head with the toe of her shoe. "I wish you had killed them. People like that, making a nuisance of themselves, showing no respect. My Eric would never have stood for it. I wish you'd killed them. I wish you'd tortured them, then killed them."

"Eric was your husband?" I said.

"We were married fifty-nine years, and even in his dying days he wouldn't have stood for nonsense like that. A week before the end he was outside our flat, yelling at the next-door kids for making too much noise. Ten years ago, that was, now."

I did the maths.

"Your husband was ex-army?" I said.

"Forty Second Commando, Royal Marines," she said. "As if that means anything to you."

"It means an awful lot to me, ma'am. My father fought in the same war as your husband, and I'm an officer in the Royal Navy, myself."

The old lady glared at me, but she didn't speak.

"Can I help you find a cab, or anything like that?" I said.

"Ridiculous," she said to herself, turning away and resuming her snail's pace. "He should have killed them. Should have tortured them..."

I watched her shambling progress for a few moments, then picked up the champagne and started towards the building. I took two steps. Then I stopped. And took out my phone.

There was something in the way they the guys had behaved that bothered me. Nothing about the encounter felt like an accident, right from the outset when they'd walked straight up to me, as if I was a target. So I called my control and filled him in. He gave no sign of whether he agreed with me or thought I was crazy, but he did put me on hold while he spoke to the police. Four minutes later he was back on the line. He said if I could sit on the guys for another quarter of an hour, they'd be scooped up by the Met and held until a couple of our people were available to have a word with them.

From what I'd seen of the guys, I would guess they'd had pretty miserable lives up to that point. And I was certain that things were going to get worse for them over the next few days. The Navy interrogators would give them plenty to think about. Whereas me, I was left with only one thought.

We were only yards away from where Melissa had picked me up on our way to Luton. She'd known what time I was likely to arrive home, having asked me to buy the champagne. And she was the only one who knew my address.

Chapter Twenty-Nine

Melissa texted me just after 4.00pm. She said she'd finally got hold of Leckie, that he was happy to help, and the meeting at her place was still on. That left me plenty of time to wonder whether she was setting me up for a second bite of the cherry. It also left me plenty of time to walk, so I left my apartment at a quarter after five and set off towards St Paul's. The area around the cathedral was clogged as usual with packs of tourists, necks craned back, gawping up at the dome. I weaved my way though them and started across the Millennium Bridge, then turned right in the shadow of the Tate Modern and dropped down to the side of the river. The Thames Path narrowed drastically as I followed it west, leaving me to run a constant gauntlet of joggers and bike riders until I was in sight of the OXO Tower.

The note Melissa had written for me gave an address on the second floor of one of the buildings directly behind the main complex, but finding the correct door took more than a little luck. I finally located it, but when I hit the call button on her intercom I didn't get a reply.

I waited a moment, then started to work my way through the buttons for the other apartments in the building. I'd only tried three when the main door buzzed open. Civilians and their attitude to security never cease to amaze me, but you can't say they're not useful.

I stepped into the hallway. Four people were waiting for someone to emerge from one of the ground floor units, so I skirted round them and made my way up the stairs. I followed the numbers until I found the door to Melissa's apartment. It was standing open an inch, so I carefully placed the bottles of the champagne on the ground, drew my Beretta, and went inside without knocking.

The main living/dining space in Melissa's apartment was lined with windows which bathed the old, golden brown exposed brickwork with light. The room was double height, and a ladder led up to a sleeping platform which spanned the entire width at the far end. An archway led to a small kitchen on the right. I heard footsteps from inside it, and then someone appeared.

It was Tim Jones. I'd been surprised to see him when we'd first met in Melissa's room at St Joseph's, too. I was glad things didn't turn out the same way, though, if only for the sake of her furniture.

"David," he said, bringing his right hand out from behind his back, complete with his Sig Sauer pistol. "Thank goodness it's you. Is Melissa with you?"

"No," I said. "I'm supposed to meet her here, at six."

"I was too. But she brought the meeting forward half an hour. She said she had some new information. Something we needed to talk about."

I pulled out my phone and saw another text from her on the screen. It said the same thing, and added that in light of what she'd found, she'd asked Leckie not to come. I must have missed it arriving in the noise from the street.

"How did you get in?" I said.

"There was no answer downstairs when I buzzed," he said. "So I waited till someone else came out, and sneaked through before the main entrance closed behind her. Then I came up here and found Melissa's door standing open."

"When was this?"
"About half an hour ago."
"Is there any sign of her?"
"No. I've looked everywhere."

"Any sign of a struggle?"

"Not that I can see."

"Have you called the police? Or your office?"

"No. She told me we had to keep this meeting absolutely secret."

"She was right," I said, turning back to my phone. "But I have a feeling the ground rules have just changed."

Before I could key the three nines I heard footsteps outside in the corridor. There were three sets. They were heavy. And coming in our direction. Fast. I paused. They continued to come closer, then stopped right outside the door. I moved to my left – the hinge side – and signaled to Jones to go right. Five seconds passed in silence. Then the door was flung back into the room, arcing around on its hinges, its handle smashing into the wall. Three men followed through the open doorway. The first came straight ahead, stopping in the centre of the room, his head snapping from side to side. The second peeled off, heading towards me. The third went to the other way, straight at Jones. All of them were over six feet tall. They were wearing desert boots, jeans, and army surplus style DPM jackets. They all had shaved heads. And they were all carrying guns.

"You," said the first guy, with his eye on Jones. "Drop your weapon."

Jones opened his fingers and let the Sig slip through, landing grip-first on the floor, next to his foot.

"Good," the guy said. "Now, both of you. On the floor. Right now."

I started to lean, as if I meant to comply with his instructions, but when my head was low enough I lunged forward, slamming it into the second guy's solar plexus. The force pushed him back a couple of steps, so I straightened my waist and whipped my neck up as hard as I could. I timed it just right, catching the guy's chin with the back of my head. His knees buckled and he went over backwards, hitting the floor hard. I followed in, kicking the gun out of his hand and stamping down on his throat before he had the chance to react.

I quickly scanned the room, and saw Jones lying face down on the floor with his arms and legs spread. The third intruder was standing over him, with a Colt Delta Elite aimed at the back of his skull. The first guy - the one who'd spoken - was still in the same spot. His arms were folded across his chest, with his gun in his right hand, and his expression looked almost bored.

"Stop," he said. "Put your hands behind your head. Then get down on your knees."

I didn't move.

"Do it now," the guy said, taking a step towards me and lowering his hands to his sides. "Because if you don't, your friend is going to get a bullet between the ears in the next five seconds."

"I want you to be very clear about something," I said. "I'd never do anything to hurt a friend, so there's no need for you to do anything hasty. But there's something I don't understand. How will the person holding my friend know whether I've done what you told me?"

"What kind of stupid question is that? He can see you."

"He can? How? Is there a concealed camera in here? Are we under covert surveillance? Have you set up some kind of on-the-fly video conferencing?"

"He's standing right behind me. He's not blind. He has a gun in his hand. And it's pointing at your friend's head. Do you want me to draw you a diagram?"

"Yes please. I love diagrams. And actually, I think a good diagram could help all of us, right now. Because that guy on the floor? He's not my friend."

"Don't try to bluff me."

"I'm not. I think he's a slimy, brown-nosing corporate schemer. The first time I met him I broke a chair over his head. Psychologically, he's toast."

"He did," Jones said. "It's true. I may never recover."

"See?" I said, taking a step towards the guy. "His bottle's gone. He's useless now. He might as well shoot him. I think you should. In fact, give me your gun, I'll do it for you."

"Hold it," the guy said.

I stopped. I was two yards away from him, and four from the guy standing over Jones.

"Now, get over there," he said, nodding towards the wall at the far side of the room.

"Over where?" I said.

"There," he said, stretching out his right arm and gesturing with the gun.

I took half a step forward and grabbed his right arm, just below the wrist. I held it immobile, the gun pointing safely at the wall, and jabbed him below the rib cage with my right hand, knocking the wind of him. Then I brought my hand up, smashing into his jaw from below. I stepped in towards him, ducked slightly and spun round so that my right shoulder slotted in place below his armpit. Then I straightened my legs and pulled down with my left hand, lifting him off his feet. I was still turning, so I pushed back hard with my left leg, building the momentum and smashing his body into the guy who was covering Jones.

The two intruders went down in a tangle of limbs, rolling sideways away from us. Neither of them kept hold of their weapons. Jones's guy ended up on his front, and for a moment he was still. The other one scuttled sideways and started to scramble back to his feet.

"Take him," Jones said, kneeling up. "I'm on mine."

"I'm not a control freak like you," I said, stepping towards the first guy, who was fully upright again. "I don't need you to kneel with your hands behind your head. You can stay standing, if you like. Or sit. Or lie down. You can even contort your body into some weird fairground sideshow position, if it makes you happy. As long as you do one thing."

"What?" the guy said.

"Co-operate. Tell me: Where is the woman who owns this apartment?"

The guy sprang forward, feinting to hit me in the face but really aiming a heavy blow at my stomach. I ignored the first, blocked the second, then snaked my right leg behind his knees and hooked his feet out from under him. He landed flat on his back, and as he hit the floor I heard a gunshot behind me. I spun round, fearing the worst, and saw Jones five feet away from me. He was on his feet. His Sig was in his hand. The smell of cordite reached my nose, and I followed his gaze down to the floor. The guy who'd been on top of him was lying there, on his back, twitching slightly, with a gaping hole where his right cheek had been.

"Watch out," Jones said, raising his gun and aiming it in my direction.

The first guy had rolled over and was scrambling for the spot where his battered old Browning had come to rest in the earlier struggle. I stepped towards him, ready to kick the gun away again, when Jones fired. The shot was uncomfortably loud in such a small space, but it did its job. The bullet hit the guy at the base of his skull. He slumped forward, face down. His body gave one long, last, violent shiver. Then he was still.

"Wow," Jones said.

I walked across and examined the guy I'd tangled

with first.

"Wow, indeed," I said. "What a great job. We started with three people who could have helped us. And we've ended up with none."

"What about that one?" Jones said, nodding towards the guy I'd just been looking at.

I shook my head.

"Damn," he said. "I thought we'd be able to talk him, to at least. I wouldn't have pulled the trigger, otherwise. What should we do now?"

"Search the bodies," I said. "I want their phones. And I want to see everything in their pockets. We might be able to piece something together. But first, I want you to call your office. Tell your control to find out if the police have been called, following those gunshots. If they're on their way, get them turned around. Then tell them to get their best cleaner out here. These bodies need to disappear. Quickly. And Tim?"

"Yes?"

"Do not say anything that could link what's happened, or this address, to Melissa. And make absolutely certain not to tell anyone she's disappeared. Anyone at all. Do you understand?"

"Yes. But why?"

I gave him a moment to think that one through.

"Oh," he said. "I get it. You think there's a leak in the department. So if Melissa's clean, we don't want them reporting that she's hiding, or they'll go looking for her. And if she's dirty, we don't want them to know we're on to her or she'll go deeper underground."

"Right," I said. "And for now, remember something else. As far as you and I are concerned, she's innocent until proven guilty."

I figured that since experience was on my side I'd search two of the intruders and just leave one for Jones, but I was still finished first. The guy whose throat I'd crushed had a spare clip for the huge Desert Eagle he'd been carrying, and that was all. I left it behind. The guy who'd done the talking had a spare clip, pictures of Melissa and me, and an old battered switchblade with a wooden handle. I took the knife and photos, and moved across to where Jones was standing. He was next to the final body, his phone still in his hand, apparently transfixed.

"Come on, son," I said. "What are you waiting for?"

"I don't know," he said, with a shudder. "It's just - look at him."

"Not pretty, I know. Do you want me to do it?"

"No. It's OK. It's just - I've never done this before."

"Well, ordinarily I'd tell you to take your time. Only right now, Melissa's missing, which means time is the one thing we don't have. So either get on with it, or step aside."

Jones crouched down and reached out his hand like a reluctant, bony spider. He didn't exactly work fast, but in the end he at least did a nice thorough job.

"Sorry," he said. "No phone. Just a spare magazine."

"Don't worry," I said. "That's the same as the others. You didn't miss anything."

"Then what are we going to do? Can we trace them through the ammo, perhaps?"

"You could try. Your people will have the resources, I guess. But there's one other thing."

"What?"

"Have you ever done a photo fit picture?"

"I've seen them. And we learned about them, in training. I've never done one, though. Why?"

"Something about this guy is familiar, and I've just figured out what it is. I was looking at his face, trying to remember how he looked before you shot half of it off. And then it struck me. Take away the fatal injury. Add hair. Change the clothes. And I've seen him before."

"You have?"

"Yes."

"Where? When?"

"At St Joseph's. He was working as a security guard."

"Are you sure?"

"I'm certain. I watched him sorting out of a bunch of yobs who were messing around in the hospital garden."

"The guy didn't look like he knew you."

"He didn't know I'd seen him. I wasn't there, in the garden. I was watching through a window, waiting to see if he needed any help. I saw a guard try to chase some kids out of there once before, and he got nowhere."

"But this guy managed on his own?"

"You could say that. If you're a fan of understatement."

"Everything's leading back to the hospital. Well, if he works - or worked - at St Joseph's, at least that gives us a place to start. We should head over there right away."

"I don't think so. I've seen the hospital security office before. And without an army of forensic guys we're not likely to turn anything up in there. We should start with Leckie, himself."

"The person? Not the place?"

"Correct. We need to know whether Leckie is the villain or the victim. These guys could have worked for Leckie, and Leckie could have sent them here to get us. Or al-Aqsaba'a could have found out Leckie was planning on helping us, and sent the guys to silence him."

"What about the photos the guy was carrying? They're only of you and Melissa. That's pretty suspicious."

"True. But you should never jump to conclusions. They already know what Leckie looks like, remember. They wouldn't need a picture of him. And they might not know you were back off the sick list."

"Well, OK. If you're sure. And we've got some time while we wait for the cleaner. Why don't I make some calls. See what I can dig up on the guy."

"You do that. I need to duck out for a while."

"Why?"

"I have some calls of my own to make."

"Oh, I see. But where can I reach you if I find anything?"

"If?"

"OK. When I find something."

"Just call me. I won't be far away. But be discrete. And be quick. Melissa's life might depend on it. And Leckie's, if he's not a crook. As well as any chance of finding the other batch of caesium. And getting a hook into al-Aqsaba'a."

"Oh. So, no pressure, then."

Chapter Thirty

I'm not normally in favour of field agents acting like they're tied to their controller's apron strings, but I figured a second attempt on my life since lunchtime was worthy of a mention. And on top of that, I had a couple of questions I wanted to ask. Questions that would best be asked without Jones being in earshot.

I made my call looking out over the Thames, and then headed for a little Italian cafe I knew on the ground floor of the main OXO Tower building, just across the way. There was no point heading back up to Melissa's apartment, specially while the cleaner would be there. That would break the golden rule: be seen by as few people as possible. And in any case, I needed time to think. I was bothered by Melissa's text about new information, followed so closely by her no-show. I guessed whatever she'd found related to Leckie in some way, but how? And where was she? Had she been snatched? Killed? Or was she lying low, waiting till it was safe to resurface?

I was half through my first cappuccino, thinking about the permutations of al-Aqsaba'a and the hospital and Leckie and MI5 and Melissa when a connection sent me reaching for my phone. I dialed Jones's number, and he answered on the first ring.

"I'm still working on it," he said. "It's not easy getting hold of people today, for some reason. So far all I've got is some basics on Leckie. His date of birth - which is the same as my dad's, coincidentally. His address - an ex old people's home in Harpenden. Snobby place, a few stops up the railway line, and handy for Luton airport if he's planning a quick getaway. His golf club. Two of them, actually. But not much about his professional life after he left Box."

"Well, keep on it," I said. "And there's something else I want you to look at. I want to know if there's a link between him and Stewart Sole."

"The guy who arranged the fiddling of the transfer records, which allowed the caesium to be stolen?"

"Correct."

"Should there be?"

"Not necessarily. But if there is, it'll go a long way towards telling us which side of the fence Leckie's really on."

"I'm with you. OK. Leave it with me. I'll see what I can find."

"Good. And I mean any connection, however small or insignificant it might seem. If their grandparents ever had a drink together, I want to know about it."

"Understood. Got to go now, though. The cleaner's arrived. Oh, there are two of them. Anyway, I'll dig up what I can. Catch you later."

I put the phone down and returned my attention to my drink, forcing myself to concentrate first on the taste. Then on the smell. And finally the contrast of the pure white foam against the rich, dark liquid. Anything to take my mind away from thoughts of what might be happening at that moment, somewhere outside that room.

The ploy wasn't very effective, but in the absence of anything better I was contemplating the need for a second cup when my phone rang. I was expecting it to be Jones, but my pulse quickened when I saw the name on the screen: MELISSA (MOBILE)

"Are you OK?" I said, snatching the handset off the table. "Can you talk?"

"I can, now," she said. "It was just another false alarm. That's the fourth this year."

"False alarm? What are you talking about? Where are you?"

"I'm on Millbank. Heading towards Parliament. I was caught in another pointless lockdown. Why? You sound worried."

"You've been in Thames House this whole time?"

"I haven't set foot outside since you left to get the champagne. I was going to bail early, to meet you and Jones, but the bonehead environmental control system thought it had picked up another airborne contaminant. As usual, it came back negative. And while they were figuring that out, no one in the building could leave. Or send an email. Or even pick up a phone."

I closed my eyes and took a moment to trace the implications of her words.

"David?" she said. "Are you still there?"

"Yes," I said. "Still here."

"Have you got any idea when you'll be getting to my place, yet?"

"Melissa, there's something you need to know about. Just hang on one moment," I said, getting up and heading for the door.

"What?" she said. "What's wrong?"

"OK, I'm outside now. I was in a café. I didn't want anyone to overhear me. Now, I'm sorry to be the one to break the news, but there's a problem with us meeting at your apartment."

I told her about what had happened with the three guys, and when I'd finished she was completely silent at the other end of the line.

"I'm sorry, Melissa," I said. "I wish there'd been a way to avoid it. Your place is really messed up. Jones is in there now, dealing with the cleaners. He was worried about you. One of us should tell him you're OK."

She still didn't answer.

"Melissa, are you there?" I said. "Are you OK?"

"I am," she said. "But what you're telling me doesn't make sense. I'm really worried, now, too."

"Why?"

"Because I didn't know you'd arrived yet. I hadn't heard back from you when I texted about the change of time. So, as soon as I got out of the building I called Jones. He told me he hadn't seen you. He said he'd gone to my building around five thirty, like I'd told him to, but no one was there. He said he waited twenty minutes, then left, assuming there'd been a change of plan."

"You spoke to him? When?"

"Two minutes ago. Right before I called you."

"But I spoke to him, it must have been a couple of minutes before that. I had another thing I wanted him to check on. He was still at your place. In fact, he told me the cleaners were just arriving at that moment."

"Something's wrong with this picture, clearly. OK. The one thing we know for sure is that he has his phone, since we both spoke to him on it. Stay where you are. I'm going to get a location on it, then I'll be right back."

I hung up, then made my way through the passage which ran through the centre of the building, emerging onto the broad walkway next to the Thames. A filthy, ragged pigeon swooped down in front of me, almost touching my head with its wings, so I batted it away and crossed to the river wall to wait.

Melissa called back after six minutes.

"He's in my apartment," she said. "Or his phone is, anyway. And he must be in trouble, to have spun me a line I was bound to see through straight away."

"Agreed," I said.

"We've got to help him. Can we risk the police?"

"No. There's no time. And it's too dangerous. Whoever's behind this clearly has a finger in your pie, and we don't know how many others. We'll take care of this another way."

"How?"

"I'm a hundred yards from your building. Leave it to me."

"No. Wait. I'm already in a cab. I'll be there in three minutes. Four at the most. And I have a key."

"OK. I'll keep an eye on things till you get here. We don't want him being carted off anywhere else."

"Good thinking. And David?"

"Yes?"

"I know how this must look. Thanks for not jumping to conclusions."

Little did she know I'd jumped to lots of conclusions, recently. And none of them good.

I switched my phone to silent, put it back in my pocket, and then spent the next two minutes surveying the immediate area for anyone else who could be watching the door to Melissa's building. I couldn't identify anyone at ground level, but there were plenty of places in the surrounding apartments and offices that would offer excellent cover. There was no way to check them in the time I had available, though. And no way to reach them without taking my own eyes off the entrance. So I contented myself with finding a spot in the shelter of the steps that led up to the higher level of boutiques around the base of the Tower, and remaining as vigilant as possible.

Melissa's cab arrived after another two minutes. She jumped out, paid the driver, and started to hurry across the twenty yards of cobblestones between the road and her building. Her black wool coat was cinched in tight around her waist, and the heels she was wearing - chosen with a day in the office in mind, I guessed - emphasised the delicately defined muscles in her calves. They did nothing for her ability to move quickly over such a slippery surface, though.

I waited till I was sure no one was following, then stepped out into the open and made my way across to join her. She saw me coming and paused a few feet from the door, her key already in her hand.

A gaggle of teenagers pushed past us in the main lobby, but we made it the rest of the way to Melissa's corridor without seeing anyone else. The door to her apartment was closed, but before we were within fifteen feet of the place we could tell it wasn't deserted. Because we could hear voices from inside. Men's. Two of them. And neither of them were Jones's.

Melissa held up her hand to stop me outside the apartment, then cupped it to her ear to indicate she was listening to them.

"Here's some free advice," a man said. "Don't try and be a hero. There's no point. No one's going to thank you for it. You know why? Cause they'll be dead."

"We're going to find them," a second man said. "Whether you tell us, or someone else does. The outcome's going to be the same. The only thing to decide is how much pain you're going to bring on yourself."

"We'll put it out there that we had to torture you for hours, if you want," the first man said. "Just tell us. Where did Trevellyan go?"

There was silence for a moment, then the sound of a fist crashing into a jawbone.

"The woman will tell us, if you don't," the second man said. "She's next on our list."

"Right," the first man said. "Maybe you should just keep quiet. We'd have much more fun working on her. Much more options, with a woman. More than just a punch bag, like you."

"And we won't even have to go looking for her," the second man said. "She'll just come walking on in here, all on her own."

"Do you know what we'll do to her, when she gets here, If you haven't already told us?" the first man said. "Maybe we should keep you alive, so you can watch."

"Memories like that should be shared," the second man said. "They're too good to keep to yourself. You know we'd have to tape it."

"And post it on the web," the first man said.

"All the pain and humiliation she's going to suffer?" the second man said. "You'll know you caused that. And you'll know you could have saved her, just by telling us one thing."

Melissa switched her keys into her left hand, and drew her Sig. Then she turned to me and mouthed, *on five*.

"David Trevellyan," the second man said. "Where is he?"

Four.

There was another moment of silence, and the sound of another blow.

Three. I drew my Beretta.

"Tell us, and we'll stop this," the first man said. "We'll stop hurting you, while you can still see, and you've still got some teeth. And we won't hurt her, either."

Two.

"What are you waiting for?" the second man said. Tell us now. Stop all this pointless pain. Save yourself. Give us Trevellyan."

One.

"Do it," the first man said. "Trevellyan didn't come back and help you, did he? You owe it to yourself. Give him up. Tell us where he is."

Melissa nodded to me, then with one fluid move she slipped her key into the lock, turned it, and pushed the door away from her. I stepped through into the apartment and moved to my left, covering the guy standing nearer to Jones, who was tied to a wooden dining chair in the centre of the room. Melissa followed me in, and moved to her right.

"Are you looking for me?" I said. "Because if you are, I'm right here. You can leave my friend alone, now."

The guy I was covering started to turn towards me, raising a Smith and Wesson. The other spun round the opposite way and lunged at Melissa.

"Stop," I said. "Drop it."

My guy froze, half way round, and let his gun clatter harmlessly to the floor. The other one, though, wasn't so sensible. He was about six two and broad in the shoulder, so maybe he fancied his chances against a woman. Or maybe he had a death wish. But either way, he took two rapid strides towards Melissa. I expected her to shoot him on the spot, but she actually lowered her Sig. She waited till he was four feet away from her. Then she stepped diagonally to her right and unleashed a tremendous forearm smash directly to the guy's face. Both his feet left the floor and he crashed down backwards, completely poleaxed. But Melissa wasn't finished. She lifted her leg and drove her foot down towards his head. I thought she was going for his throat, like I'd done to the guy who'd attacked me in that same room, earlier. But when I saw the prolonged spasm rip through this guy's body, I realised she'd taken a different option. I looked more closely, and saw it wasn't one that was open to me. She'd driven the heel of her shoe straight through his left eye and, if there was much of one there, into his brain.

Jones, the guy who'd been interrogating him, and I watched in silence as Melissa extracted her heel. She lifted her foot slowly. The guy's head followed until it was raised an inch and a quarter off the floor. Then she gently shook her ankle. His eye socket held its grip for a moment, then gave a soft slurping sound, and his skull fell back down onto the polished wood.

"That's good," she said, staring directly at the guy next to Jones. "I've seen it where the whole eyeball comes out, skewered by your heel like a kebab. Then you've got to decide: waste time picking it off, and get your fingers all covered in ocular slime; or just move on to the next home-invading bastard with it still stuck in place?"

The guy took a step backwards.

"Stop," she said. "Release my friend from the chair."

The guy pulled a switchblade from his pocket, popped the blade, and cut the four plastic ties that had held Jones in place. He handed the knife to me, then Jones struggled to his feet and staggered away from the chair, ending up leaning against the wall to help keep himself upright.

"Now, sit in the chair, yourself," Melissa said. "Then look around the room."

The guy hesitantly complied, and I followed his gaze as he wrestled to keep it away from the four dead bodies that were still lying on the floor.

"I'm going to help my friend get cleaned up," Melissa said. "We'll be gone maybe five minutes. While we're out of the room, I want you to think about your comrades. About what happened to them. And who did it. Then, when we come back in, I'm going to ask you some questions. You better be ready to answer them."

Chapter Thirty-One

Melissa and Tim were actually out of the room for closer to fifteen minutes. When they reappeared Melissa had changed into jeans and a jumper, and Tim was looking decidedly healthier. The blood had been washed off his face, his skin had regained a little of its colour, and a couple of plasters had been stuck over the worst of his cuts.

"David," Melissa said, when she caught sight of how pale the guy on the chair had become. "What happened to him?"

"Nothing," I said. "We were just swapping stories, to pass the time. I told him about a guy I once knew, in Helsinki. He tried to hold out on some information a friend of mine wanted. Then he fell out of a window. His entrails covered a twenty-foot radius. Can you believe that? The mess he made? The local kids still love to play on the stains he left on the pavement, apparently."

Melissa shrugged.

"These things happen," she said. "Maybe I need to check my window locks?"

"Good home maintenance is important," I said. "But in the meantime, this chap has some news to share with you about what he's doing here tonight."

The guy repeated to Melissa the story he'd just told me about how the two of them were the back up team for the guys who'd burst in on Jones and me, earlier. She asked the same questions that I had, about who they worked for. How they'd been recruited. How their instructions had been communicated. Where they were supposed to take us. How they'd been paid. And he gave her the same frustrating answers.

"It's a pretty standard arms-length deal," Melissa said. "Our people should be able to break into it. They'll need a little while, obviously. But they won't need this guy, if that's all he knows. We've killed four of them, already. You might as well make it five, David. Go for a clean sweep. He's of no further use to us."

I raised my Beretta and lined it up on the bridge of the guy's nose.

"No," he said. "Wait. Please. I've got something else. A name. I heard our contact say a name. Once. He was finishing a phone call one time when we met him. I don't think he knew I could hear what the person on the other end was saying. Parts of it, anyway."

"And you're telling me now," Melissa said. "That doesn't buy you many credibility points."

"I get that. I know how this looks. But I'm telling the truth. Please don't do anything... permanent to me."

"Have you got any plans to share this name with me, any time in the near future?"

"Of course. But wait. How do I know you won't kill me anyway?"

"David?" Melissa said. "Please shoot him."

"Leckie," he said. "Leckie was the name I heard."

"You expect me to believe that?" Melissa said.

"It's the truth," the guy said. "He used it twice, so I'm totally sure."

Jones made himself useful in the kitchen, brewing up some coffee, while I kept an eye on our one surviving prisoner. Melissa disappeared into a guest bedroom to make some calls. She was gone for a good twenty minutes, and when she reappeared I saw she'd put her coat back on. She was wearing shoes, too, but not the ones with the lethal heels.

"Are you sure you're OK with this?" she said, taking Jones by both shoulders before he could retreat back to the kitchen with our empty mugs.

"Definitely," he said. "Lightning never strikes twice. Did they give you an ETA for the cleaner?"

"He's nearly here. Ten to fifteen minutes, tops."

"I'll be fine, then. Leave it to me. You two get on your way. I'll catch you in the morning."

"Call me if there are any problems," Melissa said, taking me by the arm and steering me towards the door. "And not too early in the morning. You need rest. And you need to check in with the medics. I know your skull is made of concrete, but even so."

"Don't worry," Jones said. "I'll see them. And I'll sleep as late as I can."

"Tim?" I said, as Melissa disappeared into the corridor in front of me. "Keep a close eye on this guy. He seemed pretty depressed when I was talking to him, earlier. It would be terrible if his demons got the better of him and he, say, threw himself out of the window, like the guy in Finland..."

Melissa waited till she was sure the door had shut behind us before heading for the stairs.

"How are you feeling?" I said, falling into step beside her. "After what just happened?"

"I'm fine," she said. "It was hardly a unique experience."

"I know. But in your own home? Are you going to be OK, going back there?"

Melissa shrugged.

"I suppose so," she said. "The cleaner will get there soon - the real one - and he'll do a good job, I'm sure. Still, I might give it a while, though."

"That would be smart," I said. "Have you got anywhere to go?"

"I do have friends, you know. And anyway, this is London. It's not like there's a shortage of hotels. But I'll worry about that later. There are things I need to update you on first. Although, after what's just happened, they'll hardly qualify as breaking news."

"That doesn't matter. Tell me anyway."

"I will. But I could use a drink. Do you fancy an adult beverage to go with the conversation?"

The OXO Tower has its own wine bar, so there was no need to go too far out of our way. The place was a mob scene by the time we got there. The customers were mainly men in suits and women in power dresses. Some sat in pairs, but most seemed to be part of larger groups. All the tables were taken, but the moment we walked in I saw three people gathering their coats together at the end of the main, horseshoe-shaped bar. It wasn't a great spot for looking out over the river and the grand buildings beyond it, but it was ideal for not being overheard. We slipped in to their places as they were leaving, and before they were five yards away I saw one of the woman trip and turn her heel. The sole of her shoe was a vivid red.

"Look," I said. "Louboutins. You should get a pair of those, if you're going to do that eyeball trick again. It would cut down on the need for cleaning."

"In my dreams, perhaps," Melissa said. "Have you seen the price of those things?"

"No. But seriously, how much could a pair of shoes cost?"

"Oh, David, you've got a lot to learn. Let's get some drinks ordered. Then I can explain women's shoes to you."

Melissa poured over the cocktail menu for a couple

of minutes, then asked for a pomegranate martini. I ordered a glass of champagne, and wondered what had become of the bottles I'd left in the hallway outside her apartment.

"So," I said. "Tell me about the world of shoes."

"I'd love to," she said. "But perhaps I should tell you my news, first."

"Perhaps you should."

"Well, as you probably guessed, it's about Stan Leckie. After you left Thames House I made a few calls. One to him, about meeting us this evening. And several to people who'd been around the Service when he'd been. He was quick to respond. The others, less so. In fact, it took most of the afternoon before I made any progress with those at all."

"What did you find out?"

"It wasn't so much, 'what.' It was more, 'how.'"

"I don't follow."

"Remember I told you he'd been kicked out for abusing witnesses? Well, I'd drawn a picture in my head of some strong-arm tactics. Heavy duty ones, obviously, to be bad enough to get himself fired over. But I wasn't in the right ballpark."

"How far over the line did he cross?"

"Well, if you hadn't seen for yourself, I doubt you'd believe me. Remember the workhouse, in Luton? The wall, with the holes from the wrecking ball?"

"What about it?"

She stayed silent, waiting for the pennies to drop on their own.

"That was Leckie?" I said, after a moment.

"It was," she said. "That's how he broke the al-Aqsaba'a case. The original one."

"The man's a psychopath."

"Well, his tactics were extreme, that's for sure, but the outcome wasn't all bad. He did stop them killing the diplomat's baby."

"Melissa, he killed people. Horrifically. I don't see why he isn't in jail."

"He saved an innocent life, and held together a diplomatic alliance in a critical and volatile situation. Plus, no one wanted the scandal. It was much more appropriate to just usher him quietly out of the back door."

"On to the golf course. And into a comfy chair at St Joseph's, where it seems he hasn't made much progress in reforming his character."

"We don't know that for sure."

"But you cancelled the meeting with him."

"I did. I wasn't sure what this all really amounted to, but his behaviour was so extreme I felt like we needed to talk about it before taking another step."

"You were right," I said, then paused while a waitress delivered our drinks.

"Did Jones tell you the first three guys who attacked us had yours and my photos with them?" I said, when she was a safe distance away.

"That doesn't sound good," Melissa said.

"And one them worked at St Joseph's. I recognised him."

"Add that to what the guy we captured told us, and the outline of this thing is getting clearer."

"Clearer, but by no means definitive. It just narrows the options. It tells us Leckie's either a deadly threat, or he's in mortal danger."

"Agreed. But which one? And how can find out, quickly enough? The State Opening is tomorrow."

"I don't know. Maybe I should just go and ask him."

Melissa's phone started to ring before she could respond. She pulled it out of her bag, looked at the screen, then held it up for me to see.

STAN LECKIE - MOBILE

"Careful what you wish for, David," she said, then answered the call and talked for a couple of minutes.

"Well, this might put a new perspective on things," she said, double checking the call had ended. "He was calling to tell me the cameras in the corridor outside the caesium vault have failed again."

"Failed?"

"Good question. He said they're not working, anyway."

"Since when?"

"They went out of service about five minutes ago. His staff reported it to him, he immediately put out three extra teams to cover the area, then called me. He didn't know what the right procedure was, given that there isn't actually any caesium in there, now. Just the dummy container."

"Is there any sign of a break-in?"

"No. He said not."

"That doesn't mean much, though. There wasn't any damage after the robbery, either. Whoever put the container back must have known the code."

"But the code's been changed, now."

"That doesn't mean anything, either, if there's a leak."

Melissa shrugged.

"What about the independent camera your people installed?" I said.

"Let me check," she said.

Melissa speed-dialed a number at Thames House, and concluded her conversation almost as quickly.

"It's working fine," she said. "As far as they can tell. Apart from one small hiccup in the signal."

"When?" I said.

"Four minutes ago."

"What about the container? Is it still there? Can they see it?"

"They don't know. The camera's facing the door, remember. They wanted face shots of anyone going in."

"What about the tracker?"

"No signal's being received. They're pinging it right now, trying to bring it back on line."

Neither of us spoke for a moment.

"You know what that means?" I said.

Melissa nodded.

"We need to look inside that room," I said.

Melissa called Jones from the taxi on the way to St Joseph's. He was still at her place when he answered, and said he was feeling suddenly under the weather. I guessed the adrenaline level in his bloodstream had crashed, making way for the impact of the beating he'd taken to replace it.

"Just the two of us tonight, then," she said to me, slipping the phone back into her bag. "I told him - two things. Medic. Then bed."

"Wise," I said. "If this whole thing kicks off early, we don't need to be carrying any passengers."

Leckie was waiting for us at the rear entrance to the hospital when the cab pulled over to the side of the road. He stepped out of the shadows, opened Melissa's door for her, and led the way into the hospital grounds.

The three of us stayed together through the courtyard, into the Admin building, down in the lift, and all the way along the purple corridor until we reached the pair of security guards Leckie had stationed there. Then I continued on my own. I entered the code into the keypad - getting it right first time, without the impediment of the heavy gloves - and cautiously entered the room. The silence from the radiation alarm told me I didn't need to worry about caesium. Booby traps were another matter, however, so I moved no more quickly than I had done on my last visit.

My view of the room was much clearer without having to look through the fuzzy visor. At first glance it seemed that nothing had changed in the last two days, but I scanned each area nonetheless, not moving on till I was happy that everything was exactly as I'd remembered it. The broad strokes were certainly the same, but without the time pressure of the diminishing oxygen supply, or the physical barrier of the thick suit, I was able to fill in many more of the details. I could see from the every day clutter what kinds of biscuits the people who'd worked there liked, and how many of them had milk in their coffee. But the biggest revelation came from the posters on the walls. They were exactly the same style and format as the ones in Mark Jackson's office. They had similar titles, like ACHIEVEMENT, AMBITION, and INSIGHT. Only now, I could read the smaller text underneath. And I could see that the scientists held a different view of the philosophy of management. My favourite was CONSULTATION. It showed a handshake between two faceless men in sharp suits over a caption that read, 'If you're not part of the solution, there's good money to be made in prolonging the problem.'

When I was sure it was safe, I stepped further into the room and turned my attention to two things. The camera MI5 had concealed in one of the smoke detectors on the ceiling, and the cage that secured the caesium containers.

It took around forty seconds to be sure of my conclusion regarding the camera. And less than a fortieth of that time to assess the state of play inside the cage.

I didn't need any words when I rejoined Melissa and Leckie at the end of the corridor. My expression said enough on its own.

"We've got a bite?" Melissa said.

I nodded.

"What do you mean?" Leckie said. "What did you find?"

"Exactly what I was afraid of," I said. "Absolutely nothing."

Chapter Thirty-Two

There wasn't a projection screen in our customary room at Thames House, and rather than try to find one that late in the evening, Chaston just hooked a little portable projector up to his laptop and aimed it at the wall.

"The signal GCHQ sent did the job," he said, as a map of central London slowly came into focus opposite us. "They got the tracker reactivated within a few seconds of Melissa letting them know there was a problem. They've confirmed it's mobile. And any moment now, we'll see where it's got to."

Ten seconds ticked away, and then a pulsing red dot appeared in the centre of the image. It was hovering above the junction of Bressenden Place and Victoria Street, then started to move east.

"Well?" Hardwicke said. He was leaning back in his chair, his eyes firmly closed. "What's happening?"

"It's heading away from the hospital," Melissa said, leaning forward. "Towards the river. Still on Victoria Street. Right into Artillery Row. Left into Greycoat Place. Right. Now left into Medway Street. OK. It's stopped. It's still not moving. It's still stationary. Maybe it's reached its destination. Can we get in closer? We need to see exactly where it is."

Chaston fiddled with the trackpad on his laptop and the image zoomed in until the individual buildings were visible. The dot, still pulsing steadily, was inside a kind of courtyard behind a large complex which was set back several yards from the street.

"Would you look at that?" he said. "We've gone full

circle. You know what that place is?"

No one spoke.

"Well?" Hardwicke said.

"Judging by the layout, it can only be one thing," Melissa said. "A fire station."

Melissa's words hung in the air for a moment as the three of us allowed the implications to fully sink in.

"Which fire station?" Hardwicke said. "The one your trigger happy fire fighter was based at? The chap who first got this ball rolling?"

"No," Melissa said. "We never positively identified who that was. But I don't think St Joseph's is in the catchment area for this one."

"OK," the DG said. "Then, what is in its catchment?"

Chaston rattled the keys on his laptop, and the projection on the wall changed from the map to a series of search forms and finally a list of streets and addresses.

"Well, if there was any doubt about what we're dealing with, I don't think there is any more," he said. "There it is. Top of the list."

"20 Dean's Court, Westminster?" Melissa said.

"Oh," Hardwicke said.

"I don't follow," Melissa said. "What's in Dean's Court?"

"I take it you've never written to your MP, then," Chaston said. "That's the official address of the Houses of Parliament. They use it for post, and to avoid drawing attention to the real identity of the place."

"Now let's not get ahead of ourselves," Hardwicke said. "What else is on the list?"

"Let's see," Chaston said. "Westminster Abbey, obviously. The Hall. A couple of schools. Channel Four's offices. Assorted government offices. We all know what's there. It's only just up the road."

"Is our office on the list?" Melissa said.

"No," Chaston said. "But really? A fire station that covers Parliament? A container someone thinks is full of caesium? Add that to a thousand odd gallons of water, then trigger an evacuation? You could contaminate hundreds of people – MPs, Lords, maybe even her Majesty – before anyone knew what was going on. Then you've got to think about where all the water will go, afterwards. Down the drains. Into the Thames. Into the water table. And what about the people who'll have to clean it up?"

"And don't forget there's another batch of caesium missing somewhere," Melissa said. "They could be coming from both sides. Spiking the sprinklers inside the building, and the fire engine outside."

"Not a pleasant prospect," Hardwicke said. "If you're right about their plans."

"I think I am," Chaston said. "We should get people there right away."

The DG suddenly opened his eyes and moved for the first time since Melissa and I had arrived, sitting forward in his chair and glaring at Chaston.

"Why aren't they there now?" he said. "I ordered round the clock surveillance."

"Of the fire station?" Chaston said. "How could we have known to…"

"Of Parliament," Hardwicke said.

"We have people at Parliament," Chaston said. "I meant the fire station. In case they dissolve the dummy liquid in the water in a fire engine. If they leave the container behind, there'll be no way to track them."

"You meant the fire station?" Hardwicke said. "Then you should have made yourself clear. That's how misunderstandings come about."

"Yes, sir," Chaston said.

"Good," Hardwicke said, leaning back in his chair again. "Now, there's no need to draw this out. It's late. Tomorrow will be a big day. Send a team to the fire station, then all of you – go home. Get some sleep. And make sure that when we meet again tomorrow night, we have something to celebrate."

Chapter Thirty-Three

I wasn't in pain. I wasn't hungry. Or thirsty. Or too hot. Or too cold. And it wasn't noise that disturbed me. But at three minutes past three in the morning – after less than two hours in bed – my eyes snapped open and I was suddenly wide awake.

For a moment I was tempted to just roll over and wait for sleep to wash over me again. But the words that were dancing around at the back of my mind didn't want to settle back down. They came from snippets of that last conversation at Thames House. They wanted attention. And they were forming patterns I just couldn't ignore.

I reached across to my nightstand, released my phone from its charging dock, and dialed Melissa's number.

"David," she said, answering on the eighth ring. "Do you know what time it is?"

"Yes," I said.

"Then this better be important. I'd only just dropped off."

"It is. I need you to find something out for me."

"Can't it wait till morning?"

"No. I need to know right away."

"Know what?"

"Do you remember you told me Leckie had foiled an attempt by al-Aqsaba'a to kill the baby of some foreign diplomat?"

"Yes. So?"

"I need to know where the kid is, now."

"Why?"

"Specifically, if he's still in London, what school he

goes to."

"Why?"

"What did Leckie's snout tell you, right before he died?"

"They were planning something that would close down the government."

"No. That was a rationalisation. A dubious one, pushed through to fit in with Chaston's questionable logic. You told me the snout actually said, 'bring down the government.'"

"Which made no sense. No terrorist action could bring down the government. We all agreed on that."

"Depends what you mean by 'the.'"

"What?"

"Remember Chaston and the Deputy DG? The misunderstanding about 'there' meaning the fire station not Parliament?"

"What about it?"

"What if we've done the same thing? What if the snout did mean 'the' government. Just not ours."

Melissa didn't reply.

"And here's another thought," I said. "What do babies do?"

"I don't know," Melissa said. "I've never had one. Cry?"

"They do. But they also grow. And go to school. What if al-Aqsaba'a are coming back for a second attempt on the kid? The kid whose death would bring down a friendly government? Wouldn't that be more in line with their known M.O. than a grand-scale attack on parliament?"

"Stay where you are," Melissa said. "I'll call you back."

It took Melissa less than fifteen minutes to ferret out what I needed to know.

"David?" she said, when I picked up. "I hate you. And I have since the moment we met."

"Really?" I said.

"No. But I'm not happy with you. Do you want to know why?"

"Not particularly."

"Actually, you do. It's because of your questions about that kid. It turns out he is still in London. He's grown big enough to go to school. And he just happens to attend a school in the area served by the fire station where the caesium container ended up."

"That doesn't sound like good grounds for hating me."

"On its own, maybe not. But I brought Chaston up to speed. He told Hardwicke. And they agreed, with al-Aqsaba'a as a common denominator and their past record of targeting the kid, we have to regard him as a viable target."

"And your problem with that is…?"

"They want the kid under blanket security."

"Sounds wise. Isn't he guarded anyway, though?"

"He is, given the past attempt on his life. He attends school under a false name. The Met's diplomatic protection team is on him 24/7. But they've decided that's not enough, for tomorrow. They want him to have extra cover."

"That sounds like a good thing, surely?"

"It would be. Maybe. If it wasn't for one detail."

"What kind of detail?"

"The extra cover is to be provided by you and me."

"Is that a problem?"

"Let me think. I've been running with this since the beginning. I've done all the donkey work. And tomorrow, instead of being in line for a slice of the glory – not to mention the chance to clear my name – will I be at the Palace of Westminster, where the action is? No. A horde of credit-stealing, bandwagon-riding colleagues will be there. And me? I'll be stuck in a Kindergarten."

Chapter Thirty-Four

Even if you didn't know the address of the St Ambrose Academy For Boys, it wouldn't be hard to find your way to the place. Specially in the morning. All you'd have to do is follow the swarm of out-of-place, oversized SUVs that descend on it at dropping-off time.

Parking is more of a challenge, however. Melissa hardly spoke after picking me up at the Barbican and darting through a maze of backstreets in the general direction of Westminster, but as we drew close to the school she started to mutter under her breath about the lack of convenient spaces. The whole area within a quarter of a mile of the gates was either clogged with traffic or taken up with bus lanes, and I knew she wouldn't want to leave the car on a double-yellow for fear of drawing attention.

"So," she said, after finally squeezing into a bay around the back of an old telephone exchange. "How are we going to do this?"

"I don't know," I said. "Is Jones coming?"

"No. He called me, earlier. He's still sick."

"OK. If it's just the two of us, we could say we're prospective parents. We're moving back from the States, and looking for a suitable place for our charming yet precocious twins."

"Maybe. But wouldn't we need an appointment?"

"That's why we say we have twins. Have you got any idea how much a place like this costs? And with the state of the economy? Do you think they'd turn down the chance to get their hands on two lots of fees?"

"I guess not."

"It'll get us through the door, at least. And if you continue acting like Frosty the Snow-Woman we'll have no problem convincing them we're married."

The school was separated from the street by an eight-foot-high wall. It was built from stone, pitted by age and pollution, and covered in places with dark, straggly ivy. But any promise of old-world charm was broken the second you set foot through the gate. A concrete path led diagonally through beds of crushed purple slate towards a door in a single storey, glass fronted corridor that joined a pair of low slung, rectangular buildings on either side.

"Which way?" Melissa said, as she stepped inside. "Can you see any signs?"

"None," I said. "Shall we toss a coin?"

"No. Let's just go right. It's closer."

The corridor led to a large rectangular hall. There was a stage at one end, covered with clusters of collapsible music stands, and various kinds of gym equipment were attached to both long walls. The sight of the benches and ropes and wall bars mingled with a smell of dust and floor polish. It left me half expecting one of my old teachers to appear and start barking sarcastic orders at us for moving too slowly, but when I did hear a voice it had an altogether more helpful tone.

"Can I help you?" a short, white-haired woman said, emerging from a square archway in the far corner. "You look a little lost."

Melissa moved towards her, holding out her hand, but before she could speak we heard a loud whirring sound behind us, then a solid clunk. I looked round, and saw the doors we'd come in through had swung shut on their own.

"Don't worry. It's just our security system. It's

automatic. The entrances are open for half an hour in the morning, and again at home time. Other than that, except between lessons, they only unlock with one of these fobs," the white-haired woman said, holding up a black tear-drop shaped piece of plastic on a cord around her neck.

"Very impressive," Melissa said.

"Our parents are reassured by it," the woman said. "It shows how seriously we take the safety of their children. That's always been our top priority at St Ambrose."

"As it should be."

"Absolutely. Now, you were telling me what I could do to guide you?"

The woman escorted us out of the hall, past the staffroom, and asked us to stay in a waiting area while she tracked down the admissions secretary. I helped myself to coffee from a machine on a table between a pair of Barcelona couches, but Melissa went straight for her phone.

"The first batch of MPs are there," she said, when she'd hung up. "Traffic's at a standstill outside. No one's approached the sprinkler system, or any of the other vulnerable points."

"No one's going to," I said. "The action's going to be here."

She didn't reply.

"What about the caesium container?" I said. "Is it still at the fire station?"

"It is," she said. "No one's touched it since it was delivered."

The rest of our morning was taken up with a guided tour of the premises. The admissions secretary turned out to be a sharp-suited guy in his late twenties. He showed no sign of being upset at our unannounced appearance, and from the moment he set eyes on us he was in full-on selling mode. The smile didn't fade from his face, and he didn't miss a single opportunity to stress the benefits of the school. The obscure Scandinavian architect who'd allegedly designed the buildings. The mentor assigned to every child. The daily reviews, to ensure every lesson was fully absorbed. The breadth of the curriculum. The after school clubs. Music. Drama. Sport. Foreign languages. And though he didn't mention them, I also noticed the CCTV cameras that covered every inch of the grounds. The panic buttons every twelve feet in the corridors and behind every teacher's desk. The diplomat's son – known at the school as Toby Smith - playing happily in the Kindergarten. The two burly 'teaching assistants' who never strayed more than six feet from his side. And the two men dressed as electrical contractors, who were working outside his classroom with tell-tell bulges under their coveralls.

Melissa spent most of the tour with her phone pressed to her ear.

"The last MP's arrived," she whispered to me as we were leaving the Year One classroom.

"The Lords are ready," as we inspected the musical instrument storeroom.

"One Bishop's missing," as we were handed sample menus from the canteen.

"They've found him," as we left the head teacher's office.

"Black Rod's robed up," as we paused in front of the trophy cabinet.

"The Queen's ten minutes away," as we examined the selection of books in the library.

Five minutes later we were back at the waiting area, listening to the admission secretary's footsteps die away along the corridor. I wasn't expecting a further update for another five minutes, but before I could even reach for a paper coffee cup Melissa's phone rang again. She answered, and immediately I could see the tension course through her.

"A man just entered the Medway Street fire station," she said, when the call ended. "He was wearing a hazmat suit, and emptied the contents of the caesium container into the main tank of one the fire engines."

"Excellent," I said. "They're about to make their play."

"Not excellent," she said. "Because we still don't know where the rest of the caesium is."

Chapter Thirty-Five

Melissa paced relentlessly for the next three minutes, crossing from one side of the waiting area to the other, her path perfectly parallel with the lines of school crests woven into the dark blue carpet. She was holding her phone out in front of her, staring at the screen, willing it to ring. But when there was a sound, it was louder than any ringtone. And it came from the ceiling, above her.

It was the fire alarm.

"To the kindergarten," she said, a look of half surprise, half shock, on her face. "Quickly."

I didn't need to be told twice. The staff room door flew open as we rushed past, but we ignored the angry shouts telling us to change direction and carried on along the corridor towards the classrooms. The two electrical workers were on their feet, standing squarely in front of the kindergarten door, and as we approached my nose picked up the first hint of smoke. It was leaking out below the door they were guarding.

"Stop," the guy on the right side, reaching into his overall and drawing a pistol. "Armed police. Stay where you are or I will fire."

We stopped.

"Hold it," Melissa said. "Blue on blue. I'm going to reach into my pocket and take out my ID. Is that OK?"

"Go ahead," the guy said, as his partner also drew his weapon. "But do it slowly."

"What are you doing out here?" Melissa said, when they were satisfied with her credentials. "Where's Toby Smith?"

"He's fine," the first guy said. "The others are taking him out to the assembly point. It's outside, on the playground. All the classes have an allocated spot to wait in. As soon as we get word they're set, we'll go around the other way and meet them. We can't get there through the classroom, like they did. It's too full of smoke."

"We need to go now," Melissa said. "We have to move the kid. He's not safe there. The fire's a ruse to get him out in the open."

"What do you mean?" the guy said. "What do you know that we…"

Melissa's phone rang and she held up her hand, cutting the guy off and indicating she needed to take the call.

"OK," she said, hanging up a minute later. "They stopped both engines from leaving Medway Street fire station. Both crews, and everyone inside the building, are under wraps. Two other engines are en route from Victoria, in their place. ETA is four minutes. Let's make sure we have our hands on the kid before they get here."

"Are you going to tell us what's going on?" the first guy said.

"I will," Melissa said. "Off the record, anyway. But only once the kid is safe. So come on. Lead the way."

Organising large groups of kids was always my idea of hell, but the teachers at St Ambrose had it down to a fine art. We emerged from the glass corridor on to the playground and instead of the chaos I had envisaged, we found four neat double lines of children. The classes were arranged in age order: kindergarten to the left, Year One in front of us, Year Two to the right. And if the relative size of the children wasn't enough of a clue, the teaching assistants standing on either side of the diplomat's kid would certainly have been a reliable guide.

"There he is," Melissa said. "Let's get him away from the crowd, just in case."

We'd just started moving towards the youngest children when the alarm bells inside the school were switched off. Without them, we could suddenly hear the excited murmuring of the kids. The background hum of city traffic returned. And we became aware of another sound. Sirens. Several of them. At least four. And they were heading in our direction.

One of the teachers called for silence, then ordered the children to remain absolutely still. The last words had barely left his lips when the first of the emergency vehicles arrived. It was a police car, closely followed by a pair of fire engines and two ambulances. The car pulled over to the side, near the last of the Year Two children, and the fire engines swooped past it, not stopping till they were as close to the classroom building as possible. Their doors were thrown open and five firemen jumped down from each one, already suited up in their protective clothing. Like clockwork they started towards their prearranged positions, but before a single hose could be connected all ten of the men suddenly froze. They raised their hands, and I followed their gaze to two men I hadn't seen before. They'd emerged from a black BMW that had made its way up the drive under cover of the second ambulance. They were both wearing suits. They were tall, each well over six foot. And they were both holding guns.

"Nobody move," the first newcomer said. "Police. Now, listen carefully."

"They're not police," Melissa whispered to me. "They're Box. I recognise them."

"I'm speaking to the fire crew only, now," the newcomer said. "I need to know which one of you is in charge?"

The man who'd been first out of the leading fire engine raised his right hand even higher than it already was.

"Good," the newcomer said. "I need your help. Because before a single drop of water gets sprayed anywhere, we need to test it. And that won't take long, if you show me how to open the tanks."

The fireman made his way to the back of his engine and started to climb the ladder which was built in to the vehicle's bodywork.

"The hatch's up here," he said. "But you better haul your arse. We've got a fire to fight, here."

The newcomer followed him up, pulled something about the size of an iPhone out of his jacket pocket, and held it to the mouth of the tank.

"Good," he said, without looking at it, and I realised it must be a Geiger counter. "This one's clear. Let's check the other one."

They repeated the procedure, and again the agent looked satisfied.

"Clear again," he said. "Thank you. Now, please, carry on."

The chief fireman waved his hand and the others sprang back into a blur of choreographed action. I guess they were eager to make up for lost time, but I wasn't too worried about the fate of the school. I was pretty certain that whatever kind of device had caused the fire, it was designed to produce more smoke than flames. The idea was to provoke an evacuation, and that part of the plan at least had been successful. The diplomat's son had been moved exactly where someone wanted him, and even though he was flanked by four armed guards, if the caesium hadn't been intercepted, he'd have been as vulnerable as if he was standing naked and all alone.

Melissa badged the new agents, spoke to them for a moment, then started moving towards the line of kindergarten kids. I don't know if it was down to the length of time they'd been standing there, the excitement of seeing the fire engines arrive, or the drama of the armed agents appearing, but the volume of noise they were making was increasing and their lines were becoming more ragged. And the degree of fidgeting had grown much greater, too. I started to follow Melissa and as I moved, I caught sight of something flying through the air. It was looping over my head. Something oval and black, like a large egg. The line of children instinctively broke as the object plummeted towards them, and it landed in the exact spot where a tall boy with glasses had been standing. I'd expected it to bounce, but instead it cracked open and the pieces stayed where they'd fallen. It didn't make much noise, particularly in contrast with the shrieks that were coming from the nearest kids, but red smoke immediately started to spew from its cracked shell. The screaming grew louder and spread throughout the different groups of children, and the last vestige of discipline dissolved in the next split second. The smoke spread, whipped up by the rising wind, and amid the hysterical howling it became impossible to distinguish one set of panicking children from another. I could only hope that despite the chaos, the diplomat's kid was still in safe hands.

"Gun," one of the new agents shouted. "Get down."

I spun round and saw spits of flame flickering from the muzzle of his 9mm. A man, twenty feet away from me, staggered back, clutching his chest. Kids were rampaging everywhere. I spotted a second man, twenty feet away in the other direction. He had another gun. He fired two shots, and the agent went down. Then he fired two more shots, over the heads of the children. The screaming became even louder, and under cover of the frenzied movement, the man turned and started to run.

"Stop," Melissa shouted.

The man turned and fired at her. She slipped, but was straight back on her feet. She took two strides, then dropped down into a kneeling position, her weapon raised. Two more shots rang out, and this time the guy went down. He didn't stay down long either, but wasn't as controlled as Melissa. His gun arm was flailing, jerking so wildly it would have been impossible for him to hit anything he was aiming at. But it was guaranteed he was going to hit something, if he pulled the trigger again. And given the numbers, his most likely victim would be one of the children.

Melissa started moving towards him, stooping down to reduce the target she presented. The guy's gun twitched in her direction, then snapped back to his left. The other new agent was moving, too. Melissa took advantage of the distraction he'd created and charged forward, straight at the guy. He saw her coming, but it was too late to bring his weapon to bear. Melissa launched herself at his chest, sending him reeling, and the agent and I reached them just as he hit the floor.

"You take him," Melissa said to her colleague, as she regained her feet. "Make sure nothing happens. We need him able to talk."

It took a moment to spot anyone we recognised from the Kindergarten, but eventually Melissa caught sight of the boy who'd almost been hit by the smoke grenade. We started towards him, watching as he was bumped and buffeted by bigger children who were in a greater state of panic. Then Melissa suddenly changed direction. She'd spotted the two electricians. There were at the far side of the playground, standing near the boundary wall. They appeared relaxed. Detached from the madness around them.

And with no sign of Toby Smith.

"Where's the kid," Melissa said when we reached them, slightly out of breath from pushing through the crowd. "Aren't you supposed to be with him?"

"We were," the guy who'd spoken outside the classroom said. "But he had to go to hospital."

"What?" Melissa said. "Why?"

"Because of that weird red smoke," he said. "Didn't you smell it? The kid took a right lungful, and came over all queasy. So the other officers put him in one the ambulances, and off they went."

Melissa shot me a worried glance.

"Which hospital are they heading for?" she said. "Did they tell you?"

"Of course," the guy said. "St Joseph's."

Chapter Thirty-Six

I'd thought Melissa's driving was aggressive on the way to Woolwich, two days ago. But that was before I saw how she cut through the traffic that afternoon between the school and the hospital. And she wasn't just driving. She was using her phone, too.

She called Chaston, to find out if anything was happening at the Houses of Parliament.

It wasn't.

She called Thames House, to ask them to intercept the kid's ambulance.

They couldn't.

She called St Joseph's, to see if it had arrived yet.

It hadn't.

With each new frustration her right foot grew heavier until I was tempted to pick up the phone myself and pre-emptively call an ambulance for the two of us. It was starting to seem inevitable we'd need one. The chances she was taking were becoming untenably crazy. And then, after a particularly near miss with a black cab, Melissa suddenly eased off the accelerator and revealed what was really bothering her.

"Did you hear what those other agents told me?" she said. "The ones who arrived with the fire engines?"

"No," I said.

"I asked them how they got there so fast. I was thinking, it would take some serious hussle to get out of Thames House and still catch the emergency crews like that. And guess what they told me?"

"What?"

"They hadn't scrambled in response to the fire at all. They were already there, staking the place out."

"They were? Why? Have we crossed paths with another case?"

"No. Same case. Think about it. They just happened to have Geiger counters with them, and immediately test the water in the engines' tanks?"

"So why were they there?"

"They were ordered to be. By Arthur Hardwicke. Last night. You know what that means?"

I took a moment to think.

"He took your theory about the school more seriously than you'd thought?" I said.

"No," she said. "It means he doesn't trust me. If he'd trusted me, he'd have told me they were being assigned, and we could have coordinated with them. Not been surprised when they showed up, guns at the ready."

"But you're the one who came up with the link between al-Aqsaba'a, the kid, and the school. How does that make you look untrustworthy?"

"He must have thought I suggested the school link so I'd be assigned to it. And sabotage our response to it. Which is exactly what it looks like I've done."

"Not necessarily. The kid breathed in smoke. The protection detail are paid to be cautious."

"I let the kid slip through my fingers. That's the bottom line. If anything happens to him, they'll say it's my fault. They'll say I did it on purpose. Mud sticks, David."

"It doesn't have to. And it won't, if we get our hands on the poor little lad and make sure nothing else happens to him."

There were spaces left for two ambulances at the Accident and Emergency entrance to St Joseph's when Melissa pulled in, but she was in such a hurry to get inside that our car ended up blocking both of them. A hospital security guard saw us, and made a half-hearted attempt to intervene but he gave it up as a lost cause long before we'd entered the building and reached the reception desk.

"We're looking for a patient," Melissa said, flashing her ID card at the middle-aged woman behind the counter. "Name of Toby Smith. He should have been brought in by ambulance in the last five minutes."

The receptionist took her time to reply.

"Who?" she said.

"Toby Smith," Melissa said.

"You're out of luck. Sorry. There's no one with that name come in here."

"It's a complex situation. He might not have been using his real name. He's around five years old. Male. Have you had any boys that age brought in?"

"I can't tell you that kind of information."
Melissa held out her ID once again, and didn't move it until the woman turned to check her computer.

"Two boys were admitted this morning, yes," she said. "One was five. The other, six."

"Good," Melissa said. "Where are they?"

"I don't know."

"What do you mean, you don't know?"

"Where they are's nothing to do with me. You'll have to ask the triage nurse. She's the one that decides who goes where."

"OK. Where is she?"

"Round the next corner. You can't miss her."

The triage nurse remembered both the young boys who'd been brought in that day. Her words said the first one had fallen down stairs at home, but the expression on her face told us she didn't believe the stepfather's story. On another day I might have been tempted to have a chat with the guy, since she said he was still in the waiting room, but her recollection of the second kid meant that wasn't a possibility. He was the right age. The right height. He was complaining of the right symptoms. He'd been brought in by the right kind of people. Two fit looking men in their twenties. Friends of the family, they'd told her. And we could see she didn't believe their story, either.

She said she hadn't been too worried by the kid's symptoms, but had admitted him anyway so a doctor could take a closer look. She made a quick call, and told us we could find him in cubicle twelve on the main Accident and Emergency ward.

The ward was long and narrow, with a single row of beds along each side. There were twenty altogether. The spaces between them were wide, to allow for trolleys of special equipment to be wheeled in, and the floor was scuffed and scraped as a result. About a third of the beds were occupied, and beyond them we could see the two banks of cubicles. But as we approached, we could see that none of them held any patients. We checked the numbers, to be sure, and there was no doubt. Cubicle twelve was empty.

"Do you think they transferred him?" Melissa said. "Or could they have released him already?"

"I don't think it's either of those," I said. "Look at the cot. The sheets haven't been touched. They're immaculate. I don't think he was ever here."

"You might be right. But the nurse seemed so sure. I'll go and ask her to check. You stay here. Maybe the kid just needed the bathroom or something."

Five minutes crawled past, and aside from the two nurses who were bustling between the half-dozen beds that were in use at the other end of the ward, nothing happened.

Melissa didn't return. There was no sign of the kid or his escorts. I was beginning to worry, and when another five minutes elapsed and I was still on my own, I decided the time for waiting was over.

The shift must have just changed, because a new nurse was waiting behind the triage desk when I stepped back into the corridor. She hadn't seen Melissa, she said, but that didn't really help. She hadn't been there long enough. All she could do was suggest I ask at the nurses' station on the ward.

"Oh yes, I saw your friend," the ward clerk said, when I'd found the little alcove where she worked. "About ten minutes ago?"

"That's about right," I said. "Did you see where she went?"

"Out into the corridor. She seemed in a hurry, so I assumed she was leaving. I think a man was with her."

"A man? What did he look like?"

"I don't know. I'm terrible with faces. But I think he works here. I've seen him before, coming out of the admin block. I mean, I think he was with her. He might have just been going out at the same time. I'm not sure."

I didn't like the sound of that at all.

"OK," I said, pushing this new information temporarily aside for the sake of the child. "Never mind them now. What about the kid from cubicle twelve? Can you tell me where he went?"

"What kid?" she said. "Cubicle twelve is empty."

"Exactly. That's the problem. We're here to find a kid, and the triage nurse told us that's where he'd been sent when she admitted him."

"No. That's not possible. Sorry. There must be a misunderstanding. It's been a quiet morning. We've only had one little boy brought in. He had a broken arm - a green stick, actually - which we dealt with. And he's not here any more, anyway. He was discharged a couple of minutes ago."

"The triage nurse said there were two boys. It's the other one we need to find."

"Well, I don't know what to tell you. He's not here. See for yourself."

"He certainly was here. The triage nurse remembered him. Is there anywhere else he could have got to, from the corridor, without coming in here?"

"I don't think so," she said, waving to one of the nurses. "Hang on a sec. Megan? Have you seen any kids around here? We might have a wanderer."

"Not for a while," the nurse said. "No. Christine had one earlier, though. A little lad. Complete brat. Something wrong with his arm, I think. Not to mention his manners."

"No others?" the ward clerk said.

"No other patients. Does Serena's little boy count? She was heading to the staff room with him, just now."

"I didn't know Serena had a little boy," the ward clerk said.

"Nor did I," the nurse said. "But you know what she's like. Keeps herself to herself. And I assumed it was her son. It could have been a nephew or something, I suppose."

"Who's Serena?" I said.

"One of our physiotherapists," the nurse said.

"How long has she worked here?" I said.

"She's quite new. Two months? Three, maybe?" the clerk said.

"And you've never seen the kid she has with her, before?" I said.

"No," the nurse said. "You're not really supposed to bring your kids to work. But people do, sometimes, if their child care goes pear-shaped."

"Was anyone else with them?" I said.

"I'm not really sure," the nurse said.

"How can you not be sure?" I said. "Was anyone else there, or not?"

"Well, a couple of guys were near them," the nurse said. "They were quite good looking, actually. Tall. And heading the same way. But they were hanging a few yards back."

"Heading for the staff room?" I said.

"Right," the nurse said. "A couple of minutes ago."

"Show me," I said.

The nurse, Megan, took me back out to the corridor and pointed to a badly scuffed pale green door midway down the far wall.

"That's it," she said. "But you can't go in. It's more of a changing room, really, than a staff room. It's where we put our uniforms on. People might be getting dressed in there."

"Don't worry," I said. "I won't look. Now, stand back. And whatever you hear, do not follow me in. Not unless I call specifically for you."

I eased the door open and peeked inside. A privacy screen prevented me from looking any further into the room, but also made sure no one already in there could see me. I stepped through the door, let it quietly close behind me, and drew my Beretta. From there, I could also see the entrance to a closet on my right. A sign said *Domestic Staff Only*, but it would have been difficult to keep anyone else out. Because its handle had been broken. From the way its mechanism had been torn out of the wood, I'd say it hadn't been an accident. And in the gap at the bottom of the door, there was another sign of something violent. The edge of a puddle of blood.

My hand was reaching out to open the closet door when I heard footsteps on the other side of the screen. One set. They were light, and fast. Then they stopped, and a woman started to speak.

"Don't worry, my little angel," she said. "Your two friends will be back in a minute. And I have great news. The doctors don't need to see you. They don't think you need any nasty injections, after all. All you need is a nice long drink of water. That'll wash away the taste of that horrid smoke, and then you'll be absolutely fine. You can go straight back to school and catch up with your friends. I bet they're worried about you."

I took two steps to my left, rounding the screen and emerging into the changing room itself. It was a rectangular space, large, but surprisingly gloomy because there were no windows. Grey metal lockers lined three of the walls. The space between them was filled with ancient-looking wooden benches. Four rows of them. They were parallel. Two people were sitting on the nearest one. A woman, in her mid thirties, hair tied back, wearing a white polyester uniform with the St Joseph's logo on its tunic pocket. And next to her, Toby Smith.

She was holding out a large stainless steel thermos flask.

"Here, sweetie," she said. "Take some of this. It's nice and cold. Much nicer than ordinary tap water."

"Thank you," he said, reaching out to take it. "We never drink tap water at home."

"You might want to rethink that policy," I said, moving closer. "Bottled water's bad for the environment. So do not touch that flask."

The kid screamed, dived on the floor, and scrambled away from me under the bench. The woman took hold of the flask's lid and started to twist.

"Stop," I said.

She'd turned the lid half a revolution. I didn't know

how many it would take to open it. I didn't even know for sure there was caesium inside the flask. But bearing in mind Melissa's description of its effect, I was in no mood to find out the hard way. The kid wouldn't need to drink it, to be in serious trouble. She could just splash it all over him. So I pulled the trigger. Twice. And then I called for Megan.

I didn't fancy my chances of coaxing a scared five-year-old out into the open, after that.

Chapter Thirty-Seven

Nurse Megan had hesitated to enter the changing room when I'd called for her. The sight of the woman's body had stopped her in mid-stride. I was surprised, given most nurses' professional familiarity with death. But in the end her concern for the kid outweighed her reluctance to come near the corpse. She finally crept in, keeping her back close to the wall, and tried to coax the boy out from under the bench. Even her most persuasive voice was no match for his fear, though, so eventually she settled for sitting on the floor next to him and holding his hand while we waited for the pair of diplomatic protection officers – the ones who'd been dressed as electricians at the school – to arrive and take over.

The kid's removal left me with no excuse to avoid making a statement about the shooting to another pair of officers. It didn't take too long, in the end. They didn't ask anything too awkward. And I wasn't too worried about what I said, anyway. I knew that even if MI5 didn't make all record of it disappear, the Navy would.

When I was finished, I found that two more detectives were waiting to ask me about the blood I'd seen under the sluice door. It wasn't a surprise, but I was still sorry when they confirmed it had come from the officers who'd accompanied Toby in the ambulance. Their bodies had been hidden there. Both of them had been shot at close range, with a .22. Presumably the physiotherapist woman had done it, to clear her path to the kid. She'd probably lured them inside somehow, because she wasn't big enough to easily have moved their bodies. Or she'd had help, from someone stronger. Or who they'd have trusted. But whatever had happened, piecing it together wasn't my problem. The only mystery I was still interested in at that point was Melissa's whereabouts.

I hadn't heard from her since she'd gone to talk to the triage nurse. There was no answer on her phone. Or Jones's. Chaston didn't know where she was. I even tried Leckie's number. And no one at Thames House could tell me anything useful, either. As a last resort I swung by her apartment on my way back to the Barbican, but that was a fool's errand, too. The place was cold and dark and empty.

I was still wondering about her when I opened my front door, twenty minutes later. Was she missing? Had she run away? Had she been the one who'd helped the physiotherapist kill the officers? Had she left the hospital with someone, as the ward clerk had thought? If so, was it Leckie? And had she gone voluntarily? Or under duress? But as soon as I moved into my lounge and looked out over the unfamiliar silhouette of my home city, my focus expanded along with my view of the skyline. I began to reflect on the case as a whole, not just the people who'd been killed in London. What would have happened if Toby Smith, or whatever the diplomat's son was really called, had drunk the radioactive water? How long would the caesium solution have taken to eat his organs away? How would his father's government have responded to watching his slow, agonising death?

Part of me knew I should have felt good about the outcome. I'd saved an innocent kid's life. And I'd averted a critical threat to the coalition of pro-western nations. But along with the successes, I had to recognise a significant failure. I hadn't done the one thing I'd been sent to do. Expose the traitor inside MI5. Whether it was Melissa or someone else, who knew what the fallout would be? What kind of havoc had I left them to wreak in the future?

I was brought back down to earth by my phone. The screen said it was Tim Jones. I answered, but no one spoke for fifteen seconds. I knew someone was there, though. I could hear them breathing at the other end of the line.

"David?" Jones said, eventually. "Are you there?"

"Yes," I said. "Are you?"

"Are you on your own?"

"Yes. Why?"

"There's a problem. It's about Melissa."

"What's she done?"

"Done? Nothing. Why would you ask that?"

"Never mind. Just tell me what's happening."

"She's disappeared."

"I know."

"Well, I know where she is."

"You do? Where?"

"With Stan Leckie."

I took a moment to think.

"Why would she go anywhere with Leckie?" I said.

"She had no choice," he said. "Leckie snatched her."

"How do you know?"

"He just called me. He told me."

"Did you believe him?"

"Well, yes. Why wouldn't I?"

"Did he say where he snatched her from?"

"St Joseph's."

"When?"

"About ninety minutes ago."

"Where are they now?"

"I don't know."

"Can't you trace his phone?"

"That's the first thing I tried. But it didn't work. It's somehow spoofing the network into thinking it's in seventy-two different locations, all at the same time. He's ex-Box, remember. He knows all the tricks."

"What does he want?"

"Not much. Just two things. You. And me."

"Why?"

"He didn't spell it out, but it's pretty clear. He must have been working with al-Aqsaba'a on the theft of the caesium. Maybe more. He must think we've pieced it together, and wants to silence us. Even frame us."

"And Melissa?"

"He says if we hand ourselves over to him, he'll let her go."

Was Leckie using Melissa as bait? Or were they working together to lure Jones and me into a trap? The set-up would sound the same, either way. It was impossible to tell without more information.

"Well, Leckie obviously won't be letting anyone go," I said.

"Obviously," Jones said. "But we can't risk calling the police, or our own people, because he must be connected to someone on the inside, and we have no idea who that is."

"Agreed."

"He's given us two hours. Then he wants us to meet him at the old workhouse in Luton. Remember the place?"

"I do."

"Where are you now?"

"At home."

"I'm in Croydon. I'll be on the road in five minutes. Do you want me to come into town and pick you up? We could drive up there together?"

"No thanks," I said. "If the rumours about Leckie are true, we might not have two hours. Melissa might not, anyway. So drop whatever you're doing. Leave now. Go directly to the workhouse. I'll meet you there."

Chapter Thirty-Eight

One aspect of owning an apartment in the middle of the city and spending most of the year abroad is that you don't need a car. Normally, that's an advantage. That morning, however, it was the exact opposite. My ability to travel beyond walking distance and out of the scope of public transport was severely limited, and that needed to change. Quickly. So as soon as Jones had hung up, I made another call.

"Logistics Support," a male voice said.

I pulled open the centre drawer in the desk in my living room, scooped out a letter opener and a collection of other random stationary items, and prised up a tight-fitting panel that had been installed beneath them.

"I need a vehicle," I said, after running through the standard identification ritual. "And I need it outside my building in ten minutes, max."

"I'm sorry sir, but that's not possible," he said.

I took an ancient Sig Sauer .22 from the shallow space I'd revealed, and jammed it into the pocket of my jeans.

"Not possible, or not easy?" I said.

"Not possible," he said. "I keyed in your details as you told me them, and the system says you're on secondment. Which means I can't send a car for you. You're not supposed to be active."

I took out a switchblade, and slipped it into the other pocket.

"I am active," I said. "Ignore the computer. I need that car. You've now got nine minutes."

"I can't do it, sir," he said. "I can't book a car out to you when you're supposed to be on a different agency's headcount. The system won't release an asset under those circumstances."

I took a suppressor for my Beretta, and tucked that into my jacket pocket.

"Book it out to Michael Martin, Major, Royal Marines," I said. "That's what we always do in these situations. And please, hurry up."

"But you identified yourself as Commander Trevellyan, sir," he said. "You can't use someone else's name, now."

I replaced the concealed cover.

"How old are you, son?" I said. "Don't you know who Major Martin was?"

"No, sir," he said.

I threw the stationary back in.

"Key his name in," I said. "The system'll accept it. Trust me."

I heard computer keys rattling in the background.

"Oh," he said. "It worked. Bear with me, please."

The keys rattled again, more frantically this time.

"OK," he said, after a moment. "The car's on its way. ETA, it looks like, twelve minutes. Is that all right?"

"It'll do," I said. "And before you go home tonight, go to the library. Find a book about the invasion of Sicily, in World War Two. Read about the role Major Martin played. If you've got any future in this business, you'll enjoy it."

"Can't you just tell me who he was?"

"No," I said. "I can't. Because he didn't exist."

The car that pulled up outside Cromwell Tower eleven minutes later looked just like a standard, silver, 5-series BMW. There was nothing on the outside to suggest it was anything out of the ordinary. But as soon as I touched the accelerator, it was clear that the Navy mechanics had weaved their usual magic under the skin. It had taken the MI5 driver, Pearson, thirty-three minutes to pitch and roll his way from London to Luton in his big Range Rover. I shaved a full six minutes off that time. And I didn't need a moment to regain my land legs when I arrived, either.

It stood to reason that Leckie wouldn't want any random passers-by to wander onto the site and see what he was up to. He was bound to have the place guarded, or at least kept under observation, so I only allowed myself a single drive by. No one was visible at the main gate, but I saw two men standing just inside the perimeter by the hole in the wall that Pearson had driven through to park. They were wearing security guard uniforms, and they matched the company Leckie used at St Joseph's. That was smart. It told me I was on the right track, and everyone else to keep out.

I kept going for another quarter of a mile, then pulled the BMW over to the side of the road and added it to a line of parked cars. Then I called Jones. He didn't answer straight away, so while his phone was ringing I screwed the suppressor onto the barrel of my Beretta and made sure the switchblade was easily accessible in my pocket.

"I'm nearly there," Jones said when he finally picked up. "Traffic was worse than I thought. How are you doing?"

"Good," I said. "How long till you'll arrive?"

"Twenty minutes? Twenty-five, at the outside."

"OK. See you there."

I knew the textbook option was to wait for Jones. And if he'd said he was five minutes down the road I probably would have done. But almost half an hour? While there was still the slightest chance Melissa was innocent and in danger, I figured Jones could catch up in his own good time. And if she was neither, there was no point in anyone else getting caught in her web.

Chapter Thirty-Nine

The walk back to the hole in the wall would normally have taken around five minutes, but that day it took me ten. Not because I dawdled. But because I didn't stay on the pavement. I only followed it as far as the rear corner of the wall. Then I checked for cameras. Or sensors. Or anyone watching. The coast seemed to be clear, so I took a moment to find suitable hand and foot holds in the weathered stone surface and pulled myself up high enough to peer over to the other side.

There was no one in sight, so I slid over the top of the wall and dropped down behind a rough stack of rustic, reclaimed bricks. They'd have been worth something in a buoyant economy, but as things stood, it looked like no one could even be bothered to steal them.

The patch of scrubby ground between where I'd landed and the heap of rubble I'd seen last time was clear, so I drew my Beretta and crossed the open space. I got to the far side, unnoticed. I knew that if I skirted round to the right of the mound, I had a chance of moving deeper into the workhouse's grounds without encountering anyone. If I'd just been there for covert surveillance, that's what I'd have done. But standing back and watching wasn't on the agenda, this time. I was there to get Melissa out, and whether that meant rescuing her or arresting her, I couldn't afford anyone blocking my exit route. Or raising an alarm. Or calling in reinforcements. In fact, in the circumstances, an early look at the opposition could be beneficial. It could tell me what kind of organisation I was facing. And if I could find someone who was prepared to spill a few beans, a lot more besides.

I moved round to the left of the mound and, as expected, I saw the two security guards. They didn't see me, though. They were looking in completely the wrong direction. I guess they were expecting me to approach them from the street, because I closed to within ten feet before either one of them reacted. And by then, it was far too late.

Sometimes the best way to loosen a person's tongue is to draw things out for as long as possible. Put them off balance. Disorient them. Twist their perception of the situation so much they end up thinking that talking's their own idea.

Other times I just rely on brute force and ignorance.

I raised the Beretta and shot the first guy right between the eyes. Blood and bone fragments showered the side of his friend's head as he turned to see what was happening. Then I stepped closer to the first guy's crumpled body and fired another shot into his skull.

"Is Leckie here?" I said.

The guy who was still alive turned to face me. The scarlet spatter stood out vividly against his suddenly pale skin, and even such a gentle movement sent it dribbling down towards his chin.

"What?" he said.

"Stan Leckie," I said. "Is he here?"

"I don't know who that is."

"The guy from the hospital. St Joseph's."

"Oh. Yes. He is. He hired us. He brought us here."

"Is there a girl with him?"

He gave another nod, and I noticed his pupils were growing wider by the second.

"Where are they?" I said.

The guy stuck out his arm and pointed to the area at the back of the main building. That's what I'd feared, but my heart sank nonetheless.

"How many other people are with you?" I said.

The guy looked blank, and didn't respond in any way.

"There's you, this dead guy, the guy who hired you, and a girl," I said. "How many others are here? Answer in words this time."

"None," he said finally, in a surprisingly low, gravely voice. "We were told to guard the gate."

"What about the other gates?"

"There's only one other gate. It used to be the main entrance. It's blocked now. And there's no one on it. Are you called Trevellyan?"

"I am."

"I was told to say, he's expecting you. The guy from the hospital. And he thought you'd come in this way."

"What were you supposed to do about that?"

"Stop you. And take you to him. He said he was putting on a show, specially for you to watch."

I thought of the three holes punched in the solid stone wall, and wondered if this guy had been on the gate that day, too.

"How generous of him," I said. "Only, I'm afraid there's bad news. The show's going to be canceled."

"It is?" he said.

"It is," I said, raising the Beretta again. "Which means your gate keeping services are no longer required."

Chapter Forty

I made my way across the parking area towards the gap between the back of the main building and the old workhouse asylum. It looked like only one car had been there recently, based on the tyre tracks in the soft ground. One car, and one other vehicle. Something wide. And heavy. And that rode on caterpillar tracks.

I retraced my steps, looped back around the hill of rubble, and found my way to the passageway that Melissa had used as shelter from the sniper. That should have given me a view through to the main building, in theory. But in practice, it didn't. The far end was blocked by something. A mobile crane. One that had seen better days. Its maroon bodywork was dull and dented, and all the windows in its cab were broken. It was certainly in bad shape cosmetically, but I couldn't tell what state its mechanical parts were in. All I could see was that its boom was extended at a sharp angle. Whether anything was attached to it was a whole other question.

Approaching the crane from the passageway was out of the question, so I pulled back again and worked my way round to the route Pearson and I had taken to reach the west wing of the main building. Common sense told me I'd be no use to anyone with a volley of bullets inside me, but the delay this detour caused was agony. It felt like it would have been quicker to crawl across the Sahara Desert. The only saving grace was that the security guard I'd spoken to seemed to have been telling the truth, and I didn't encounter anyone else lurking around the far boundary of the grounds.

I slipped into the west wing through the same

entrance I'd used last time, and wasted no time in leaving the room and crossing the hallway. The inside of the building smelled worse than before, and the door at the bottom of the stairs - which I hoped would lead to the main part of the building - was very reluctant to open. When it finally gave way the air quality didn't improve, but I stepped through anyway and found myself at the start of a long, straight, bleak corridor. I turned to my left and made straight for where I hoped the entrance to the central block would be. I kept going until I reached a doorway. It led to a hallway that was identical to the one I'd come from, so I crossed my fingers and took it. I could see daylight to my left, so I followed it to the remains of a window, trying to ignore the uneven black stains on the floor and fresh, satanic graffiti on all four walls.

Another line of anaemic bushes gave me a degree of cover as I made my way along the outside of the building, parallel to where I'd been before. This time, though, a view of the battered crane had replaced the informant and his motorbike. For a moment I wondered whether he'd really approached Leckie, who'd staged his murder in front of our eyes so he'd look innocent. Or whether the whole episode was a stunt from the beginning, to distract us from Leckie's real goal. And then such hypothetical thoughts were pushed away. But not by me, deliberately. By the sound of breathing. It was human. Heavy. And close.

I continued past a patch where the plant cover thinned alarmingly, and kept one eye firmly on the crane. And I was encouraged by what I saw. For two reasons. There was no sign of anyone in the cab. And nothing lethal was attached to the heavy cable that was dangling from its jib.

The breathing grew louder the closer I crept to the end of the wall. I paused for a moment, to bring my own respiration under control. Then I stood up straight. Raised my Beretta. Stepped around the corner. And came face to face with Melissa.

She was standing with her back to the wall. Her arms were stretched out on both sides, at shoulder height. Her wrists were held by crude iron shackles that stuck out from the stonework. There was a vacant pair of shackles to her left, between us. And to her right, the line of three craters whose previous occupants had been pulped by a swinging mass of steel.

There was only one question in my mind. Was she trapped there, herself? Or was she there to trap me?

The reason she was facing me rather than looking straight ahead turned out to be simple. She was straining with all her might to free her right hand. I could see the iron digging into her flesh. Her skin was tearing, and blood was dripping down to the ground from her wrist.

I felt like I had my answer.

"Melissa, stop that," I said, stepping closer. "You're hurting yourself. Let me help."

"David, what are you doing here?" she said. "Get out of the way."

I could see tears in her eyes, but before I could reach the shackle she gave a last almighty heave and tore it free from the masonry.

"Jones called me," I said. "He told me there'd be a trade, for you. Are you OK?"

"So far," she said, raising her blood-soaked hand. "Don't worry about this. There was a method. Look closely - the wall was damaged when that nearest hole got smashed in it. You can see little cracks running across. They reached the place where my right wrist was attached, so I figured it would be the easier one to get free."

"That's smart. Do the cracks reach your left one?"

"No, sadly, they don't," she said, wrapping her fingers around the enormous spike that was still attached to the dangling shackle. "So it's time for phase two. Dig for victory. I'll soon get this other one loose."

"It'll take ages," I said. "See how deep that thing went in? Here. Let me help."

"Not a chance. You need to take cover, somewhere, and..."

Her next words were interrupted by the sound of a huge, dog-rough diesel engine spluttering into life. It was coming from the crane. We spun round together, to look, but I still couldn't spot anyone in the cab.

"What's he doing?" Melissa said, glancing nervously at the gaping holes to her right.

"Nothing," I said. "He's just trying to scare you. The wrecking ball isn't even attached. He didn't have time. And if he pokes his head out to take a shot, it'll be the last mistake he ever makes."

As we watched, the crane's jib started to move. It was turning anti-clockwise, away from the asylum building, and kept going until it was sticking out sideways at ninety degrees, the cable swinging harmlessly in impotent circles below it.

"Don't worry," I said. "Leckie's just putting on a show. He wants to rattle you."

"What do you mean?" she said. "Leckie's..."

Then the crane itself began to move, drowning out the rest of her words. The track nearer us was locked, but the one on the opposite side must have been engaged because the entire vehicle was slowly rotating. It kept turning, practically on the spot, tearing up the ground beneath it, until it was facing directly towards us. All of a sudden the lack of a wrecking ball didn't seem like such an obstacle.

The Beretta was in my hand, but I had no shot into

the cab. Moving closer wouldn't help, unless I could make it all the way to the crane's bodywork, climb up on it, and fire through the broken window. But that wasn't a viable option, either. I'd be too exposed for too long to stand a realistic chance. The only way to stop whoever was at the controls would be to gain some height. Not too much, or the cab's metal roof would protect him. The first floor window would probably give the right angle. But getting there quickly enough was the problem. I could climb back in through any of the ground floor windows, but as far as I knew, the only staircase was at the far end of the wing. I'd have to run all the way back there, go up one floor, and run all the way to the front again. I could move fast, when the occasion called for it. But it would still take too long. The crane would be able to reach the building in half the time. That would leave a square hole in the stonework, rather than another round one. But the distinction would be purely academic as far as Melissa was concerned.

"You pull," I said, leaning closer to her ear and taking hold of the spike that was still hanging from her right wrist. "I'll work on the mortar. Together we've got a much better chance."

Melissa started to strain against the shackle, and within a couple of seconds blood was beginning to seep from a fresh wound on her left wrist. I had nothing to show for my efforts. I was trying to dig away at the point where the iron stem disappeared into the masonry, but was making no impact at all.

"Time for brute force and ignorance, again," I said, letting go of the metal and casting around the immediate area for a suitably sized piece of brick or stone. "I need something to hit that thing with."

I spotted an ideal brickbat about twenty-five feet away, and as I moved across to grab it the sound of the crane's engine grew suddenly louder. The driver must have been revving it hard. I turned to look, and it gradually returned to idling speed, like a petulant beast that demanded attention. I stood perfectly still and watched for half a minute, and the note didn't change. Then I took a step towards Melissa. The noise instantly increased, and the crane began to move. Slowly at first. Almost imperceptibly. But my eyes weren't playing tricks. Its speed was increasing. It was heading directly at Melissa. And the shackle was still holding firm.

The crane's speed peaked at maybe four miles an hour. The kind of pace that would drive you insane if you were caught behind it on a public road. But to me, at that moment, it felt like a meteor couldn't travel faster. Or be harder to knock off course. I couldn't shoot the driver. I couldn't get to a place where I even had a chance of shooting him. And even if I could be sure of killing him - if the rock in my hand was magically transformed into a grenade, for example - there was no guarantee that would stop the crane's relentless, grinding, forward progress.

Melissa was thrashing wildly from side to side now, pulling with all her strength. Blood was pouring from her wrist and I caught a glimpse of shiny white bone gleaming through a wide gash in her skin. The crane had already halved the distance between its starting position and her. She had twenty seconds left before it would crush her against the stone, no more, and the way she was acting showed she knew it. She put her right foot on the wall at waist height, then her left, so that all her weight was on her wrist. Then she started slamming herself backwards, bending at the waist and pushing with her legs like a naughty toddler trying to escape a parent's iron grip. It must have been absolute agony. And it was all in vain, because despite everything she tried the shackle refused to yield.

I knew there was a risk of her being hit by a ricochet or a fragment of flying stone like the informant had been, but we were both running out of options. So I raised the Beretta and aimed for point where the shackle was anchored to the wall. I fired. And missed. She was in a blind panic now, gyrating like an ancient berserker, and I'd pulled the shot for fear of hitting her directly. Which gave me an idea. It was a desperate one. Something that might make her hate me for the rest of her life. But with ten seconds left to save her, I didn't think I had a choice.

I took a step to my right, to change the angle. Then I fired again. And this time I hit my target.

Melissa's left wrist.

Chapter Forty-One

The bullet severed Melissa's hand and she fell back, hitting the ground hard before I could get close enough to catch her. The best I could manage was to grab her under the arms and drag her sideways, a second before the crane slammed into the wall. Dark arterial blood was pumping from the mess of ragged, torn skin and splintered bone of her now shortened left arm. Her face was pale, almost green, and her eyes were glazed and unfocussed. I pulled off my belt and looped it round her bicep. The crane's engine had stalled in the impact, but I could hear blocks of dislodged stone still raining down on its bodywork. I pulled the makeshift tourniquet tight, and kept on increasing the pressure until the flow of blood from her wound had slowed to a dribble. Melissa groaned, just once. Then I heard two other sounds. Footsteps, close behind me. And a shotgun cartridge being crunched into place.

"Leckie?" I said, slowly raising my hands.

"Is she all right? Don't let go of her. We've got no time. We need to..." he was saying when I dived away to my right, rolling over and reaching for the little .22 to replace the Beretta which I'd dropped when I was stopping Melissa's bleeding.

A gun fired behind me. But it wasn't the deep *boom* of a shotgun. It was the lighter *snick* of an automatic pistol. I spun round, still on my knees, and saw Leckie lying face down on the ground. About fifteen feet away. He had a single bullet hole in his smart blue overcoat, located neatly between his shoulder blades. Another man was standing behind him, twenty feet further back. It was Tim Jones. He was breathing heavily. His face was bruised and battered. And his Sig Sauer was in his right hand.

"So much for Stan Leckie," he said, striding forwards and putting two more bullets into the back of his head. "May he rest in pieces."

"I guess you weren't as far from London as you thought," I said.

"I guess not. And you're welcome, by the way. I'm happy to help you. Specially after you came back to Melissa's to help me, yesterday."

"Let's just call it square," I said, standing up, tucking the .22 into the back of my waistband and retrieving my Beretta. "Now, where's your car?"

"Over there," he said, nodding towards the hole in the perimeter wall. "Why?"

"Melissa's hurt. We need to get her to hospital."

"Where is she? What happened? Is it serious?"

I guessed it was natural he'd ask. If he'd arrived after the crash, he wouldn't have seen the crisis develop. Or how it was resolved. And the crane would have obstructed his view of Melissa from the spot where he'd stood to shoot Leckie.

"She lost a hand," I said, leading the way to where she was lying. She'd rolled over into a fetal position since I'd moved, and was hugging her injured arm to her chest. "And a lot of blood. It looks like she's going into shock."

"Leckie did this?" he said. "The bastard."

"No. She lost the hand because I shot her."

"You did? Why?"

"Because there was no time, she was moving, and the shackle was too narrow to hit."

"Wow. That's hard-core. But they're very narrow, David, those shackles. You can't blame yourself for this, you know."

Jones's patronising tone reminded me of the conversation I'd had with my control when he told me I was being seconded to MI5. That was the morning after I'd hospitalised Jones himself, ironically. How had my control described my actions? As doing more harm than good? I'd dismissed his words, back then. But now, looking down at Melissa's crumpled body, I couldn't be so sure he was wrong.

"I know," I said, consciously shaking off the doubt. "I don't blame myself. It was the only way to save her. Now, we better hurry. She needs treatment, fast."

"I'm with you," Jones said. "What do you want me to do?"

"Drive us," I said, hoisting Melissa onto my shoulder. "My car's too far away."

"No problem," he said. "Come on. Follow me."

I fell in step behind him, trying to balance my urge to hurry with the need to not shake Melissa around too roughly as we moved across the treacherous ground. Jones reached the car comfortably before me, paused for a moment, then opened the front passenger door and reclined the seat to its limit.

"You know, David, you've been through a lot today," he said. "You've saved two lives, already. Why not let me take care of things from here? There's no need for you waste your time in another hospital. I know you hate them."

I didn't reply until Melissa was in her seat with the belt fastened around her.

"That's a generous offer," I said. "I do hate hospitals. But no thanks. I think her chances of pulling through will be a little higher if I take her."

"Why?" he said.

"Because otherwise, I think it won't be long before I get another distraught phone call telling me that despite your best efforts, she bled out en route to the hospital. So you'll be staying here, and I'll be taking her."

"I don't think so."

"I do. And I just have one question before we go. Who was driving the crane, just now?"

Jones was silent for a moment.

"Stan Leckie was driving it," he said, finally. "Of course."

"A word of advice," I said. "If you're going to lie convincingly, you need to not hesitate so much. And don't elaborate. Answer quickly, simply, and try to keep your eyes still."

"I didn't hesitate. I mean, I didn't understand the question. I was trying to figure out what you meant."

"You were? I'm intrigued. Which part of the question was particularly confusing?"

"It's not that. It's because you already knew Leckie was driving it, so I couldn't understand why you were asking."

"Leckie was driving. What was he trying to do?"

"Kill Melissa."

"Just Melissa? Or me, too?"

"Both of you."

"I can understand Melissa. She was chained up. She couldn't get away. But me? I was mobile. And he had a shotgun. Why didn't he just shoot me, instead of leaving me free to release her?"

"He must have wanted to use his trademark method."

"So, not only to kill us, but to make sure the world knew who'd done it?"

"I guess."

"You're quite new to this game, aren't you Tim? Have you crossed paths with many killers?"

"Not too many, no."

"Because here's a word to the wise. There are lots of reasons for killing. Money. Revenge. Panic. Covering your tracks. But announcing your own guilt? Inviting the police to catch you? That's not high on many murderers' lists."

Jones didn't reply.

"And there's another problem," I said. "Leckie wasn't threatening me with that shotgun. He was about to tell me something. And then you conveniently shot him."

"Leckie was guilty," he said. "He was tied into al-Aqsaba'a up to his elbows, and I can prove it."

"Maybe you can. But can you prove who was helping him? From inside MI5? Or are you trying to do the opposite?"

Jones didn't answer.

"I don't have time for any more nonsense," I said, after five seconds of silence. "Where's your phone?"

"In my pocket," he said. "Why?"

"Take it out," I said, leveling my Beretta on the bridge of his nose. "Call your mother. Tell her goodbye."

Jones didn't move.

"What's wrong?" I said. "Don't you have a mother?"

"No," he said. "I do."

"Then don't you care about her? Don't you think she'd appreciate the chance to say goodbye to her son? Because if you don't tell me what I want to know, I'm going to do to you what you did to Leckie."

Jones started to move his mouth, but it was a couple of seconds before any sound came out.

"OK," he said. "You win. It was me. I was driving the crane."

"You were?" I said. "How did you get in place to shoot Leckie so soon after you crashed into the wall?"

"I didn't wait for the impact. I jumped out as soon as

it started moving."

"So why didn't I see you?"

"The crane was between us."

"It couldn't have been, or you'd have been on the other side of Leckie when you shot him."

Jones shrugged.

"I could call your mother for you," I said. "After you're dead. And explain how you were a traitor. How does she feel about Islamic extremists, by the way? Is she a fan?"

"It's not like that," he said, as a sharp red dot appeared on his forehead. "No one was supposed to get…"

I dived forward, trying to knock him to the ground, but I heard the bang while I was still in the air. When I landed on him his body was already slack. The red dot had been replaced by a neat, black-edged hole. The back of his skull was missing. And what had passed for his brains were soaking into the dirt next to his corpse.

Chapter Forty-Two

My suspicion about the crane driver had been proved right, but a little more dramatically than I'd planned. I rolled off Jones's body and scrambled closer to the car, desperate for cover, and trying to steal a couple of seconds to think. I knew from experience that where you found one traitor, a second usually wasn't too far away. A young, naïve one to do the donkey work, and be thrown under the bus if necessary. And an older, wiser head to lie low, pull the strings, and walk away untarnished. Jones fitted the first bill. But who could his puppet master be? I doubted it would have been someone I hadn't come across before, because they wouldn't be close enough to the case to influence it in any major way. The problem now, though, was they were close enough to influence me, permanently. If I could just figure out who it could be, that might give the tiny edge I'd need. I had precious little else to work with, beside a critically injured girl I had to get to the hospital.

I heard stones rattle, somewhere in front of the car. Someone was moving. Changing their angle. Coming closer.

I ran back through the people I'd met since first arriving at St Joseph's. The things that had happened. The discussions we'd sat through as a result. The opinions that were expressed. The decisions that were taken. And then a couple of subtle phrases and an unexpected set of orders suddenly tied themselves into Jones's last words, making a shaky kind of connection in my brain. That may not have been significant. But the red dot reappeared. And that was. Because it was hovering over the centre of my chest.

The vague connection was all I had. There was no choice but to gamble.

"It's a little ungrateful to shoot me, don't you think?" I said. "Considering how much I helped you, today?"

The red dot started to twitch. Then it moved. Across my body. Up the side of the car. And onto Melissa's abdomen.

"You didn't know the fire at the school was just a diversion, did you?" I said.

The dot stayed resolutely still.

"Your plan would have backfired, if I hadn't been there to save the boy," I said, deciding it was time to go all in. "Wouldn't it, Mr Hardwicke?"

The dot disappeared, and more stones rattled directly in front of the car.

"Do you have any evidence for such a wild claim, Commander?" Hardwicke said, emerging from behind a mound of rubble. The front of his coat was covered with mud and brick fragments. The vague, distracted look that had always been on his face at Thames House had been replaced with a focused, angry stare. And the rifle in his hands was still pointing straight at Melissa. "Because otherwise, you'd struggle to make anyone believe you."

"How about this?" I said. "We take the girl to the hospital, and once she's safe I'll hand everything I have straight over to you."

"Agent Wainwright? I like her. I'd have liked to see her walk away from all this. And I would have let her – you too – if only you'd gone through with your threat to shoot Jones. Everything would have fallen on him and Leckie. But you had to start asking questions. And I can't take the risk you haven't been asking them elsewhere."

"I haven't."

"Put your gun down, and pick her up."

"Why?"

"Because she's in the wrong place. I want you to move her."

"So you can kill her?"

"You set that particular ball in motion. I'm just going to let nature finish its work."

"And me?"

"Interesting question. If you'd asked me yesterday, I'd have said you had a bright future ahead of you. Today, I'm forecasting rain."

"Then, I'm not seeing the incentive to help you."

"OK. Try this. If you don't help, I'm going to shoot you in the spine. And I'm going to aim low, so you don't die straight away. So you lie there for a while, paralysed. Then I'll take your belt off Wainwright's arm, and your final sight will be her blood pumping out of the wound you inflicted and mingling in the mud with what's left of Jones's brain."

I didn't move.

"Oh," Hardwicke said. "I see. You're thinking of calling my bluff. Well, that's your choice. But do you really believe I couldn't get people over here to dress the scene any way I want it? Or that I couldn't just leave your bodies here, and think of a way to explain how the chips happened to fall? Because let me tell you – I've achieved a lot, today. And I'm not about to see it all go south."

Hardwicke raised his rifle and lined it up on my stomach. A whole new can of worms was opening before my eyes, but I had no time to deal with it. Getting Melissa to hospital was my priority, which meant putting Hardwicke on ice, at least for a few hours. But that was easier said than done. He was armed. He was too far away to rush. And he was completely unstable. My options were limited. I decided my best shot was to keep him talking, and try to work an angle as quickly as possible.

I put my Beretta on the ground, released Melissa's seat belt, and lifted her back on to my shoulder.

"I suppose it's quite ironic, in a way," I said.

"What is?" Hardwicke said.

"I was brought in to work against you. And here I am, helping you."

Hardwicke laughed.

"My poor boy," he said. "You don't understand. I was the one who requested you. I brought you in to help me, and that's what you've been doing from the start. Didn't you know?"

"No," I said. "What else did I do?"

"There's a group of busy-bodies in parliament who are trying to foist external investigators on the Service, for breaches of security. I've been fighting them for two years. And now, you've given me the ammunition I need to back them off for good."

"I did? How?"

"We had two bad apples in our barrel. Jones, and Wainwright. It should have just been Jones, but that number doubled because of you. Wainwright became collateral damage. But anyway, it proves our existing methods work. And if they're not broken, why fix them? It's just a shame you had to give your life to expose the vicious traitors."

"All this so you could avoid some semi-retired ex-superintendent looking over your shoulder?"

"No. That was just the icing."

I felt a little tension come back into Melissa's body.

"What else was there?"

"Have you got any idea how much press you get for saving a sweet-looking little kid? Let alone what public displays of success do for funding?"

"You thought al-Aqsaba'a was going to use a fire engine to spray the kids at St Ambrose with the caesium solution? Which is why you dropped the hints at that late night meeting at Thames House, when the container showed up at the fire station, and everyone thought Parliament was the target. And ordered the other pair of agents to be there, even before we'd caught on to what was happening."

"That's right. That whole Parliament thing was bizarre. It suited me for a while, after you all misunderstood that snitch's warning. Frightening MPs is never a bad thing. The only thing they care about is themselves. I thought you lot would get back on the right track eventually, but Leckie having the container moved made things worse. He was trying to nudge you towards St Ambrose, but he'd forgotten the fire station serves both places. And I have to admit – the way time was running out, I was getting a little nervous, myself."

"That's a hell of a lot of trouble you went to."

"Actually, it wasn't. Leckie did all the heavy lifting."

"Did you plant him at the hospital, specially for this?"

"No. I'd have planted him in jail, but that would have aired too much dirty laundry. So I told him I'd let him walk away, but only if he kept his head down. I made it clear. One squeak of trouble, and he wouldn't end up in a cage. He'd end up in a box."

I could feel Melissa's stomach muscles working against my shoulder, now, almost as if she was trying to wriggle further down my back.

"And this scheme was his idea of a quiet retirement?"

"No. He was approached by al-Aqsaba'a. They had some evidence about the people of theirs who'd got on the wrong side of his demolition ball, apparently. They offered him a deal. Procure the caesium, or they'd hang him out to dry."

"How did you find out?"

"He came to me. Offered them to me on a plate. I'd take the glory, and in return I'd ensure the evidence would never see the light of day."

"A tidy arrangement. Only it seems you both were trying to embellish a little."

Hardwicke smiled.

"I've never been a fan of leaving hostages to fortune," he said.

"Maybe Leckie knew that," I said. "Maybe that's why he moved the final act to the hospital?"

"Maybe. I honestly don't know. But knowing Leckie like I do, I bet there was more to it. He never accepted having to leave the service. Deep down, he thought we were weak. He thought everyone should behave like he did. So I wouldn't be surprised if he'd planned it that way all along. Then instead of glory, we'd be disgraced. There'd be calls for the service to toughen up. And he'd imagine himself being welcomed back with open arms."

"Doesn't sound too rational."

"Psychopaths seldom are."

Melissa's hand seemed to be clawing at my waistband, which was strange. There'd be no danger of her slipping off if she'd only stay still.

"And what about the evidence al-Aqsaba'a were blackmailing him with?"

"That'll be what the second stolen batch of caesium was for. A frame. I bet he'd have planted it at one of their houses, or mosques even, and blackmailed the blackmailers. I'd have liked to ask him about it, actually, but Jones's finger was a bit too itchy."

"Jones was working for him?"

"Jones was working for both us. Only he didn't realise it."

"How did he get hooked up in the first place? They never served at the same time. I checked."

"That made them the ideal combination. There were no grounds for suspicion. So I had a mutual friend introduce them. Jones was pretty useful, for a while. You know, Leckie actually had him convinced they were doing the right thing? And he certainly helped keep my blood pressure down. When that idiot fireman damaged the vault door? The fake burglary? That could have been stressful, otherwise."

Then the penny dropped. I realised what Melissa was doing.

"There never was anyone coming to collect the caesium from the thieves, was there?" I said.

"Of course not," Hardwicke said. "It had to be recovered, so everyone would think none was missing."

"The thugs who jumped me outside my building?"

"Leckie's idea. He thought you were getting too close. Jones arranged it, though."

Melissa tapped me twice in the small of my back. She must have got what she needed.

"And the idiots who came after us at Melissa's apartment?" I said.

"Leckie again," Hardwicke said. "He was starting to panic. And lose faith in Jones."

"Why did Jones take a beating, to protect me?"

"The way I heard it, he had no choice. He didn't know where you'd gone."

I took a moment to think, and realised that was true. I'd left Jones alone so he wouldn't overhear my phone calls, and I hadn't told him where I was heading because I'd had no clear idea myself.

"It was what you could call an irrevocable breakdown in their relationship," Hardwicke said. "Jones got scared. He realised Leckie was getting ready to cut his losses. So he decided to get his retaliation in first."

"And he was prepared to sacrifice Melissa to do that?" I said.

"I don't know. Maybe Jones snatched her from the hospital. Maybe he tricked her. But it really doesn't matter, now. He's dead. And he's just as useful to me that way. Just as the two of you are going to be. Now, turn around."

"Really?" I said. "I thought it would be harder than that."

"What would?"

"Doesn't matter. You really want me to turn around?"

"I do. Because I'm going to shoot you in the back. That way, when your people find you, they'll think you died running away from someone."

"Well, if you're sure," I said. "Everybody ready?"

Melissa tapped my back. I pivoted on the spot, 180 degrees, and almost simultaneously I heard two gunshots. It was like an old fashioned duel, I thought, bracing myself for the impact of a bullet.

None came.

"Are you OK?" I said, turning back to face the spot where Hardwicke had been standing.

"I'm fine," Melissa said, almost in a whisper.

Hardwicke was lying on his back. His eyes were screwed shut, and he was clutching his chest and writhing. I stepped closer and kicked the rifle well out of his reach, then gently lowered Melissa's feet to the ground. I kept a tight hold under her arms, taking most of her weight, and she kicked him hard in the side of the head. His writhing subsided, but she waited for him to open his eyes before doing anything else.

"Goodbye," she said finally, holding his gaze. "Sir."

Then she lined up the .22 and fired two more times.

Chapter Forty-Three

Melissa dropped the gun, turned, and walked away from Hardwicke and Jones's bodies as if they were nothing more than rotting tree trunks. She moved slowly at first, then picked up speed and I realised she was heading back towards the main building. I thought she must be making for the wall she'd been chained to, but she didn't get that far. Instead, she stopped when she reached the spot where Leckie had fallen. She paused there for a moment, her head tipped down like she was praying. Then she knelt, stretched out her right hand, and placed it over the blood-sodden hole in the back of his coat.

I stepped up alongside her, and saw she was crying. She wasn't making a sound, but large heavy tears were cascading down her cheeks and dripping off both sides of her chin. Some had landed on the remains of her left wrist, which she was still clutching to her chest, diluting the blood and carrying it further down her arm.

"It's my fault he's dead," she said, without looking at me. "He came here to save me."

"It was Jones who brought you?" I said.

She nodded.

"How?" I said.

"At the hospital," she said. "When I went to look for the nurse, to ask about that stupid kid. Jones was there. He pulled a gun on me."

"He was lying when he told me Leckie had you?"

"Of course. He said that to lure you here. He wanted to kill us both, and let the blame fall on Leckie. Only he didn't count on Hardwicke being here."

"Hardwicke was driving the crane?"

"That's right. It was like him forging Leckie's signature. Jones wasn't expecting that."

"But Leckie was here to save you?"

"Yes."

"Not to kill anyone?"

"No."

"So you were in on his plan, too?"

"No," she said, pulling her right hand back and spinning round to face me. "Absolutely not."

"Then why keep you alive? The wheels were coming off his whole scheme. If you weren't with him, wouldn't it have been better to put you and Jones in the frame?"

"Maybe. But he would never have done that. Not to me, anyway."

"Why not?"

"Because," she said, standing and moving backwards, away from me. "He was my father."

"Stan Leckie was your father?" I said, rooted to the spot.

She nodded.

"Are you serious?" I said.

"One hundred percent," she said.

"And you chose not to share this with me? You didn't think it might have been a useful thing for me to know?"

She didn't reply.

"Did anyone else know?" I said, wondering why my control hadn't briefed me.

"No," she said. "They didn't. I'm sorry. I only found out myself four days ago."

"How did you find out?"

"Remember the time I told you I was following a

lead in Leytonstone? Well, I wasn't. Leckie had called me. He'd asked me to meet him near the Serpentine. He claimed to have information about the case, for my ears only. But when I got there, he dropped this bombshell on me. It was a lot to take in. I needed time to figure out what it meant. You have a father?"

"Yes."

"Did you know him when you were growing up?"

"I did."

"Then you can't know what it's like to spend your whole childhood with such a void in your life. My mother told me he was dead."

"Why?"

"She's a lawyer. She was very rich, even back then. She didn't need his support. Their paths briefly crossed, one time, but it was never something that was meant to last. If they'd told Box about me, there'd have been implications for Leckie's work. A kid's a liability for an undercover operative, obviously. There was nothing between them, so they didn't see the point of making it official. It was easier, and safer for everyone. And just as well for me, given how his career panned out."

"It was a coincidence, you working for Box too?"

"A complete coincidence. He said he liked it, though, cause he could keep an eye on me."

"So why tell you now?"

"Because you and I were getting too close to finding out what he was doing. Despite everything, I was his daughter and he didn't want me to get hurt. And he couldn't ask Hardwicke to pull me off the case. You can't wear a different aftershave around a guy like that without him putting two and two together."

"And the meeting with his snout. Here, at the workhouse. That came up straight afterwards."

"It did. He was trying to help. He wanted to throw me something that would keep me out of harm's way, and make me look good at the same time."

"And something that would keep his misdirection on the rails. He wanted Hardwicke's eyes firmly on that school."

"That too, I guess. Look, I'm sorry I didn't tell you straight away, but it was a lot to process. I've been all round the houses. I've been in shock. I've been confused. I've been angry – I even met my mother and screamed at her for lying to me. I've been relieved. I don't even know what else I've been. I've just been a mess, I suppose."

"How do you feel now?"

"That's the funny part. My mother had told me my fictitious dead father was a good man. A good lawyer, if such people exist. And I felt empty and alone. Now, I know my father was what? A scheming psychopath? A man who killed people with wrecking balls and barbed wire? And you know what? I feel happy."

I didn't comment, but not for the first time in my life I was glad I'd brought a switchblade with me.

"And here's why. Do you know what's really important about my father? Two things are. First, he really, honestly believed what he did was right. He saved innocent lives, too, remember. And second, he could have walked away from this mess alive, with everything he'd worked for intact. But he didn't. He came here to save me. And he died for me. Imagine that. Someone being prepared to give his life for yours. It's humbling."

I didn't reply.

"The same goes for you, I realise," she said. "You didn't have to come back here. I should thank you, too."

"Even after what I did to your hand?" I said.

"You saved my life. Twice. In one afternoon. Right

now I'd consider marrying you."

I looked away.

"That might be difficult," I said.

"Why?" she said.

"You've got nowhere to put the ring."

Melissa was still for a moment, then she peeled her left arm away from her chest and held it unsteadily in front of her, with the bloody jagged remnants of her wrist just below eye level. At first I could see her physically battling her neck muscles, forcing herself not to turn away. Ten seconds ticked past. Twenty. Thirty, and she still didn't flinch.

"Don't worry," she said, after forty-five. "I'm not serious about the wedding. But there's nothing here I can't deal with."

"Really?" I said.

"Absolutely," she said. "Look. I may have no hand, because of you. Probably no job, either. But that's better than having no breath in my body. My father just gave me back my past. I'm certainly not going to squander my future. I'm going to be a lot more careful how I spend my time, now, in general. And I think you should be, too."

"I'll try."

"I'm serious. No repeats of the last few days. Not the crazy parts, anyway. Like what just happened here. Promise me."

"I can't promise. It depends on too many things."

"What kind of things?"

"People keeping their thieving hands off my boots, for a start."

MORE HARM THAN GOOD

With Special Thanks To:

Bill Cameron – Cover Design
Stacie Gutting – Copy Editing
Janet Reid – Literary Representation
Tom Robinson - Publicity

Printed in Great Britain
by Amazon